The Little Girl In The Wardrobe

THE
LITTLE GIRL
IN THE
WARDROBE

C.J. GRAYSON

TANZY & BYRD THRILLERS 4

JOFFE BOOKS

Joffe Books, London
www.joffebooks.com

First published in Great Britain in 2025

© C.J. Grayson

Cover art by Nebojša Zorić

ISBN: 978-1-83526-967-1

PROLOGUE

Warrington

Selena Goldberg sipped her rum and Coke and gazed through the restaurant window. She had a great view of the street: bright lights and gaudy colours of shopfronts and takeaways opposite. She wasn't too pleased about the tables being so crammed together — the restaurant was busy for a Tuesday, occupied mostly by couples and families, although a few dined alone, no doubt away on business. Elbow to elbow with a pregnant stranger conducting a loud and tedious dissection of the menu with the waiter, she was grateful the man on her other side was quiet, at least. A busy restaurant meant the food would be good, she reminded herself, as her stomach rumbled.

'What time's the meeting tomorrow?' asked Corey, picking up his lager and taking a swig.

'Ten o'clock. It'll last a few hours.'

She tried to hide her irritation. Corey knew exactly when the meeting was, of course — he just wanted to complain again about her dragging him along with her. He hadn't been married long and clearly wanted to be back home with that new wife of his. He didn't seem to care that, as his boss, she was offering him a valuable opportunity to better himself.

1

'I still don't understand why we need a new security system,' Corey said.

Selena resisted the urge to pull a face at him, and instead leaned forward so that she could hear him over the noise of her neighbouring diner.

'I know you don't like me to say that West Manor used to be a lunatic asylum,' he went on, raising his voice, 'but the Victorians knew how to build a secure facility. Impenetrable fences, only one way in and out, and a friendly guard at the gatehouse. Plus all the CCTV you could want.'

'West Manor's guests are the crème de la crème,' Selena reminded him. 'They come to us for privacy — that's our selling point, after all. They don't want to worry about getting papped as they arrive for rehab or anxiety therapy or a meditation workshop. Anyway, it's part of the job to keep up with changes in security — locks, cameras, and all the rest of it. And it's good for your personal development to come along to meetings like this with me.'

All excellent points she had made before. She drained her glass to cover up her annoyance for having to explain this again.

'Go easy with that, Selena. Don't forget you're driving.'

Since when did her employees get to dictate what she drank? She set her empty glass down and indicated to the waiter that she'd like another.

Corey slowly shook his head. 'Well, all I'm saying is I think we're doing a good job. Even the patients themselves don't know who's staying in the next suite.'

'Guests, Corey, not patients.' It was time to change the subject. 'Since we're talking work, do you think Reggie needs any help? He's been a bit slow with the repairs to the north wing. I know he's snowed under.'

'Yeah, maybe. Probably not on his game since his sister died.'

'Perhaps it's too much for just him. Maybe we could employ someone else to give him a hand. He's been spending a lot of time in the basement.'

Corey laughed. '*His* basement, I call it. Really it's his office, isn't it?'

'Well, it is, but . . .'

'He's just working on something, I bet. He's always messing around with something. That ramp he built for wheelchairs to get down into the garden was impressive.'

A tanned waiter in a clean black apron appeared at last, and elegantly set Selena's pizza down first, along with another rum and Coke, then Corey's lasagne. 'There you go. Enjoy.'

They both smiled and tucked in. The woman to Selena's left was now chatting volubly to her dining companion about a buggy she wanted to buy. The man on Selena's other side was tapping away at his phone with a scowl on his face, but the good food was worth the close quarters.

'How's the pizza?' asked Corey, smiling.

'It's good.' She took another bite. 'What's funny?'

He raised a finger and pointed to her chin. 'Little bit of pepper sauce there.'

She wiped it off, her eyes darting around to see if anyone else had noticed. When she ordered pizza, whichever flavour, she always asked for extra-hot pepper sauce and mustard. The taste reignited memories of her childhood, her family sitting around campfires on summer nights back in Trinidad. Bliss.

After they'd finished, they settled the bill and made their way out to the car park.

'You sure you're okay to drive?' he asked her.

She raised a hand as they approached the car. 'I've only had two. I'll be fine.'

They both climbed in and buckled up. Unfamiliar with the route back, she typed the hotel postcode into Google and put the phone on the holder.

The man who'd been sitting at the next table walked in front of their car, the creases in his leather jacket reflecting their headlights. Why was he looking at her car like that?

'Scary-looking dude,' noted Corey as the man climbed into a black Range Rover parked a few spaces over.

Selena was paranoid. Really she shouldn't drink — it just made her anxious. 'Yeah,' she agreed. 'He doesn't appear very pleasant at all.'

She pulled out of the car park and followed the satnav route, thinking about tomorrow's meeting and mentally calculating how many doors she would include in the quote. In her rear-view mirror, she noticed the Range Rover driving behind her. Every time the lights shone in her mirror they blinded her. Thoughtless, inconsiderate clown.

'Selena, you might want to slow down. You're going over forty. And you've had two drinks.'

She didn't respond, still mulling over her plans for the next day.

'Selena!' Corey slapped his hand on the dashboard and braced himself.

She snapped out of her thoughts, but it was too late. She hit the man who'd stepped out onto the road. His body bounced up over the car, cracking the windscreen.

She slammed on the brakes. 'Shit.' She looked around, peering through the rear windscreen.

The Range Rover behind had stopped too, its headlights illuminating the outline of the man on the ground.

'God, what have I done?'

She jumped out of the car and ran over to the man to check him.

No pulse. He was dead. She covered her mouth in disbelief.

'Selena,' Corey said. 'What have you done?'

She pulled out her phone.

'We have to ring for help,' she said. But she didn't call anyone.

Frozen, staring at her screen, she heard the door of the Range Rover open. The driver walked over, eyeing the man on the ground, his body all mangled and twisted. He looked to be quite elderly. 'That was a nasty one. Is he okay?'

'He's dead,' Selena said.

'You saw what happened?' asked Corey.

4

The man nodded. 'Unfortunately for you, yes, I did.'

'Oh God . . .'

'Fortunately for you, I can pretend I never saw a thing, and we can all go on our merry little way.'

'What do you mean?'

The man in black peered around the street. 'No CCTV. No witnesses. Nobody's watching. So if *I* didn't see anything, then no one did. And I know you've had a few drinks too. Let's be honest, it wouldn't look good to the police.'

Selena studied him, trying to fully grasp what he was saying. 'Drive away?'

'Bingo.'

'We need to call an ambulance.'

'What's the point? You said it yourself, he's dead.' He looked down at the body. 'Go now before you change your mind and do something silly.'

Selena eyed Corey. What did he think about the man's suggestion?

'You don't have long to decide,' the man in black said. 'Someone will see you here.'

'Come on, Corey,' she heard herself say. 'Let's go.' It was as if someone else was speaking for her.

She ran to her car door and clambered in. Corey quickly jumped in the passenger seat, closing the door.

'We shouldn't be doing this, Selena,' he said.

In the rear-view mirror, she could see the stranger staring after them. She set the gear in first and drove back to the hotel in silence.

* * *

For a week, Selena found herself checking the news every five minutes for reports of hit-and-runs, missing pensioners — the national news at first, and then sites and forums local to Warrington. She stumbled across an article regarding a man in his eighties who'd died on the same street as the restaurant they'd eaten at. Her heart sank. The report said passers-by had found him dead in the middle of the road, evidently from a hit-and-run. Police were asking for anyone who had any information to come forward. After several days, she'd almost convinced herself that nothing would come of it, until her phone rang one quiet morning. Selena frowned at the number she didn't recognise, though this wasn't unusual in her line of work, so she answered.

'Hello.'

'Selena Goldberg?'

'Speaking. Who's this?'

'I'm just a concerned citizen in Warrington. I thought I'd bring it to your attention that I witnessed a hit-and-run the other week.'

Selena froze, unable to speak or think. Her mind just shut down.

'Selena?'

'Who is this?' she whispered, feeling dizzy.

'I'm someone with video evidence of the event, and I'm willing to turn it in to the police. I'm not sure they'll be too happy knowing you killed a man and simply drove off.'

'I don't know what you mean.' Her heart was racing.

'I was driving behind you.'

'You were in the Range Rover?'

'That's me!'

'You're the one who told me to drive off!'

'And now I'm using this to blackmail you.'

'I don't know what you're talking about.'

'Well, I'll see what the police have to say about that. Good—'

'Wait!' She lowered herself onto the living room floor, unable to stay on her feet. 'What do you want? How did you get this number?'

'Easy enough to find out who you were. I was sitting next to you in the restaurant that night. "West Manor's guests are the crème de la crème,"' he mimicked.

Selena stifled a groan. Why had she been talking about work in such a crowded place?

'I need you to do me a favour.'

'What?' asked Selena.

'Nothing fancy, just a few nights' bed and board for some . . . relatives of mine. Ultimate privacy. No outside callers. That sort of thing. Do you think you can do that for me?'

'Yes, I'm sure I can,' she replied, physically shaking now. 'What do I call you?'

'You can call me Jarrett Banks.'

1

Wednesday morning
Emergency control room, Durham Constabulary Headquarters

Just after 9 a.m., Josephine McClaine lowered the phone beside her keyboard and rubbed her eyes. It was her fourteenth call of the morning, and only an hour into her shift.

'God . . .' She was looking forward to lunchtime already. Coasting on less than four hours of sleep thanks to the teenagers partying all night next door, she wearily smiled at the PC walking by with a coffee in her hand.

She readjusted the headset so it felt more comfortable and waited for the next call. Last week had marked ten years since she'd joined Darlington Emergency Services as a dispatch operator. Most of the job was routine, but some days were testing, like yesterday, when she'd received a call from a ten-year-old boy called Jack, saying his dad was trying to hurt him. She'd kept little Jack calm while she'd dispatched police units to his house to arrest his violent father.

'Want a coffee, Josie?'

She swivelled to Simon, the operator at the next desk.

'Coffee?' he said again.

She definitely needed it. 'That would be lovely, Simon. Thank you.'

As he disappeared from view, her phone rang.

She cleared her throat, pulled herself in, and pressed accept on her headset.

'Durham Constabulary, where are you calling from?'

No answer.

'Hello? Where are you calling from?' She frowned at the screen, checking if the call was connected. 'Hello?'

'I — I . . .' the caller said.

'Hello, is anyone there? Can you hear me?'

The call disconnected.

She sighed. Simon had said the phones were playing up this morning, but it was the first time she'd experienced it.

'I got you some biscuits too.' Simon startled her as he leaned over, placing a cup of coffee and two chocolate digestives beside her keyboard.

'I'm trying to be good,' she said, tempted by the biscuits.

'Well, just stare at them, then.' He stood, smiling. 'But I'm not sure they'll eat themselves.'

Grinning in appreciation, she picked up her coffee and took a sip as he dropped into his chair and put on his headset, ready for his next call.

Josie eyed the biscuits, not wanting to have one in case a call came in while she was chewing. After waiting a while, she thought, *The hell with it*, and grabbed one, quickly snapping it in half and eating it. Just as she finished, the phone rang.

'Durham Constabulary,' she answered. 'Where are you calling from?'

She waited a few seconds for a reply that never came.

'Hello?' She turned to Simon in frustration, pointing to her headset.

The call disconnected.

'Si, are you still having phone issues today? That's the second call now where I couldn't hear anything.'

He scowled and leaned in. 'Was it the same caller?'

9

Josephine opened the call history and noted it was the same number as the previous caller.

'Got a location?'

She clicked on the call ID number, which brought up the mobile number and a GPS point the service provider had automatically provided, informing them the call was made somewhere on Haughton Road, Darlington.

'Might be a bad signal.'

'Ahh, it's ringing — try again.' He pointed at the incoming call on her screen from the same number.

'Durham Constabulary, where are you calling from?' Josie said calmly.

'Help . . .'

'Hello? This is the police. Can you tell me where you are?'

'Help me,' said a quiet voice.

She frowned, staring at the GPS location. 'My name is Josie. How can I help you?'

'Help me,' the voice said.

During her years doing the job, she'd become very good at gauging different voices and guessed this voice belonged to a young girl, no older than ten.

'You need the police?'

'Yes.'

'Can you tell me your location?'

'I can't . . . I don't . . .'

'It's okay, we can trace the call if you stay on the line. Help is coming. Can you describe what's happening? Hello?'

The line went dead again.

'Ahh, Jesus, come on!' she cried, banging the edge of her desk with her palm. She turned abruptly to Simon. 'We need someone to have a look at this ASAP. Whoever this is, they clearly need our help.'

Simon dashed away from the desk in search of someone to help with the communication issues.

The phone rang again. The same caller.

She tapped the accept button. 'Hello? Are you there?'

'Please help me, Josie.' There was a desperate edge to the girl's voice.

'I'm here to help you. What's your name, dear?'

There was a mumble, but nothing Josie could understand.

'Say that again, please.'

'Anya.'

'Okay, Anya, it sounds very quiet where you are. Are you not able to speak very loudly?'

'No. Please help. He's coming.'

'Who's coming, Anya? Are you in danger?'

'He has a knife. He killed her.'

2

Wednesday morning
Emergency control room, Durham Constabulary Headquarters

'Anya, listen to me.' Josie took a short, sharp breath to compose herself. 'You need to hide. Can you do that for me?'

Silence.

'Anya! Are you there?'

'I'm . . . I'm here.'

'Are you able to hide in a safe place?'

'I think so.'

'Okay, go do that now,' she told the girl. To her left, Simon had been watching her intently and pulled up his chair, adjusting the settings so he could listen in to the call. On the monitor were the caller's number and GPS location. A flashing cursor blinked inside a black text box on the screen. Josie needed to fill in more information, which would be automatically passed on to the police responders on their way to the address.

'Are you safe now, Anya?' Josie asked softly, her hands flexing and clenching just above her keyboard, a calming technique she often used during stressful calls. She navigated through the system, sending emergency units, both police and ambulance, to the house.

The sound of footsteps came through their earpieces, followed by a light knocking, and then it went eerily quiet.

'I'm inside a cupboard in a bedroom,' Anya told them through short, frantic breaths.

'Good, that's great, Anya. Well done.' A notification appeared on Josie's screen to inform her that the police had been dispatched to the caller's location.

'Aww, my head really hurts.'

'Did you hit your head?'

'Yeah.'

'The paramedics are on their way. But, listen, I need you to stay exactly where you are so we can talk a little more. I need some more information from you. Please, keep your voice quiet, if you can.'

'Okay,' Anya whispered, her words slurring. 'I feel kind of sick.'

Josie frowned. How badly was the girl hurt? She didn't want to make her talk too much in case the man found her, but she didn't want Anya to pass out either.

'Anya, can you tell me what happened?'

'I heard something downstairs. Her eyes were open. She wasn't moving. Someone was near the door staring at her. He had a knife in his hand. I saw the blade.'

'Did he see you?'

No answer.

'Anya, did he see you?' Josie asked calmly.

'I don't know, I — I went back upstairs. I don't know what to do. Please help me.' Josie heard the sound of suppressed sobs.

'How old are you, Anya?'

'I'm — I'm nine.'

'Okay, that's brilliant. You're doing so well. You're so brave.' Anya started to weep.

'I know it's hard, but keep as quiet as you can, Anya.'

'There's blood on the tiles.'

'It's okay, Anya, just hold on. Is there anyone else in the house with you?

'Just me now. And him.'

Anya's location was on Haughton Road in Darlington, just opposite Darlington College. The police should have been there by now. Josie tapped the edge of her desk with her fingers. Beside her, Simon looked deeply concerned.

'Okay, Anya. Police are very close.'

Josie typed some notes into the text box, and pressed ENTER, knowing the responding units would access them as they arrived, giving them the best chance to defuse the situation.

Josie and Simon frowned at the map, watching the tiny blue dot representing the nearest car approach the house. The red pin on the map identified Anya. They were close.

'Anya, hold on,' she whispered. 'You're doing great.'

'I need to—'

Josie frowned when Anya didn't finish her sentence. 'Anya?'

'The bedroom door is open,' whispered Anya. 'He's in the room with me.'

With wide eyes, Josie saw the police car on the screen had stopped. The police would be breaking down the door at any moment.

'Just stay quiet, Anya,' whispered Josie, her breathing now quicker. She could feel herself with the girl inside the cupboard.

'He's walking around the room.' A sudden short gasp came through. 'God, he's at the cupboard door.' Her voice was barely a murmur.

'Hold the door closed, Anya. The police are in the house. I need you to—'

She heard the sound of a creaking door, followed by a blood-curdling scream that filled their earpieces, loud enough to freeze them into their chairs.

'Anya!' Josie gripped the edge of her desk. 'Anya, are you there?'

Anya didn't respond. The line went dead. The red dot disappeared.

3

'It's up here on the left, Josh. Just over the bridge.' PC Louise Degnan studied a zoomed-in map of Darlington on the car's interior screen. She scanned the notes that Dispatch had entered from the emergency call moments earlier.

PC Josh Andrews guided the marked Vauxhall Astra past a queue of cars. The road was slippery from the earlier downpour, making driving more challenging. The skies were dark and threatened more rain. After nipping back onto his side of the road, he lifted his foot from the accelerator, aware of the dangers of oncoming traffic over the railway bridge.

'What's Dispatch say?' he asked, focusing on the road.

Degnan frowned at the notes on the screen. 'Nine-year-old girl hiding in a cupboard in her bedroom. A woman has been stabbed in the kitchen. The intruder is still there with a knife. The girl is called Anya.'

'It's one of these along here,' said Degnan, staring at the houses further down on the left, opposite the college.

Andrews slowed. 'Which one?'

PC Degnan concentrated on the screen, trying to figure out where the dot was flashing. The row consisted of approximately twenty houses, set back from the main road on a smaller turning. Most were semi-detached properties, with a row of five terraced houses bunched together on the right.

'I'd say it's this one.' Degnan pointed at a house with a black door. 'It has to be.'

'Let's go, then.' Andrews stopped the car.

They jumped out, dashed to the rear of the Astra, and opened the boot. Andrews quickly grabbed two stab vests and handed one to Degnan, who wasted no time putting it on.

They raced across the concrete towards the house, batons in hand. Nearby cars on Haughton Road had slowed, the nosey drivers trying to see what was happening. An elderly lady walking a small dog on a lead had also stopped to observe Degnan and Andrews run past her, desperate to ask what the commotion was about.

Degnan's long dark hair swung as she passed the blue Volvo XC60 on the driveway and reached the front door.

She tried the door handle, but it was locked. 'Just had an update,' she told Andrews, pointing to her earpiece. 'They said there was a scream, but the call's been disconnected.'

PC Andrews charged the door with his shoulder, reliving his younger rugby days. The doorframe cracked but stood firm. He tried again, this time putting more weight into it. The lock shattered and the door swung inwards, slamming into the hallway wall. Andrews darted for the stairs to the left, climbing them two at a time, Degnan close on his heels.

'Police, police, police!' he shouted. 'Make yourself known.'

The stairs led to a small landing. The first door to the left was a bathroom, judging by the white tiles Andrews could see from the open door. He peered in quickly, seeing no one, then backed up, going to the next.

'Police!' shouted Degnan. 'Anyone here?'

The door to the next room was half open, so Andrews pushed it with his left hand and raised his baton in his right. 'This is the police! Make yourself known!'

The room had dark red walls, which gave the room an oppressive feel. A set of wardrobes sat in the alcove to the right, and shelves of books filled the opposite alcove near the window. A double bed was to their left, up against the wall that backed onto the bathroom. On the chimney breast, a TV was fixed to the wall, turned off, with a narrow shelf a few inches underneath it, filled with tiny ornaments and random pieces of gold jewellery. The floor was messy: crumpled clothes and several see-through boxes filled with more clothing.

'Anything?' Degnan asked, a step behind him, unable to see the full room.

'No.'

They backed out and continued searching. The next door was shut. Taking a breath, he turned the handle and pushed it open. The room smelled of lavender mixed with something else, like cheap perfume or wax melts. Andrews scanned the room, absorbing the small, colourful vanity unit in front of the chimney breast. The alcoves were filled with two built-in wardrobes, symmetrical to each other in both size and design. A single bed with a pink bedspread with an outline of Barbie was pressed up against the wall. The centre of the room was clear, bar a rectangular pink fluffy rug and a small pile of folded clothing.

'This must be Anya's room,' said Degnan.

'Anya, are you here?' Andrews shouted.

After no response, he turned to Degnan. 'Check the other room at the front.'

'Okay.' She slowly stepped out onto the landing.

Andrews moved further into the room. 'Anya, are you in here?'

He angled over to the left set of wardrobes and, with bated breath, slowly opened the door.

'Louise.'

'Yeah?'

'In here.'

4

The time on the dashboard was 10.26. Detective Inspector Max Byrd frowned at his reflection in the rear-view mirror. Today he looked more like fifty-two than forty-two. He was exhausted — his son, Alan, was eight months old and wasn't a big fan of sleeping. Byrd and his partner Claire had agreed that because she looked after him during the day when he was working, he'd get up at night with Alan to give Claire a restful sleep. Byrd felt like he was sometimes operating on two cylinders instead of four.

'You coming, boss?' asked PC Amy Weaver, cheeks pink in the March chill. She was already out of the car, ducking under the cordon that was strung across the driveway of the semi-detached house. Byrd followed her wearily past the small crowd of onlookers, wishing he could borrow some of her energy. PC Andrews was at the cordon, hair swept neatly to the side.

Byrd looked back at the people watching. 'I see we've attracted an audience.'

Andrews nodded. 'Interested locals concerned for their neighbours, I suppose.'

'Yeah, or nosey buggers with nothing else to be doing,' Byrd said.

They chuckled.

'What's going on?' a man asked from behind the cordon. 'Is Steve all right?'

Leaving Andrews to deal with the questions, Byrd and Weaver headed for the closed front door. One of the senior forensic techs, Jacob Tallow, was standing in front of it tapping some notes into an iPad.

Byrd nodded at Tallow, a six-foot-four monster who towered gawkily over Byrd's six foot one. He was an average-looking sort, with a long face and longer neck, but he wasn't ugly to the right person — his wife clearly didn't think so.

'How're the kids doing, Jacob?'

Tallow had told Byrd about an issue his eldest son was having with a bully at school.

'Hey, Max.' He peered up from the iPad. 'He punched him right in the mouth,' he said, pride in his tone.

Byrd grinned, happy to hear it. He hated bullies. The lowest anyone could go. 'What's it like in there?'

Tallow sighed. 'Put some overshoes on and take a look — we've collected our samples and taken photos already. I told you it wouldn't be long before we'd have one of these again. It's been too long for this town.'

Byrd smiled and shook his head. 'Yeah, there's never a dull day in Darlington, right?'

Once Byrd had placed overshoes and latex gloves on, he entered the silent property, a familiar smell hanging in the air: death. Something awful had happened here.

As he stepped into the hallway, he almost bumped into PC Degnan standing at the base of the stairs, studying the carpet. She was five foot seven, and in good shape from almost daily gym and spin classes. Her face was oval and pretty, with bright blue eyes behind thin-framed glasses. Her hair was dark, tied back into a ponytail, as she often wore it for work. Degnan had transferred from Manchester several months ago after moving to Darlington with her family, something to do with her husband's new job as a doctor at Darlington Memorial Hospital.

'Hey, Max,' she said quietly.

Byrd could see by her pallor she'd witnessed something disturbing. 'You okay?'

She managed a slight nod.

Byrd pointed towards the kitchen. 'What's in there, Louise?'

'Something I'm glad I don't see every day. Otherwise, I'd be finding another bloody job.'

Byrd briefly put a hand on her shoulder. During his career, he'd taken courses on how people's emotions are portrayed through their body language. Within Darlington, there was no one better at judging how someone felt based on their physicality.

'Where's Josh?'

She pointed down the hall. 'In the kitchen with Emily Hope.'

It was apparent she didn't want to go back in there.

'Were you the first responder? Can you tell me what happened?' he asked.

'PC Andrews broke the door down, and we went straight upstairs. Dispatch notes informed us the caller, a child, Anya, was in a wardrobe. We found her in the front bedroom, semi-conscious. She's taken a bad knock to the head at some point.'

'Where is she now?'

'The paramedics took her straight to the hospital.'

'Any sign of intruders when you arrived?'

'No sign of anyone besides her mother.' She lifted her gaze towards the kitchen. 'A window was open in the back bedroom. Judging by the sloping roof, someone could have climbed out and dropped down into the garden.'

Byrd raised a finger to scratch his large nose. 'Have you cleared the whole house?'

'We checked the place over for intruders and any more survivors. Forensics have given us the go-ahead to come in and out, but I think they have more to do.' She sighed, inhaling the warm, stagnant air around them. 'I need some air, boss. I'll be back in a minute.'

They heard heavy, purposeful footsteps behind them. 'Excuse me, guys.'

Byrd and Degnan moved aside for the towering Tallow to pass, dressed in his white paper suit, carrying his iPad. His mask was now pulled down under his chin to reveal the beard he'd been growing. According to his wife, he looked better with one.

'Come on then, Amy, let's have a look at what we've got.'

'Not so fast, Max,' a voice said from behind. 'I can't let you have all the fun.'

Byrd turned to see Detective Inspector Orion Tanzy walking in, wearing dark blue jeans, black shoes, and a dark-coloured softshell jacket zipped up to his chin. *Makes a change from his grey parka*, thought Byrd, but he didn't comment. 'Hey, Ori.'

Tanzy was an inch taller than Byrd and much slimmer. He was a black belt at judo and trained several times a week, and it showed in his physique. His hair was very short, a few shades from being bald, and he sported a finely trimmed goatee. Tanzy, heavily tanned and originally from South Africa, had emigrated when he was just four years old.

Byrd led the way to the kitchen — all modern decor and clean lines. A rectangular table sat in the centre, with a fruit bowl and a cluster of magazines, undisturbed except for a spatter of blood. A door leading to the back garden was open. By the chrome sink was a pile of dirty pots and pans, as if someone had been about to start on the washing up. On the immediate left was a row of cupboards, both top and bottom, with a built-in cooker and hob with a silver extractor fan fixed above it. By the back door was a pair of men's walking shoes and a pair of pink wellies, much smaller in size, no doubt belonging to nine-year-old Anya.

Behind the table, Tallow crouched, the thin elastic strap of his face mask stretched across the back of his head. A few feet to his right, facing the detectives, was the other senior forensic, Emily Hope, and the trainee forensic tech, Amanda Forrest. Hope was on her knees but peered up at them at the doorway before nodding and returning her focus to her work.

Emily Hope was petite, both in height and physique, but she had a massive personality, taking no shit from anyone and usually saying what was on her mind. She was two years younger than her partner, Tallow, who was thirty-nine, but she was definitely the boss in their working relationship. Even with her tattoo-covered arms and no-nonsense temperament, her curious sea-green eyes had the power to lure you into her world, even if you didn't want them to. Recently, she had bleached her pixie-cut hair.

She stood, which, next to Tallow, made her seem the height of a child, but she'd got used to it after years of working together. She enjoyed going out at weekends, less so Tallow's comments when she rocked up on a Monday morning looking rough, but she liked the perks of being single. The pair were polar opposites in every way.

'How are we getting on?' Tanzy asked.

The trainee, Forrest, looked at him, as if considering the question, but no one replied. Tanzy accepted their silence, assuming they were still pissed off with him because of their disagreement a few weeks ago, when Tanzy had turned up at a crime scene and suggested something that the forensic team didn't like — in fact, Hope had told him to fuck off. Byrd had asked him kindly to leave, which he did. They hadn't spoken since.

'We've taken a short video of the room and countless photos,' said Hope, her voice flat. 'You're welcome to come in and look around.'

Was that sarcasm, Byrd wondered? He couldn't tell if she was smiling behind her mask.

The detectives peered down at the woman on the floor between Hope and Tallow. She lay on her back, slightly twisted. Her still eyes stared up at the ceiling. Her mouth hung slightly open. She was wearing a faded purple dressing gown tied around the middle with a belt that had probably loosened during the commotion, revealing the damage to her stomach and chest: dozens of stab wounds. The forensics were keeping a healthy distance to avoid the crimson pool that had spread from beneath her on the tiled flooring.

'Who the hell's done this?' Tanzy shook his head slowly.

'What are your thoughts?' Byrd asked, noticing Hope frowning at the body before them.

'When did the call come in from the young girl?' Hope asked.

Byrd checked his watch: 10.48 a.m.

'Anya spoke with Dispatch around nine thirty.' Byrd cocked his head. 'Why?'

'Because . . .' She paused a beat, eyeing the body on the floor. 'This hasn't just happened. This woman has been here for over twelve hours at least.'

5

'Twelve hours?' said Tanzy, frowning. 'How is that possible?' He turned to Byrd, who was standing to his left. 'But the call came in less than two hours ago?'

'That's what Degnan said, yeah,' replied Byrd, equally baffled. 'The message from Dispatch was that Anya had seen her mother's body in the kitchen, and someone was standing there with a knife. That same person was still in the house until shortly before the police arrived — that's why Anya hid in the wardrobe upstairs.'

'It doesn't make sense,' added Tallow, slowly rising to his feet. 'Not one bit.'

'This blood here,' said Hope, pointing to the floor, 'has hardened. If this woman had only been dead for a couple of hours, the blood would be much thinner, not congealed like it is.' She angled slightly towards Tallow, who was gently squeezing the arm, checking how the blood reacted to the pressure of his fingers. 'Jacob?'

'Yeah, I agree. The blood would return to the surface if she'd died recently. See here.'

Byrd and Tanzy leaned over to get a better look.

'When squeezing her forearm, the pressure point should turn white,' Tallow said, 'then slowly return to her natural skin colour. But there's no colour change at all. This usually happens past the twelve-hour mark.'

'Interesting,' commented Byrd with narrowed eyes. 'You're confident she was murdered more than twelve hours ago?'

Both forensic techs nodded without hesitation.

'Absolutely.' Tallow slowly found his feet again, visible pain in his eyes.

'You all right, Jacob?' asked Forrest, a small, plump girl with long dark hair and a round face.

'Touch of joint pain. I'll live, Amanda.'

Byrd and Tanzy spent the next several minutes inspecting the scene. There were no signs of a weapon that could have caused the wounds on the woman's stomach and chest. Nothing else in the kitchen seemed out of place, although the unwashed dishes suggested an evening meal of spaghetti rather than breakfast.

'Three plates,' pointed out Byrd. 'I wonder if the third diner was the killer?'

'We'll leave you to get on,' said Tanzy. 'Is it okay if we start on searching the house?'

When they received a nod from Emily, the detectives slowly backed out into the hallway, stopping at the base of the stairs.

'So it happened more than twelve hours ago, but Anya's call only came in a couple of hours ago?' Byrd shook his head. 'Something's off, Ori.'

'It is, Max,' Tanzy agreed.

PC Degnan appeared through the front door. The colour had returned to her face. A sea of people stood watching from the cordon beyond.

'It's a circus out there,' she told them as she closed the door.

'Anything to get the good folks of the town out and about,' said Tanzy. 'Is Andrews okay?'

'He's getting a bit of information out of the neighbours, I think. They're quite a chatty bunch.'

'Makes a change. Very well, let's leave him to it. You and Weaver can do a full search of the house. See if any documents identify the mother and daughter,' said Byrd. 'Look for anything. Photos, certificates, utility bills. I want names and dates of birth. Oh, and somebody outside was asking if "Steve" was okay. Could be the father? We need to find out who and where he is.'

As Weaver and Degnan moved away to start their search, Byrd looked thoughtful. 'Statistically, there's a good chance it was the father,' he said. 'Late-night argument with the mother, turns violent — daughter comes down in the morning and finds her mother's body.'

'Maybe.' Tanzy took a long, deep breath. 'But the girl didn't say that, did she? She said she found the killer standing over the mother in the kitchen. Wouldn't you say, "My dad's killed my mum"?'

'Sounds like she hit her head pretty badly,' Byrd told him. 'She was barely conscious when the police arrived. Maybe the dad killed the mother, saw the kid, knocked her on the head and thought he'd killed her too — did a runner. Then the girl woke up, hours later, thinking it had all just happened, and called the police.'

'But that doesn't explain why she thought there was someone in the house when she was on the phone, why she hid, why she screamed just before the police arrived, does it? And if there is a man living here, then where the hell is he now?'

6

Wednesday mid-morning
Haughton Road, Darlington

Byrd and Tanzy removed their overshoes and stepped outside for some much-needed air. The crowd at the cordon had grown, and people were asking what had happened, but PC Andrews wasn't telling them anything.

'What are you thinking?' Tanzy moved away from the door.

Before Byrd could reply, Tanzy's phone beeped with a text message.

'Is that Pip?' asked Byrd.

'Yeah.' His wife had asked him to bring milk home after he finished.

'Is Jasmine over her sick bug?'

'Yeah, much better. She didn't want to go back, but she's okay now.'

'Good.' Byrd looked around. 'We need to start knocking on doors, see who this family is.'

Not far from them, PC Eric Timms was speaking with a well-dressed woman in her early forties. The gawky officer

27

looked almost too thin, Byrd thought, but he knew Timms trained in MMA several times a week, and was packed with muscle under his uniform. Byrd certainly wouldn't fancy going toe to toe with him.

The detectives made for him, ignoring the arrows of questions from the cordon. Timms introduced the woman as Emma Slater, who lived four doors down. 'Ms Slater knows the occupier, Mia Mitchell, and her daughter. She also says Steve Mitchell, Mia's husband, lives here, but that he's often away on business.'

Byrd swivelled towards the blue Volvo on the driveway. 'Is Steve's car here now?'

'No, that's Mia's. Steve drives a black BMW. I don't know what type, but I'd recognise the registration plate if I saw it.' Emma Slater's accent indicated she was a local. 'He's been away for a couple of days. Not sure when he's due back.'

'Have you got a number for Steve?'

'Sorry, I don't. I'm not that friendly with them. We often speak in passing. They're pleasant enough. I — I just . . .' She gently moved from side to side. 'I can't believe what's happened to them. How's little Ella?'

'Ella?' Tanzy frowned.

'Yeah, their daughter.'

'We were told the girl's name is Anya,' Byrd said, frowning too. By all accounts the girl hadn't really spoken when the police had arrived, as she was drifting in and out of consciousness. But she must have been whispering when she'd called emergency services. Had the dispatcher misheard her name?

'Steve and Mia's daughter is called Ella. I should know. We've been neighbours a while now.'

Tanzy and Byrd exchanged a brief glance. Just then, a voice from the cordon reminded Byrd of something more pressing.

'Ms Slater, might we walk towards your house, please?' he suggested. 'Some of those journalists are filming.'

Emma Slater agreed with the idea.

'Did you see anything strange here this morning or last night?' asked Tanzy as they walked. 'Or hear anything unusual?'

She pushed her lips out in thought. 'No. This morning I heard the police siren and saw the car pull up. But I wouldn't have noticed anything last night — I was in my office at the back of the house till quite late, working. I'm a solicitor. Plenty of unsociable hours, unfortunately.'

Tanzy remembered the teatime dishes in the sink. 'But perhaps earlier in the evening — around teatime, late afternoon? You didn't see Steve Mitchell's BMW here then?'

'I came home from the office around six thirty, seven-ish. I work in Duke Street, so I pass their house on my way. There was no BMW when I got home.'

'Okay,' said Byrd. 'Is there anything you can tell us about Mia or Steve Mitchell? Any recent disturbances or anything unusual?'

'Around here?' She smiled. 'No. No, it's a quiet street, this one. We're quite lucky, to be honest. The people are lovely. I've been here for eight years. I think I've heard Steve and Mia argue once in all that time. That was when one of them left the door open, and their poor daughter wandered out and nearly made it to the road. They were playing hell with each other.'

Byrd nodded, listening to her closely. He peered up at her house. Behind the net curtain, he could see a child-shaped silhouette in the window above the door.

'That's my niece up there. She's dying to come out and see what all the fuss is about.' Emma flicked her wrist to see the time. 'Excuse me, I have to start work. I'm sorry I can't be any more help.'

'No, that's fine. Thank you for your time,' said Tanzy. 'You have a good day.'

Timms paused beside the Mitchells' front door after Emma had gone inside. 'Something was on there, wasn't it?'

Tanzy scowled at the exposed bracket fixed to the wall. 'Yeah. It looks like something for one of those doorbell cameras, doesn't it?'

Timms nodded. 'But now the doorbell isn't there any-more. Like it's been removed.'

'Not everyone likes them — they make a beeping noise when you walk past that drives Pip insane.'

'Would have been useful for us if it was still there.' Timms smiled at Tanzy, and they all put their overshoes back on before going into the Mitchell house. PC Degnan was descending the stairs.

'Find anything?' Byrd asked.

'Yes. Mia Mitchell, aged thirty-nine, Steve Mitchell, aged forty-one, and their daughter Ella, nine years old. They've lived here a while, judging by the collection of utility bills in the folder under their bed.'

'Any indication of their jobs?'

Degnan nodded. 'Mia's just started a business selling per-fumes from home. Steve works for a medical company called Medico. The logo is a person holding a heart. I'll see if I can contact him through them.'

'Good work.' Byrd turned to Tanzy. 'I'll have a look upstairs, Ori.'

At the top, he popped his head inside the bathroom. He went over and gently opened the wall cabinet to see if there were any pills or medications inside, but found none. The rest of the bathroom looked normal, with bath salts and shower gels on the side of the bath, a toilet to the right, and towels hanging to the left on a chrome towel rail near the vanity unit. He caught his reflection in a mirror on the wall, which confirmed he needed a haircut. *Looking more like Dad every day*, he thought.

Backing out of the bathroom onto the small landing, he could hear Tanzy talking downstairs with Forensics. He went into the next room, seeing no signs of struggle or anything out of place. He did notice the window and frowned, wondering why it had been pushed so far open. He rounded the bed, stood at the window and leaned out. Below was a slanted roof that led to a long, narrow garden enclosed by a six-foot fence.

He knew from past experience that the house backed onto a small service road, though he hadn't been down the road since these houses had been built.

Before he turned away, something caught his eye at the end of the garden. Between the vertical gaps in the fence, someone was watching him.

7

Wednesday mid-morning
Haughton Road, Darlington

In the kitchen, Tanzy crouched close to Mia Mitchell's body, but far enough away so he didn't disturb the pool of dried, clotted blood around her. He cast his gaze about the room, trying to think where the killer might have dropped the murder weapon.

He slowly stood, peered around, and pulled open a drawer. 'Already done that, Orion.' Tallow scowled at him.

Tanzy offered him a faint smile, and went over to Hope, who was inspecting the cuts on Mia's stomach. Tanzy himself had been stabbed years ago and remembered the pain like it was yesterday, but he couldn't imagine the pain this woman must have endured. Whoever killed Mia was probably smart enough to have taken the weapon with them. So far, nothing they'd seen here matched the cuts on her chest and stomach.

A moment later, Byrd pounded down the stairs, shot into the room, and raced towards the back door.

'This is a crime scene, Max, not a fucking running track!' shouted Tallow.

'Max?' Tanzy followed him out. 'Where are you going?'

Byrd was already halfway down the garden.

'I saw someone watching me,' he explained, heading for the gate at the far end.

'Who was it?'

Byrd inhaled sharply. 'I don't know. A man. Quite tall, stocky build.'

He reached the gate and pulled it open. Beyond it was a small service road.

Byrd peered around as if bewildered.

Whoever was there had gone.

* * *

The crowd out front had thinned, people bored of asking what was happening and being fobbed off by PC Andrews, who was still at the cordon, doing a grand job of keeping them back. Up the street, PC Weaver and PC Timms were knocking on doors, speaking with as many neighbours as possible.

Tanzy went left towards Weaver while Byrd headed right towards Timms.

'Anything useful?' Tanzy asked Weaver, as a neighbour closed the front door.

'Nothing so far, boss.' She turned to him, her bright blue eyes reflecting the late morning sun.

Weaver's usually straight blonde hair was curly today and looked longer than usual. Tanzy wondered if she'd had extensions, like Pip used to have. He remembered how awkward they were when they were removed. 'Which doors have you knocked?'

She pointed along the short street. 'Spoke with most of them, but some aren't in, probably at work.'

He nodded. 'We can always come back.'

They caught up with Byrd and Timms near the front of the house where the cars were parked. Timms echoed Weaver: no one had seen anything useful.

'Let's head back for a briefing,' said Tanzy. 'We'll catch up with Forensics soon.'

* * *

Ten minutes after they returned to the station, they were all seated in the meeting room on the first floor with coffee. The room was well lit, with windows along one wall offering a view of passing cars on St Cuthbert's Way. Byrd sat at the table closest to the door, listening to Tanzy's recap of the morning's events and watching the officers react to the information.

Not everybody here had been at the scene: DS Leonard had just returned from a short break away with friends, and looked fresh and raring to go. Then there was the new DCI, Mark Corbridge, who stood at the front of the room with a frown on his face. He was dressed smartly in a dark suit that would have fit him better if he were thinner. He was bald and clean-shaven and wore thin, black-framed glasses.

'Interesting start to the day,' the DCI began. 'We need to find Steve Mitchell, that's the priority.'

Byrd nodded in agreement, weighing the new DCI up. A month ago, the team had said their goodbyes to DCI Fuller, who'd had enough of Darlington. The stress of the job had been too much for him and the workload had caused him troubles at home. Byrd knew that Fuller had told Superintendent Barry Eckles that both he and Tanzy were ready to step up to DCI. But when Eckles had spoken to him, he'd been reluctant to go for the promotion. He didn't fancy overworking himself like Fuller had. Clearly Tanzy had felt the same.

Perhaps that had been a mistake. Now Corbridge had arrived and, despite his invaluable experience as a DCI in Birmingham for twelve years, Byrd didn't like him. Corbridge was unpredictable, veering from jokey to prickly all in one meeting. In his first month here, he'd had run-ins with both Byrd and Tanzy.

PC Weaver raised a slender hand.

'Yes, Amy.'

'Sir, is Steve Mitchell our number-one suspect?'

'Amy, I know as much as you,' he replied sternly. 'If not less. You've actually been to the house. Do you want to come up here and do this?'

Byrd curled his lip, noticing her face redden, and decided to stand. 'Please show our officers some courtesy, sir,' he said. 'I know you're new here in Darlington, but if you're going to stand there and try to make people feel little and embarrassed, then I'll run this meeting.'

'*Excuse me?*' the DCI said, a look of surprise on his face.

'That may be how you ran things in Birmingham, but here—' Byrd extended a finger and stabbed the air near his feet — 'is not how we do things. Whether you're the super-intendent or the night cleaner, we have respect for everyone.'

A wave of stunned silence filled the room. Byrd's face was hot but he did his best to maintain eye contact with Corbridge. He'd overstepped the mark. *That's what months of sleepless nights do for your career*, he thought ruefully.

'You know,' the DCI said in his Brummie accent, 'that's the first time a DI has ever spoken to me like that.'

Byrd nodded, waiting for the repercussions.

'And do you know what?'

'What's that?' asked Byrd.

'I love it.' He nodded twice. 'For you to defend your team is admirable. And I respect that, Max.'

Byrd bobbed his head, but held his gaze.

Corbridge turned away from Byrd and focused on Weaver. 'Amy, I'm sorry if I made you uncomfortable. I apologise.'

She awkwardly smiled but said nothing.

'Thank you, Max. Sometimes I need reining in. Let's proceed.'

Satisfied with himself, Byrd lowered in his seat beside Tanzy, who couldn't help but smile.

'So, what do we know?' the DCI asked, moving on like nothing had happened.

Before anyone answered, the door opened. PC Josh Andrews entered. He'd stayed at the house with Forensics to secure the scene.

'Better late than never,' said Corbridge.

Andrews paused at the door.

'Sit down, Josh,' Byrd told him, knowing the DCI was on the wind-up.

Andrews stood in the doorway. 'Sir, there's someone here to see us.'

'Who?'

'Steve Mitchell. He turned up at the house and didn't know what was happening. I've brought him here to be interviewed. I — I wasn't sure what else to do.'

DCI Corbridge nodded. 'Good work, Josh.' He looked over to Byrd and Tanzy. 'You two want to take this one?'

Tanzy and Byrd stood and headed for the door without a word.

Wednesday afternoon
Darlington police station

The man pacing the interview room wasn't quite what Tanzy had expected. Steve Mitchell was tall, at least six feet, and physically athletic. He was clean-shaven and wore thin, blue, square-framed glasses that, if anything, made him look younger than forty-one, which they'd learned from the documents back at the house.

'Mr Mitchell?' Tanzy projected his voice across the small room.

Steve Mitchell jumped and spun towards them, clearly on edge. 'What on earth is going on? Why are the police at my house? Why are—'

'Mr Mitchell, please take a seat.' Tanzy motioned to one of the chairs at the table. Steve complied and the detectives sat opposite him.

'Mr Mitchell,' Byrd started, 'can we start by—'

'Where are my wife and daughter?' he interrupted.

Byrd collected himself. 'My name is Detective Inspector Max Byrd.' He motioned to Tanzy. 'And this is my colleague,

Detective Inspector Orion Tanzy. Can *we* start by asking a couple of quick questions?'

Mitchell shook his head. 'No, I'm asking the questions here. Where is my family?'

'This will go much smoother if we can communicate,' Tanzy replied. 'We'll get to know what's going on much sooner, and it will benefit everyone.'

Mitchell glared at Tanzy. 'Fine. Ask away.'

'Can we see some identification, please?' asked Tanzy.

Mitchell showed them his driving licence. The photo looked years old.

'Happy?'

Byrd nodded. 'I understand you weren't at home last night, Mr Mitchell? Where have you been?'

'I've been away on business in London for three days. I'm a medical salesman. I've literally just got back.'

'What is it you sell?'

Mitchell sighed, obviously feeling his time was being wasted. 'I sell medical equipment to hospitals around the UK. Sometimes I'm away, doing presentations to various hospitals and medical centres, but this particular conference spanned three days.' He took a heavy breath. 'Now, please, tell me what's going on.'

'We received a phone call from your house this morning,' said Tanzy, 'saying a man was in your house. And that this man attacked your wife.'

Mitchell gasped, leaning forward, his hands coming up to his chin. 'God . . . Is — Is Mia okay?'

There was an uncomfortable silence between them.

'Your wife, Mia, is . . . I'm very sorry to inform you, but she's dead, Mr Mitchell.'

Mitchell's eyes glazed over as he placed both hands over his mouth. 'What?'

The detectives waited, allowing the unbearable news to sink in.

'She's . . . dead? How?'

'Our forensic team believe she was attacked with a knife.'

'There's something strange, though,' added Byrd. 'Despite what the caller said, Forensics believe your wife, at the time she was discovered, had already been dead for over twelve hours.'

'That's impossible. I spoke with her on the phone last night. She was making something to eat.' Mitchell shook his head. 'Where's Ella?' he asked, almost in a whisper.

'She's at Darlington Memorial Hospital. We found her hiding in a wardrobe, but she's had a nasty bump to the head.'

Steve scowled. 'Is she okay, though?' He peered up through gaps between his fingers. 'I need to see her.'

'We'll take you there, Mr Mitchell,' Byrd said. 'I know it'll be difficult, but we'll need you to identify your wife too.'

Steve Mitchell dropped his head into his hands again. 'Okay.'

'I'll call the hospital to let them know we're on our way.'

9

Wednesday afternoon
Darlington Memorial Hospital

On their drive to Darlington Memorial Hospital, Steve Mitchell sat silently in the back of the car. Byrd glanced at him several times in the mirror, but he seemed in a daze, obviously digesting the news about what had happened to his wife and daughter.

Byrd parked in one of the few remaining spots in the car park, and they made their way over to the entrance, feeling the sudden change of temperature in the air. The sky above had become darker, and rain was imminent.

The sliding doors parted with a *shhhh*, and they felt the heater's warmth above the door, blowing hot air down into the entrance area. Inside, they passed a paramedic standing beside an elderly lady on a trolley, her face covered with a ventilator, a sad look in her eyes that told the detectives whatever illness she had, she'd been through hell with it.

Byrd had already spoken to the pathologist, Arnold Hemsley, who was expecting them, so they quickly signed in and were allowed through the automatic double doors. Byrd looked back at Steve Mitchell, whose eyes were streaming with tears as they walked down the corridor. Up ahead, a twenty-something dark-haired woman wearing a white lab coat flashed them a welcoming smile, expecting their arrival.

She led them down a series of corridors to a metal door that was open a few inches. Inside, they could hear light footsteps and the pinging sound of small metallic tools being picked up and dropped. The woman pushed the door open slowly.

'Dr Hemsley? The police are here.'

'Ah, come in, please,' he replied somewhere inside the dark room.

They entered to see Arnold Hemsley standing beside a body on the trolley before him inside the square, brightly lit room. Mia Mitchell was completely covered. Byrd kept his focus on Steve Mitchell. Often, in murder scenarios, there was a high chance the spouse was involved. Byrd studied his face and the way he moved. If Mitchell showed any sign of guilt, Byrd was confident he'd spot it.

Hemsley was a slight, bald man in his fifties who'd been hardened by a lifetime of working long hours and eating very little. Smiling thinly, he revealed his cigarette- and coffee-stained teeth, and the crow's feet lining his eyes deepened. He placed the surgical instrument down on a narrow metal stand, then walked around the table that Mia Mitchell occupied, removing his latex glove and extending a hand. Byrd and Tanzy shook it firmly. Byrd's father had always said you could judge a man's character by his handshake.

Steve Mitchell was frozen to the spot, staring at the body under the white cover.

'This is obviously very difficult for you, Mr Mitchell. Please take as long as you need.' Hemsley's voice was soft and carried an air of authority and understanding. 'I will pull back the cover and reveal only her face in a moment. We just need a simple nod to confirm this is your wife, Mia Mitchell.'

Steve Mitchell stepped closer to the trolley.

The pathologist removed the cover.

Mitchell's eyes widened, but he didn't look away. 'Yes, that's Mia.'

'You can have a few moments with her, but please don't touch her,' said Hemsley, as he backed away a few steps. The detectives did the same out of respect.

After several minutes of absolute silence in the room, Steve slowly turned to Byrd and Tanzy, tears falling down his cheeks. 'I'm ready to go and see Ella now.'

The detectives thanked the pathologist and left the room, finding the female assistant, who walked them back to the small reception area.

Tanzy kept an eye on Mitchell in the main corridor, who appeared a little grey and unsteady on his feet. Tanzy stayed close in case he needed physical support.

'This way,' said Byrd softly, leading them to the lifts. It was hot inside and it felt like there was no air to breathe, so when the doors opened, it was a relief to all of them. They hung a right towards the children's ward, and Tanzy spoke into the intercom, explaining who he was and why they were there.

The door buzzed open, and they went in. A paediatrician appeared from the room to the left and guided them down the hall to ward number four. The distinctive smell of hospital food and disinfectant lingered in the air. The doctor paused outside the room and pointed through the internal window.

'It's quiet today, so it's just her in there. Probably for the best — she's very jumpy. She has a concussion and wasn't in a state to talk when she first came in, but she's beginning to improve.'

The girl lay on her back with her head and upper body slightly raised, propped up by the incline of the hospital bed and several pillows for added comfort. She was watching the grey blanket of clouds gently floating by through the vast window that spanned the room's length. Byrd noted she appeared in good health.

'Her right wrist is potentially fractured, so we've given her something to numb the pain and have elevated it for now.

We'll need to send her for an X-ray to know for sure. Besides that, she's recovering from shock and needs rest to recover from the head injury, so she shouldn't be questioned for too long.' He raised a hand to check his watch. 'Before I go, though, are you aware she was wearing a GPS ankle tracker?'

Byrd frowned. 'An ankle tracker?'

The doctor nodded. 'Appears to be an anklet, but it's a tracker. We had to remove it to treat an injury on her leg, but it was designed not to be removed by the wearer.'

'The anklet? No, I thought it was jewellery. It didn't look like a court-sanctioned monitor,' he added. 'Have you come across anything like that before?'

'Not one that was so difficult to remove. But I've seen a few like it — they're fitness monitors, usually. Counting steps, heart rate, distance covered, that sort of thing.'

'Thanks, doc.'

The GPS tracker certainly raised a question, but Byrd was happy to see the girl they'd been worrying about. She had a round face with long dark hair that fell down over her shoulders. Byrd thought about both the emotional and physical pain she must be going through.

Then he realised something was off. Most parents would have shot in there by now. But Mitchell was still standing next to him, staring at the child in the bed, a look of despair on his face.

'What's the matter?' asked Byrd.

'There — there has to be some mistake,' whispered Mitchell. 'That girl in there? She's not my daughter.'

10

'She isn't Ella?' repeated Byrd.

'That girl lying on that bed is definitely not Ella. She's not my daughter. I don't know who she is or what she was doing in my house, but it isn't Ella.'

'Are you absolutely sure?' Byrd asked, but he knew Mitchell wasn't faking his horror. He remembered the confusion over the child's name. The call dispatcher hadn't misheard after all.

'I know what my daughter looks like.' Mitchell produced his phone. 'Let me show you.' He navigated through the photos. 'Here, look. This is Ella.'

Byrd focused on the photo of Steve, Mia and their daughter Ella. They were on a beach, smiling at the camera with the sun and sea behind them. Byrd had to admit the girl lying on the hospital bed was not the one in the photo.

It didn't happen very often, but he was lost for words.

Mitchell pointed to the room. 'Who the hell is that, and what was she doing in my house?'

'Could she be a friend of Ella's?'

Mitchell huffed. 'I don't know. I just want to know where Ella is.'

'Let's see if we can find out,' Byrd said.

* * *

By the time Byrd had handed Mitchell over to a family liaison officer, Tanzy had called in social services and managed to get a social worker assigned as an appropriate adult so they could question the child. When Byrd got back to the room, Tanzy was perched in the uncomfortable chair beside the bed talking with the girl, while Pamela Walker, a social worker whom Byrd had met on previous cases, looked on. As Byrd and Pamela shook hands, Tanzy smiled up at them.

'This is Anya,' he told Byrd. 'Nine years old, from Warrington.'

'What's your surname, Anya?' Byrd asked gently.

A small frown. 'I . . . I don't know.'

'That's the concussion,' Tanzy explained. 'Don't worry, Anya, the doctor tells me it'll come back to you soon.'

'But I need to remember *now*,' she whispered. 'I need my dad to come and get me. If I stay here *he'll* find me.'

'Who will — your dad?'

'No, the nasty man,' she said, almost folding into herself. 'He makes us do bad things at the big house.'

'What man?'

'The man who knocked at the door and fought with Ella's mam.'

'No one's going to find you. You're safe here,' Tanzy reassured her.

'I just want to go home.'

'What happened after the man knocked at the door, Anya?' asked Byrd.

'I was upstairs with Ella. Then the man came in . . .' Her face was grey, and Tanzy wondered if they had asked too many questions when she was supposed to be resting. 'But I didn't want to do it. He's trying to make us do things we don't want to.'

'What was the man making you do?'

'He wanted me to help him kill them . . .'

11

The day before
Tuesday late afternoon
Haughton Road, Darlington

It was just after 5 p.m. when Ella opened the back door to the garden.

'Where you going, Ella?' Mia asked, looking at her from the oven.

'Just outside, Mam.'

'Have you cleaned your room?'

Ella's pet lip appeared, fully aware she hadn't completed the only task her mother had given her.

'Ella, go tidy your toys up like a good girl. It'll save you having to do them later.'

Defiant and trailing her feet, Ella slowly moved away from the back door, through the kitchen, and up the stairs.

Less than twenty minutes later, Ella appeared in the kitchen.

'All done?' asked Mia, standing at the cooker.

'Yes, Mam,' replied Ella, traipsing past her, still obviously in a mood about it.

Mia wandered over to the back door and watched her daughter in the garden, feeling content. Their garden was long and narrow. The section closest to the house was a small decking area with a rectangular table and a seating arrangement over to the right. Beside one of the chairs was a heat lamp, and next to the table was a firepit with black ashes at the bottom. The rest was grass, covered sparingly in Ella's toys: footballs, a hula hoop, a skipping rope. The list went on. Towards the back was an activity set, including a slide, swing, and monkey bars. She watched Ella head straight for the swing and smiled as she gently swayed back and forth.

Mia turned back to the kitchen, focusing on making their tea and thinking about Steve, whom she'd just been talking with on the phone. He was working long hours and phoned when he could, which Mia appreciated. He was coming back tomorrow, and she couldn't wait.

* * *

Ella was swinging gently when she heard something behind her. She put her feet down and turned to find a girl of about her own age standing on the other side of the back fence, watching her through one of the gaps. The gate in the fence provided access to the rear parking area, something the Mitchells seldom used for their own car, as they had plenty of space out front.

'Hello?' Ella got off the swing.

The girl silently stared through one of the gaps.

Ella didn't recognise her. 'What's your name?'

The girl with long dark hair and brown eyes smiled at her but remained silent.

'My name's Ella,' she told the girl. 'What's yours?'

'Anya.'

'Do I know you?'

Anya shook her head.

'Where do you live?'

48

Anya turned and pointed to the house behind her.

'I've never seen you before.'

'We just moved in,' Anya told her. 'Can I play with you?'

Ella nodded but wondered why her voice was so shaky. 'Are you okay? You seem scared.'

The girl shook her head. 'I just want a friend to play with. Can I come in?'

'Erm, I don't know. I'll have to ask my mam. Wait here.' Ella skipped to the kitchen and asked her mother if the girl could play in her garden. Frowning, Mia peered down the garden, seeing the outline of the girl just beyond the fence. 'Do you know her?'

'She's called Anya. She lives in the house at the back. She's just moved in.'

Mia couldn't exactly say no — she was always telling her to make friends at school. She nodded. 'Yes, okay then, Ella. She can come in and play for a little bit. Go have fun and make a friend.'

Ella smiled widely, ran down the garden and unlocked the gate. Anya, her new friend, walked in with a big smile on her face and a sparkle in her eyes. She briefly looked back at the man watching her through the fence.

He slowly nodded and watched her closely with narrowed eyes.

12

The day before
Tuesday late afternoon
Haughton Road, Darlington

Anya and Ella played at the bottom of the garden, taking turns on the slide and swing. Anya asked what school Ella went to and the name of her teacher. Ella told her about their class project, making a mini garden using crafts, and that the winner would get a prize and a certificate.

Ella didn't have many friends around Haughton Road. It wasn't exactly a place where kids could play out on the street, what with the constant flow of unforgiving traffic. She had wished many times for a little sister to play with.

She noticed something around Anya's neck. 'What's that?'

'Oh, this?' She raised a small hand, delicately pinching the necklace between her thumb and index finger. 'My mam gave me it.'

'That's nice.'

'Aww, I'm so hungry.' Anya rubbed her tummy, glancing behind her towards the fence again.

'What do you keep looking at?' asked Ella. 'Who's back there?'

50

'No one. I . . .' She trailed off. 'I'm just hungry, that's all.'

Ella frowned. 'Do you want to come in for tea?' She pointed to her house. 'I can ask my mam if you like?'

Anya nodded. 'Could I?'

'I'll ask.' Ella dashed up the garden and into the kitchen, almost out of breath. Mia wasn't there but came in from the dining room a moment later, holding a pack of wipes and a bottle of cleaning spray.

'Ella,' Mia said, then stopped. 'Where's your friend?'

'She's in the garden. She said she was hungry, Mam. Can she have tea here?'

Mia thought about it, then gave her daughter a slow nod. What would be the harm?

'Of course. Go ask her if she likes spaghetti bolognese. If so, tell her tea will be done in twenty minutes. Are you having fun out there?'

Ella, without answering, excitedly dashed back out into the garden.

'My mam said you can have tea at ours.'

'Thank you.'

'We're having spaghetti bolognese.'

Anya looked behind her again to the fence.

'What's wrong?' Her new friend appeared upset about something. 'You never had spag bol?'

The girl shrugged and started swinging more while Ella went on the slide. The sun had dipped behind a passing cloud, and the garden was suddenly a shade darker and a few degrees colder.

Anya lowered her hand and lightly touched her anklet.

'What's that?'

'Have you got any scissors?' she whispered.

'Scissors. Why?'

Anya turned back to the fence once more. 'It doesn't matter.'

They played a little more, again taking turns on the slide and swing.

'What's that?' Anya asked.

51

Ella followed her gaze and frowned. 'Swing ball?'

Anya nodded.

'You've never played swing ball?'

'No . . .'

'It's so much fun — want to play?' Ella approached a small rectangular garden box by the fence, lifted the lid, and grabbed two plastic rackets. 'Here, take this.'

The girl took one. 'How do I do it?'

They played swing ball until Mia leaned out and called them in. On their way up to the house, Ella asked, 'So what school do you go to? You didn't tell me.'

But Anya didn't seem to hear her.

'What's your name?' Mia was standing at the cooker, stirring the mince and sauce in the pan with a wooden spatula. The smell of herbs and pepper lingered in the air.

'Anya,' she whispered, her voice almost not reaching Mia. The girl appeared suddenly shy, stopping near the door, her arms down by her side, her hands knotted in a ball.

'Hey, come on in, don't be shy. Where would you like to sit?'

Ella walked past her, stopping at a seat at the table. 'I normally sit here, Anya. But seeing as you're our guest, you can have my seat for today.'

The girl thanked her and shuffled towards the table, cautiously pulling out the chair and eyeing the empty plates and cutlery in front of her.

'Where's your dad?' she asked Ella.

'Oh, he works away,' Mia said, concentrating on the mince in the hot pan. 'He'll be back tomorrow.'

* * *

Once Anya and the girl had disappeared into the house, the man decided to make his move. He'd enjoyed watching them play, laughing, and getting along so well — the plan was taking shape.

It wouldn't replace what he'd lost, but he could certainly try to make things more like the way they were. Maybe Anya had given him a second chance, a chance to carry on doing what he'd done for so long.

Time would tell, of course. He was merely experimenting at this stage.

He backed away from the fence, walked down the small service road, made a left, and walked around the front of the house.

Confident the plan would work, he knocked on the door.

* * *

The girls spoke quietly among themselves while Mia plated up the food, occasionally checking her phone as she did so. She'd started an online account only last week, selling fragrances and perfumes from a merchant near Doncaster, who'd informed her via email that he'd shipped the first batch, arriving tomorrow.

'I just need the toilet, Mam.' Ella pushed her chair out.

'You know where it is,' Mia joked, smiling as she left. 'Do you like onions, Anya?'

Anya shook her head. 'I need the toilet too.'

'It's okay, just head up the stairs. Ella will show you where it is.'

Mia smiled as the little stranger followed Ella. While preparing the final touches to the meal, she thought about Steve. She knew his job was demanding and she and Ella missed him dearly when he was away, but it wasn't so bad. One of her friends' husbands worked in the army and was barely ever there, so she considered herself lucky he was only away possibly a few times a month at the most, not months at a time, only being able to speak with them on the phone or on Facetime.

She carried the plates over to the table, looking forward to seeing the girls enjoy the meal. She loved making spaghetti bolognese. It was so simple but satisfying.

A knock at the door pulled her from her happy thoughts.

'Just a second,' she said out of habit, not that the person knocking would be able to hear her. She walked down the hallway. 'You girls all right up there?' She angled her head towards the stairs.

'Yeah, Mam,' replied Ella from the landing.

She unlocked the door and saw a man standing on the step. He was thin and looked to be in his late forties, with wispy hair and an ageing face.

'Hey,' Mia said. 'Can I help you?'

'Is my daughter here?'

'Anya?'

He nodded. 'She said she was playing out, but I'm unsure if she was playing in your garden. It's hard to judge which house it is from the back.'

'Oh, yeah, she's here. I'm just about to give her some tea. Is that all right?'

The man nodded. 'Oh yeah, that's fine. She's a good little eater. I hope you've made plenty.'

Mia held the door half open, staring at him.

'Could I just see her for a moment? I need to tell her something.'

Mia opened the door further. 'Sure, come in. She's upstairs with Ella.' She moved back so he could enter, then called up the stairs. 'Anya, your dad is here to see you.'

* * *

'You need to help me,' Anya quickly told Ella, joining her inside the bathroom. 'I'm in danger.'

Ella frowned, unsure what to say.

'Please, he'll be coming for me.'

'Who will?' asked Ella, worry plastered over her face.

'He's making me do things I don't want to. I need to get away from him and get help. Have you got a phone?'

'I don't have a phone. Do you not have one?'

Anya shook her head.

Ella narrowed her eyes and rocked her head back in thought. 'Mam's is downstairs probably. She has a landline in her bedroom, but she doesn't use it. Where's the man?'

'He was watching us in the garden. He wants me to do something bad, but I can't.

'What does he want—'

The knock at the door downstairs silenced her.

'Shhhh.' Anya raised a quick finger to her lips. She lightly shoved Ella out of the way, gently opened the bathroom door, and crept out onto the landing. Peering around the edge of the banister, she watched Mia Mitchell open the front door. 'Oh, no . . .'

* * *

Mia had shouted but heard nothing back.

'Anya, your dad is here. He needs to tell you something.'

'Where is she?'

She turned to the stranger standing in her hallway. 'She's upstairs.'

Mia took a few steps up. 'Ella? Anya?'

'He isn't my father!' she heard Anya shout. 'He's a bad man. He's going to hurt you.'

Mia scowled. 'He's a what man?'

'Don't let him inside the house!' screamed Ella, appearing at the top of the stairs with Anya. They both looked petrified. 'He's here to hurt us! He's killed people!'

The door slammed. Mia turned back. The man was at her shoulder. He barged into her, knocking her hard into the wall. Anya and Ella both screamed as her face struck the fancy wooden panelling, causing a sudden flash in her vision, rattling her head. She fell back onto the carpet.

'Anya, get down here!' shouted the man, taking the first step, then the second.

'No, no, no,' mumbled Mia, opening her eyes and clambering to her feet. She threw her arms around the man's waist and pulled him back so hard he came crashing back down on top of her, banging the back of his head on the edge of the unit positioned under the hanging coats. His weight knocked the wind out of her lungs — it felt like a piano had fallen on top of her.

He yelped in pain and tried to wriggle free from her grip, but she held firm, frantic hands clinging on.

'Mam!' screamed Ella at the top of the stairs.

Mia had surprised herself with her actions, but her daughter's voice encouraged her, so she tried to get back to her feet while holding onto him. She needed to stop this man from getting to her daughter and Anya.

'Get the fuck off me.' He swatted his clenched fists at her grip.

Mia lost hold of him and he dashed for the stairs again. She grabbed an umbrella and swung it hard into the side of his knee with so much force that she heard something crack.

He groaned and toppled back down towards her. This time, she dashed out of his way and pounded down the hallway towards the kitchen, away from him. She needed her phone.

She spotted it on the worktop near one of the sauce-covered spatulas and charged towards it. Behind her, she heard his wild footfall, chasing her down.

'Shit, shit!' she screamed as she grabbed the phone. And that's when she felt the hot, searing pain. At first, she didn't understand it, couldn't work out what it was. The feeling was so alien she couldn't associate it with anything she'd felt before. With wide eyes, she looked down at his hand, holding the knife, half of the blade inside her stomach. There was blood on her T-shirt, dripping onto the white tiled floor.

The man removed the knife and continued stabbing her over and over again, until she heard nothing more.

* * *

After killing the woman, he stood studying her lifeless body. Blood was starting to spread over the white tiles. Her eyes were open, staring vacantly at the ceiling above. It was a beautiful sight. Not exactly how he'd planned it, but this was an experiment.

He breathed deeply, and closed his eyes to cherish the moment.

Sudden sounds upstairs brought him back to the present. Footsteps pounded frantically down the stairs.

'Shit,' he muttered. 'The girls.'

In a panic, he dropped the knife and dashed out of the kitchen, saw them at the front door, desperately trying to open it. He charged for them, managing to grab Anya before she escaped, and pulled her back into the house, her head catching the side of the door frame. In doing so, he tripped on the hallway rug and released her, falling against the stairs and catching his head off the second step with a clatter.

'Fuck!' he screamed.

He found his feet and scrambled outside. *Shit*, he thought, *they've gone*. The sun had set behind the college opposite. Staring left and right, he couldn't see the girls anywhere on the small road in front of the row of houses.

'Where the fuck are they?'

The last thing he wanted to do was to lose Anya. If she told anyone what she knew, he'd be in serious trouble.

Bringing his hands to his face in frustration, he saw the blood on his palms and froze. The woman's blood from the kitchen.

'God,' he whispered, looking around to see if anyone had noticed him or the blood. Dozens of cars were passing on the main road, battling through rush hour. Lucky he was set back a little. He needed to get away now before someone spotted him. Shoving his hands into his pockets, he briskly walked up the street and back to his van. He'd look for Anya later.

13

Tanzy and Byrd's stomachs turned at what Anya had told them: that the man had wanted her to help him kill them.

'Why did he want you to do that?' asked Byrd.

'He makes me do bad things. I don't want to.' Anya's face looked even greyer. A passing doctor paused at the door and came in and checked her chart.

'Did he say what would happen if you didn't do as he said?' Byrd asked quickly.

She nodded three times.

'You can tell us,' Tanzy said encouragingly.

'That he'd never let me leave. I hated the big house.'

'What's the big hou—?'

'I'm sorry, Detectives,' the doctor said, 'but you'll have to save your questions for another time. This girl is very sick and she needs to rest.'

'Just one last thing, please. Anya, do you know where Ella is?'

She shook her head. She spoke in a rush, as if she was afraid she would forget it all. 'Ella's mam ran into the kitchen,

58

and we ran downstairs and out the front door to escape. But he grabbed me and pulled me back. I hit my head on the door frame. When I got outside, I couldn't find Ella. I felt really sick so I hid behind some bins. I could hear him calling my name, so I just stayed really still — I think I passed out. When I woke I was really cold, and it was dark, and I realised I'd lost my necklace, so I went back into the house. And that's when I heard someone in the kitchen. I saw him, holding a knife. I went upstairs and called the police.'

'Ori,' Byrd said. 'A word outside, please.'

When they were outside the door, they turned to each other, both of them pale. Tanzy said what they were both thinking. 'We need people looking for Ella. She's out there alone somewhere. She'll be so scared right now.'

14

At that moment, Pamela leaned out of the room. She was about fifty, dressed smartly in grey and black. She looked anxious, but, as Byrd recalled from previous meetings, that was her usual expression.

'I expect you'll be on your way now?' She managed to make it sound like an accusation. 'I'd better stay and monitor Anya, in the absence of a parent. If she feels well enough later on I'd like to interview her, hear the story from her side, and see what she remembers of her family and living situation. Is there anything you need to ask her that you haven't already?'

'We'd like to know the same as you,' Byrd said, scratching his chin. 'Perhaps you'll have more luck than us in getting the particulars. Like who, and where, her family are. Full names. And what she meant by "the big house" — you heard that?'

Pamela nodded. 'I'm not promising anything.'

'Understood. We have team members contacting Warrington police to see if they have any missing children that fit her description. I'll keep you informed.'

'She's scared,' Pamela told them. 'It's not just trauma. This man she was talking about really frightens her. She thinks he's coming for her.'

'A constable will stay on the ward to keep an eye on her. We'll give her some space, let her get her X-ray, and be back later for an update.'

Pamela thanked them and returned to the ward while Tanzy and Byrd lingered in the corridor.

PC Timms arrived less than ten minutes later, appearing through the door at the end of the corridor.

'Thanks for coming, Eric.'

'She in there?' Timms asked.

Tanzy nodded, then gave him a basic briefing on the situation.

'We would appreciate you staying here until you're relieved,' Tanzy added. 'We don't know how this will pan out. We need to brief the team about Ella Mitchell back at the station. We've already sent the photo of her to our media outlets, so they'll be posting about that anytime now.'

* * *

As they were driving back to the station, Tanzy's phone rang. It was PC Degnan.

'Boss, we've had a call from someone living three houses down from the Mitchells on Haughton Road — one of the ones who was out when we were knocking on doors. They say they have a camera in their garden, which can see into the Mitchells' garden. They have something important to show us.'

'What's on it?'

'They're asking for you to go to the house. It's something you need to see.'

Tanzy hung up. 'We need to head back to the house, Max.'

Byrd frowned his way. 'How come?'

'We might just have something.'

15

Susan Brown's house had a similar layout to the Mitchells', but the hallway was dated. Nasty patterned wallpaper lined the walls and swirls of Artex covered the ceiling, and a musty smell, like decades-old wood polish, pervaded the house. But as they followed her into the kitchen they found it was newer, recently installed.

'I'm sorry if you knocked before,' Susan said. 'I was sleeping — been on night shift. Emma, one of my neighbours, told me what happened.' She shook her head at the awful news. 'Can I get you a coffee or something?'

'No, thanks,' replied Byrd.

She looked at Tanzy, who shook his head but smiled politely.

'So, we had a camera put up last year after having some trouble with some teenagers next door. I checked the footage to see if I could see anything that would be helpful to you.' As she spoke, she was already firing up her iPad.

'Here we go.' She angled the screen so they could see better. 'This was yesterday teatime.' She pressed play.

'See her?' said Susan, pointing.

They followed her finger. A girl was playing on a swing towards the right of the screen.

'That's Ella Mitchell. Lovely kid, she is.'

'The camera covers a lot of ground, doesn't it?'

She briefly smiled at Tanzy's observation. 'Top-of-the-range piece of kit.' She focused on the screen. 'Oh, watch this . . .'

On the footage, Ella moved slowly towards the back fence of the garden and stood still for a while.

'Is she talking with someone?' Byrd frowned, leaning closer.

'Just wait . . .'

They observed Ella run back up the garden, and then a moment later, she ran back to the fence again.

'Watch what she does,' Susan said.

Ella opened the rear gate, and another girl — Anya — entered the garden.

'They play for a bit, and then it seems they go inside the house.'

'Does that other girl look familiar to you, Susan?' asked Byrd.

'No, I don't think so.'

'Did they come back out?'

'No, we don't see them again. The other girl must have left the house by the front door.' She offered a slight shrug.

'Interesting,' said Tanzy.

'There's something else you need to see.' Susan clicked another file and opened it, starting from midnight. She moved the cursor forward on the time bar to just after 9 a.m. earlier that day. 'Now watch.'

On the screen, a man appeared through the garden gate.

'The gate must have been left open,' noted Tanzy.

'So, it looks like he goes in.' She skipped forward nearly ten minutes. 'And then he comes back out a few minutes later, running towards the fence as if he's panicked about something.'

'He's not there very long, is he?' Byrd said.

'No.'

'When he comes into the picture again, it looks as if he's jumping down,' Tanzy said. 'Rather than just coming out of the back door.'

'So, he went upstairs, panicked when Anya screamed and he heard the police arriving, and left through the window.'

'Looks like it.'

The detectives thought back to what Forensics had said about Mia Mitchell, that her body's condition suggested she'd been dead longer than twelve hours. Unfortunately, this camera only proved that Anya arrived yesterday at teatime, and there was a man there the next morning. It didn't confirm Anya's story about someone coming into the house through the front door and murdering Mia Mitchell.

With Susan's blessing, they grabbed a copy of the footage and returned to Byrd's car.

Tanzy put his seat belt on. 'Interesting this, Max.'

They set off towards the station.

'Either that man killed Mia and then came back the next day . . .'

'Or he wasn't the one who killed Mia Mitchell,' Byrd finished. 'He ran out of that house in a panic — I'd say he wasn't expecting to see Mia's body in the kitchen.'

'But he knew about the gate. And whoever Anya was afraid of must have seen her go into that garden.' Tanzy sighed. 'We need to find the man who was there last night.'

Byrd smiled thinly.

'What is it?'

'I agree that's how it seems,' replied Byrd. 'But the camera only shows a man there this morning. There is no definitive evidence suggesting a man was there last night. The only account is that of a traumatised nine-year-old girl who sounds like she's telling tall tales — light on description, heavy on accusations.'

'I wouldn't hedge my bets on the nine-year-old being able to do this, Max.'

Byrd shrugged. 'I'm not saying that, but who's to say it wasn't a woman?'

'Maybe.'

'Regardless of what really happened, based on the girl's head injury, can we trust what she's saying right now?' Byrd glanced Tanzy's way. 'Mia Mitchell can't confirm her story. And without speaking with Ella Mitchell, she can't confirm it either, wherever she may be.'

That got Tanzy thinking.

Byrd shrugged. 'He's not saying that, just that maybe it was a woman.'

'Maybe.'

'Regardless of who, really, it happened. So if on the one hand injuries cause a rape when she's completely not guilty . . .' Mia stared at him, needing the next bit '. . . then why not rape, when she's guilty, he gets a gentler sentence, anyway. It may be.'

'That got your thinking.'

16

Wednesday morning
Haughton Road, Darlington

Corey Tills watched the flashing dot on his phone's screen. Anya was nearby, but as he looked at the houses in front of him, he couldn't work out which one she was in. He moved along the short row.

'There,' he said.

He studied the house for a moment and saw no signs of life in any of the windows. The dot on his screen had been hit and miss most of yesterday, coming and going, never settling in one place. He couldn't stand watching this dot — it made his head ache. He must have dozed off watching it yesterday evening, and then woke up with a terrible sick feeling that Anya had been on her own all night and it was all his fault. Not his fault, he reminded himself. Selena's fault. Ever since Selena had got him into this mess he'd not been sleeping properly. If only he could just call the police and come clean, get Anya to safety. But then he'd go to jail for preventing a burial or assisting an offender, or perhaps even for manslaughter, wouldn't he? He'd googled the possibilities often enough in the many sleepless nights since the hit-and-run in Warrington.

But right now, the dot was unmoving and finally stable. It looked like she was in a house rather that out on the street. He found a map of his location and zoomed in, noticing a road behind the house. He returned to his car and drove around the back, parking in the small area between the two houses.

He got out and peered through the gap in the fence at the house he thought it was. Confident there was no one watching, he opened the gate and made his way up the garden, keeping his eyes on neighbouring windows in case anyone spotted him.

Reaching the back door, he checked his screen again. The flashing dot was close to his phone's location. He lowered the phone and tried the handle. The door opened.

'Bingo.'

He came to a sharp halt, seeing the woman on the tiled floor before him. Her body was twisted, her chest and stomach peppered with knife wounds, surrounded by a pool of dark, curdled blood.

'What the fuck?' he whispered.

There was a knife beside the woman. Corey studied it for a moment — had Anya done this? He bent down and picked it up. Judging by the colour of the woman's skin, the body looked like it had been there a while.

He heard a sound from somewhere in the house.

'Anya, is that you?' he said slowly, drawing out the word 'you'.

He stared into the hallway. Then, a flurry of feet climbed the stairs.

'Fuck's sake, Anya,' he whispered. He put the knife into his coat pocket and headed for the hallway. 'Anya?'

He went upstairs slowly. Reaching the top, he popped his head into the bathroom, then checked the room at the back, seeing a double bed up against the left wall, a television fixed to the chimney breast opposite and, through the open window in front of him, the garden he'd just walked up to gain access to the property.

He opened the door to the next room.

'Anya, are you in here?'

The only place she could be hiding was the wardrobe. Corey reached for the handle and cautiously pulled it open. Inside, Anya held a phone to her ear, presumably speaking with someone.

Corey frowned at her. 'Anya . . . where the hell have you been?'

She let out a scream that made his blood curdle, and he was forced to cover his ears with both hands.

'Jesus, Anya . . .'

Seconds later, police sirens were heard coming from Haughton Road. He looked out and saw a marked Astra pull up outside the house.

'Shit!'

Two uniformed police constables jumped out and raced for the door.

Remembering the dead woman lying in the kitchen, he dashed out of the room and into the back bedroom, where he pushed the window open and clumsily escaped onto the kitchen roof, nearly falling as he did so, and dropped down onto the decking.

He ran back to his car.

Once inside, his phone rang.

'Yeah?' he answered, panting hard, wondering if he'd been seen.

'Have you got her?' Selena asked.

'No. The police have just turned up. I escaped before they came in.' His heart was beating so quickly he could barely get a breath. 'God, that was close.'

'Corey, where is she?'

'She was in the wardrobe at the front of the house. She just screamed, and the police turned up.'

'Is she okay?'

'She was shaking.'

'Why didn't you grab her? We need her back here.'

'Because a dead woman who'd been stabbed about twenty times was lying on the kitchen floor. The place is a fucking mess.'

Silence.

'You there?' Corey pulled the phone away from his head and checked the signal strength.

'Did she kill the woman?'

'Well, it certainly wasn't me.'

'Was there anyone else in the house?'

'Not that I saw,' he replied. 'Listen, I'll have to go. The police will flood the place once they find the dead woman.'

'We need her back here, Corey. If she doesn't come back, there'll be hell to pay.'

'I know, I know,' he said. 'The tracker has been all over during the night, but she didn't look in great shape — I'm sure they'll take her to hospital. I'll get her out of there.'

'Just make sure you do. If you lose her—'

'If *we* lose her, you mean?'

A beat of silence, then, 'If *we* lose her, well, let's just say we don't want to find out what'll happen.'

'I understand.' He hung up.

* * *

Across town, in her office in West Manor, Selena Goldberg placed her phone back on her desk. She let out a frustrated sigh. 'Fuck, I don't need this right now.'

She was worried about Anya — a child of nine shouldn't be wandering the streets alone.

'Alone,' Selena muttered to herself anxiously. 'If Anya's alone, where are the others?'

17

Wednesday evening
Darlington police station

Byrd knocked on DCI Corbridge's office door, unsure if he'd still be there. Depending on the workload, he was usually gone before 6 p.m. Today had been a big day for the Durham and Darlington Constabulary, though, so Byrd had a feeling he'd be in.

'Come in,' the DCI said from the other side of the door.

Byrd opened the door and Corbridge peered up at them, half his face hidden behind the computer monitor.

'You guys still here?' he asked. 'Good to see.'

'We practically live here,' joked Byrd, but knew it wasn't far from the truth.

'What can I do for you?'

'Just updating you, sir. We haven't been able to question Anya again — the doctors say she's still very woozy from the concussion and struggling to remember things. It would be dangerous to push her further. I'm afraid we still don't have a surname for her.' Byrd told Corbridge he'd arranged for PC

Andrews to swap with PC Timms so he could stay late at the hospital and change over with the night-shift PC.

'Andrews happy to do that?'

Byrd nodded. 'Josh is fine with it.'

'Commitment. Love to see it.' He drew in a lungful of humid office air. 'Anything else?'

They told him of the footage from Susan Brown's camera, and the man captured crossing the garden. 'But if the time of death is correct, this man may not be the killer,' Tanzy added.

Corbridge considered this. 'What about the front door? Could he have accessed that last night? Just because the camera hasn't picked him up doesn't mean he never used the front door.'

'We thought the same,' Byrd said.

'And Ella Mitchell? Anything from our press release?'

'Ella's picture is the landing page on the news sites, as you'll have seen. No credible tips so far. But it's early days yet — someone must have seen something.'

'Have you released an image of Anya too? See if we can get her parents in that way?'

'No — the doctors say she'll recover her memory in the next few hours, so we have to follow safeguarding protocol and wait for more information from her, for now.'

'Very well. Hopefully, we'll see Ella sooner rather than later. Any hits on Anya from the Cheshire police?'

Tanzy shook his head and pressed his lips together. 'Unfortunately not. No missing kids fitting her description.'

'She must be linked to one of the local schools? Might be an avenue to pursue. Difficult without a surname, though. Where is Steve Mitchell?'

'Family liaison officer dropped him off at his sister's,' said Byrd. 'Got his contact number if we need it. I told him I'd ring him tomorrow.'

'Bloke's no doubt going out of his mind.'

The silent head bobs agreed with him.

'Anyway, let's see what comes back from the news tonight. Ella Mitchell is out there somewhere — I want her found. And get to the hospital first thing. Let's see if a good night's sleep gets Anya to reveal any new information that could help us. The last thing I need is the super on my arse about this.'

18

Byrd arrived home just after 8 p.m. feeling shattered. It had been another long day with another crime scene and another headache to fend off. He turned off the BMW's engine, let his head rock back into the headrest, and yawned. The street was calm and quiet, just how he liked it. It was one of the reasons he'd moved to Low Coniscliffe.

One of his neighbours was walking his dog on the opposite side of the road. He glanced over, waving courteously like he did every time he went by. Byrd liked him. The man was always cheery and had time for people in the village. He had his own gardening business and carried out most of the work for the local residents, so being an arrogant arsehole probably wouldn't do him any favours from a business perspective.

He peered down the dark street, looking forward to the days he would arrive home with the sun gently dipping in the sky, the air warm enough to sit out in the garden with Claire and Alan and see it go down.

Once through his front door, he removed his jacket, hung it on the wall hook to the right, kicked off his shoes, and straightened them out so Claire wouldn't moan about it.

Since having Alan, Claire had begun keeping everything unusually clean and tidy. Everything needed a place. Byrd had put it down to her wanting the house to be spotless for Alan, minimising germs. Byrd certainly didn't mind coming home to a clean house — there were worse habits a partner could have, that's for sure.

He wandered down the hallway, feeling the heat from a nearby radiator, and entered the kitchen with his laptop bag hanging from his shoulder. Gently nudging it off, he placed it on the table in front of Claire, who pulled her attention from her Kindle and looked at him.

'I don't think that's the right place for that, is it, Mr Byrd?'

Smiling, he bent down and kissed her. 'Nope, but I couldn't wait to kiss you. It's been on my mind all day.'

'You're such a terrible liar.'

Grinning, he picked up the bag and put it neatly against the wall under the hanging coats so it wasn't deemed a 'trip hazard'. Claire had decided the hook near the front door was for coats they wore daily, and the coats they seldom wore could go here or be hidden upstairs in a wardrobe. Byrd, not fussed with arguing, had agreed. It wasn't worth challenging the trivial things in life.

'How's Alan Shearer?' he asked, knowing it would wind her up.

She frowned at him. 'Alan *Byrd* is okay. I've just fed him.'

'Hopefully he sleeps better tonight, dreaming of his first goal for the Toon.'

She looked up at him, used to his constant references to football and the never-ending idea of their son playing for Newcastle United when he was older. 'You look tired.'

'Believe me, I *feel* worse . . .' He glanced around the orderly kitchen. 'What have you two been doing today?' He grabbed a mug from the top cupboard and set it down on the worktop.

'Went to a singalong group at Cockerton Library this morning, then looked around town in the afternoon for a dress.'

'Another dress?'

'If you don't want me to go to the police dinner next month, it's fine. I'll happily watch Netflix instead.'

'Find anything you like?'

'No, but I bought three.'

'*Three?* You only need one for the event, not *three*,' he replied, pouring hot water into the mug.

'And I'll do a sexy catwalk in the bedroom and let you decide which one fits me best.'

'What about the other two?'

'I'll take them back . . .'

He rolled his eyes, finished making the coffee, and brought it to the table.

'Thanks.' She took a quick sip. 'I've been talking to Pip. She bought one too. Got hers from Binns, so she says.'

'Sure, Ori will be happy about that, the cost of their stuff.'

They both laughed and enjoyed each other's company for a while. Claire told him about their day and how Alan interacted with other babies. 'He's coming on so much, you know.'

Claire spotted something in Byrd's expression.

'What's up?'

'Nothing,' he said.

'There is.'

'I'm just sad not to see it, that's all.' He sighed lightly.

She lovingly placed her hands on top of his. 'But you *do* see it, Max. You're here most weekends and here every night. Everyone needs to work.'

'I wish my parents were here too. They'd have really loved him.' He stood up quickly as if he'd forgotten something that needed his immediate attention.

'Where are you going?' she asked, frowning up at him.

'With all this baby talk, I need to go see him. I'll be down soon.'

'Wanna carry on watching *Fringe* when you're back down?'

He said yes as he left the kitchen, went upstairs, and slowly opened Alan's door. The green walls were filled with big canvases of jungle animals, and the baby's name was fixed in huge letters above his cot. A soft brown rug was positioned in the middle of the floor, and white Ikea wardrobes took the rest of the space.

Byrd silently peered into the cot. Alan was on his back, sound asleep, with a dummy in his mouth. His small chest rose and fell to his calm, rhythmic breathing.

'Hello, little man,' he whispered.

He stared at Alan for ages, watching him — the shape of his tiny face, nose, and biteable cheeks.

'Max?' whispered Claire from behind. 'I'm waiting for you.'

He looked at his watch and realised he'd been watching Alan for over half an hour. 'Jesus, sorry, lost track of time. I'll be down soon.'

Byrd moved away from his sleeping son and went to their bedroom to shower and change before settling in for the evening.

19

Corey Tills pulled his old red Volvo XC90 into the hospital car park just after 9 p.m. He found a space near the back and turned off the engine, knowing what he was about to do would be challenging. He'd waited until it was dark, since the hospital would be quieter, with fewer witnesses.

He checked his phone, noticed a text message.

Make sure everything goes smoothly. Don't attract any attention.

He sighed, put his phone away, and stepped into the cool March air. He walked across the car park, confident he was far enough away from the camera fixed to the side of the hospital he'd noticed on a previous visit. He took the path next to the trees and the small garden area towards the entrance.

Entering the hospital, he calmly walked along the corridor to the lifts. Reaching them, he chose the stairs, keeping his head down in case there were cameras in the stairwell. He stepped onto level two and angled right, spotting a woman sitting on the small seating area beside the coffee machine to the left, peering down at her phone. She didn't look up as he passed.

He came to a locked security door.

'Shit,' he muttered. He'd forgotten about this door.

Noticing the camera attached to the intercom, he quickly backed away. He returned to the corridor and went to the toilet for temporary cover. He needed time to think of something.

He pulled his phone out and sent a text message.

The security door is locked. I can't get in.

He hit send, and there was an immediate reply.

I don't care how you do it — just get in. If they find out what's happened, we're in trouble.

Corey took a breath and waited. There must be a way. Without making a sound, he unlocked the door and looked along the corridor. The woman on the bench had vanished. He closed the door and locked it again, keeping his ear to the wood so he could listen for any sounds out in the corridor.

Moments later, he heard footsteps pass the toilet. He peered out, seeing a man and a woman walking towards the security door of the children's ward.

'We're here to see Annie in room six, please,' the woman in front said into the intercom.

Corey kept clear of the camera and waited patiently. When the door buzzed open, he followed the couple inside, thanking the man for holding the door open for him.

That was easy — now for the challenging part.

In the first room he passed a small boy playing on the floor while a woman, presumably his mother, sat a few feet from him on the closest chair, distracted by her phone.

Corey looked forward and continued. All he had to do was find Anya. It sounded so simple, but there were several rooms to check and a nurses' station — they'd ask questions if he appeared like he didn't belong.

Up ahead, he spotted a camera on the ceiling pointing his way. He kept his head down as he moved down the corridor.

Shit. He stopped suddenly. A uniformed police officer was sitting on a chair further down the corridor. That must be where Anya was. At least he didn't have to search for the right room, but the police officer threw a spanner in the works. Could he out-muscle him if it came down to it? Probably not — the officer looked fit and capable.

Unsure what to do, he found a toilet further down on the left, went in and locked the door.

'Come on, think,' he whispered, staring at himself in the small square mirror fixed to the wall. He couldn't stay in the toilet for ever because the officer in the corridor would get suspicious, if he'd taken enough notice. Corey couldn't risk that.

Then an idea came to him.

It was risky. Very risky.

He flushed the toilet, washed his hands, and dried them before opening the door. Instead of taking a right towards the police officer, he took a left, walking down the corridor as if he knew where he was going, and took another left at the T-junction. He tried the handle of the first door, and it opened into an unoccupied room — just a bed, a chair, and a TV.

This could work, he thought.

A minute later, he left the room and closed the door, then wandered down the corridor, past the officer sitting on the chair and the nurse at the desk, who was too invested in the contents of the magazine in front of her to notice him.

All he had to do was be patient.

Just before he reached the exit, the fire alarm rang out, the sound abruptly filling the corridor. He stopped as if not expecting it and made a show of looking concerned. A nurse appeared. 'Excuse me.' She dashed past him down the corridor.

'Is that a drill?' he asked the desk nurse, who shook her head.

'You should make your way to the fire assembly point in the car park,' she told him.

Corey moved away slowly as if complying, almost bumping into a man wearing overalls and a tool belt who had appeared at the end of the corridor.

'Is that on this ward?' the caretaker shouted over the constant ringing.

The nurse was already inspecting a live information panel on the wall near her station.

'Yes,' she said, then gazed around. 'But there's no smoke?'

The caretaker moved towards her as a stream of patients and hospital staff flowed past, making for the fire assembly point by foot, wheelchair, and, in one case, on a bed. Corey stepped to one side, unobserved, watching the commotion unfold. Anxious voices flowed over him as the continual alarm rang out.

Corey gritted his teeth, eyes on the police officer. The man had stood up and gone into Anya's room, but he came out again without the girl, looking uncertainly at the duty nurse and the caretaker.

'Down here, there's smoke!' the caretaker called from at the far end of the corridor, seizing a fire extinguisher. The officer left his post and ran to help the caretaker, his shoes slapping the lino as he disappeared around the corner.

'Bingo,' Corey said.

He ran to the room the officer had been guarding and opened the door. Anya was sitting on the edge of the hospital bed, staring at him with wide eyes.

'Corey,' she said, with a gasp of relief. 'What's that noise? Is there a fire?'

'Yeah. Let's get you out of here!' he shouted above the wailing of the alarm.

To his surprise, she jumped off the bed and ran to him.

20

Tanzy stepped through his front door and found his house quieter than usual. He placed his car keys in the bowl to his left, removed his shoes and hung his coat with the others on the wall. He was still getting used to the layout of the new house and thought a little wistfully of his old home in Newton Aycliffe.

One morning some months ago, Pip had woken Tanzy at 5 a.m. to tell him they needed to move to Mowden right away to be in the catchment for the best secondary school. He'd told her to go back to sleep, but had somehow been persuaded to view this 'perfect' house — and he had to admit it was nice. And then the whirlwind of moving began, along with everything that went with it. At least that was over, Tanzy thought. He'd not told Pip he'd turned down a promotion to DCI when they were in the thick of it. At the time he'd been so busy with the move he couldn't see how he'd have time for the job. Now he wondered if he'd been in too much of a rush to refuse the responsibility.

With his laptop bag hanging over one shoulder, Tanzy strolled into the kitchen. Pip was washing up at the sink, wearing her PJs and purple fleecy hoodie. Her newly dyed dark hair would take some getting used to, that was for sure.

'Hey, Ori. Good day?'

'The house is quiet,' he said, unable to hear his children anywhere. Usually there were signs of them somewhere — clattering around, watching television, or listening to music at volumes that pushed the limits.

Tanzy set his laptop bag on the table and leaned in for a kiss, but she pulled away. 'What's up?'

'Nothing.' She shrugged lightly as she continued to wash the dirty plates from teatime, rinse them, and place them on the drying rack.

Fair enough, he thought, not having the energy to argue with her. Pip was hit and miss. Sometimes she'd be the life and soul of the room, other times, not so much, sinking into the shell she often found herself in nowadays. Tanzy had been so proud of her coming off the drink, had supported each and every minute of her alcohol-free life. But in recent months, he'd noticed a change in her: her sparkle had faded.

Tanzy didn't understand why. He'd tried talking it through with her, but she said she was okay. Eric and Jasmine had started asking what was up with their mother, and he decided to discuss it with her now.

'Kids asleep?'

'Jasmine is. Eric is watching his telly.'

Tanzy popped the kettle on, grabbed a mug from the side, set it down, and dropped a spoonful of coffee in it. 'How was your day?'

'Was all right.'

He waited. 'Just all right?'

She sighed and dropped her shoulders. 'It was good. I got some work done and sent it off. I had a meeting earlier with my manager.'

'And?'

She shrugged. 'Went all right.'

'*Just* all right?'

She nodded.

Tanzy took a short, sharp breath. 'Pip, what's going on?'

'What do you mean?' She frowned, turning to him.

'Come and sit down, love. Just for two minutes, okay?'

She gave the slightest of nods and dawdled over to sit with him. Tanzy slowly dropped into the seat beside her and studied her for a moment.

'What's going on with you, Pip? Over these past few months, you've been different.'

'We've spoken about this,' she replied. 'I've told you I'm okay.'

'But you're not. Even the kids have noticed a change. They're asking me about why you're sad.' He fell silent, letting that sink in. 'I don't know what to tell them.'

She stared at him, absorbing his words, and her expression indicated that they reached somewhere in her heart.

'Are . . . are you drinking again?' he asked, not wanting to but needing to.

'Of course I'm bloody not!' she snapped, suddenly loud.

'Okay, okay.' He held out his hands in apology for the difficult question. 'Then, what is it, babe? Are *we* okay?' He gestured between the two of them. 'I know we don't have sex all the time, but—'

'We have it enough, I think.'

'You've turned me down a few times recently. I'm not trying to pester you, I'm just concerned.' He knew everyone had the right to say no when they didn't feel like it, but Pip hadn't been interested in sex at all lately — almost to the point where Tanzy wondered if there was someone else in the picture.

'I'm tired, that's all,' she countered, unable to meet his eye.

He'd heard that a lot recently. 'Pip, if things aren't how they should be, just tell me, and we can work on it.' He tilted his head. 'Am I working too much? Not spending enough time with you and the kids?'

'It's not that . . .'

'So, what is it then, babe?' He leaned closer to her, gently grabbing a slender hand. 'Tell me.'

'I feel like a failure.'

The kitchen went quiet. How could she think that? 'A failure? Why?'

She shrugged again, her small, narrow shoulders rising and falling. 'I don't know.' She buried her face in her hands as if hiding would make her problems go away. 'I can't help how I feel, Orion.'

Tanzy hadn't told her, but since her noticeable change in mood over the last few months, he'd looked into how the human body reacts to overcoming issues with alcohol, learning that sometimes — not always — the person feels really good about their achievements of overcoming the temptation but, after a while, the joy of the accomplishment lessens and they often slip back into thinking that the alcohol will make them feel happy again, hence why some alcoholics never become free of the habit.

He touched her forearm tenderly. 'I know, Pip. I want you to know that, whatever you're going through, I'll always be here.'

She wiped a tear from her eye.

'The kids need their smiley mammy back.'

Letting out a sudden chortle, she leaned forward and squeezed his hand, giving him a light kiss.

'So, tell me about the meeting today. I want to know.'

Pip had started a new job with *Northern Heights* as a print layout designer. It wasn't exactly a burgeoning industry — newspaper sales had suffered hugely since the growth of the internet and social media — but Pip seemed to enjoy the work, tapping into her creativity. But now Tanzy wasn't sure if her new job was another possible reason for how she felt. Was it too stressful for her? Was someone at work upsetting her?

'My manager says I'm doing well. She's pleased with my new design. She thinks the changes will attract more readers, which is good.'

'Well done.' Tanzy beamed with happiness. She'd come so far.

'But it's hard.'

'Why?'

'Because print can't really compete with the online side of the business,' she explained. 'There's always a chance they'll ditch print altogether if circulation isn't good enough. And I think what's left of the team are wondering if a redesign is worth the expense.'

'But it is worth it, right?' Tanzy softly squeezed her arm. 'If the readers think the paper looks old, they won't buy it, will they? I'm proud of you, Pip.'

She smiled, the good old Pip returning briefly. 'How was your day? You're back late.'

She was right. He wondered if his staying late at work had contributed to her current state of mind.

Tanzy sighed tiredly. 'Never a dull day in this town.'

'Wanna talk about it?'

He shook his head. 'Not really. Just usual stuff.'

Pip smiled, and Tanzy felt happy to see it. She got up and returned to the sink to finish the remainder of the washing up. He padded over and stood behind her, wrapping his muscular arms around her and placing his hands on top of hers.

'Love you, Pip.'

Smiling, she angled her head to his and turned to kiss him. 'I'm gonna get a shower. I stink.'

She briefly studied his thin, tanned face, then caressed his bald head with a wet, soapy hand. 'Still a handsome devil though, aren't you?'

'Suppose you could do worse.' He kissed her and went upstairs to check on the kids.

21

Wednesday evening
Darlington Memorial Hospital

With the fire alarm still ringing, Corey had a fighting chance of getting Anya away from the children's ward without much fuss. He glanced back down the corridor. Nobody was chasing them. People were obviously too distracted by the fire he'd started a few minutes ago.

The one thing you could count on when dealing with police is they'd always help people — a courageous strength the public needed, but in this instance, a weakness that Corey had exploited for his own benefit.

He pushed through the security door, which had temporarily disabled its metallic lock due to the fire alarm, and together they dashed past the lifts towards the stairs.

'Where are we going?' she asked him.

'Getting you out of here.'

The alarm had quietened by the time they reached the ground floor. They took a left and headed for the exit. Along the corridor, a stocky man wearing a security uniform walked towards them, holding a walkie-talkie to his mouth. With a frown, he spoke into it.

Corey avoided eye contact with him and moved as casually as possible.

'*A girl from the children's ward has gone missing. Name's Anya, surname unknown. Keep a look out,*' a voice said on the radio. '*Dark hair, thin, wearing a white hospital gown. She's not in her room. She has a pot on her wrist.*'

'Shit,' whispered Corey, glancing down at the girl by his side, who looked up at him with wide eyes, hearing the same message.

The guard slowed, eyeing them both curiously. 'What hair colour did you say?' he said into the walkie-talkie.

'*Dark hair. She's thin. Nine years old. Her name is Anya.*'

'Keep walking,' Corey whispered to her. 'Just keep going.'

'Are you from the children's ward?' The security guard moved to block their way.

Corey and Anya stumbled a little, then veered left around him.

'Sir, excuse me!' said the guard firmly, then scowled at Anya. 'What's your name?'

'Move out of the way, please,' Corey said.

'I'm asking the girl her name.' He spread his arms wide.

'And the girl isn't telling you, so let us pass.' Corey eyed the space on either side of him, judging which side was bigger.

'I'm going to have to ask you to wait here.' The guard brought the walkie-talkie up to his mouth and pressed the button. 'Security to the ground floor, I have—'

He let out a sharp wail as Corey kicked him in the groin as hard as he could. The guard crumpled to the linoleum floor, dropping his radio.

'Come on, Anya, let's go!' shouted Corey, but she didn't move. He swept her up in his arms and ran into the cool March night. Outside, he could see people gathering at the fire assembly point.

'You're not taking me back to him, are you?' she asked. 'He's a bad man.'

'Back to who?'

She didn't answer. He raced along the path and jumped off the kerb, scrambling towards the red Volvo.

'Get in the front,' he said, opening the door and pushing her inside. He held her in the seat while he strapped the seat belt over her, then raced around the front of the car and climbed in.

'Right, let's get you b—'

Corey gasped suddenly as he was pulled back into the headrest, the tremendous force around his throat crushing his windpipe. He couldn't move. Throwing his hands up, he clawed at whatever was choking him, desperate for air, but it wasn't letting up.

* * *

Anya panicked. There was a man in the seat behind Corey, pulling a cord around his throat, the ends gripped firmly in his hands.

Corey coughed and gagged, frantically trying to get his fingertips under the taut cord, but the other man was too strong.

'Die, you fucker!' screamed the man in the back.

Anya screamed and grabbed the door handle, but it was locked. She cowered against the passenger window, covering her ears to block out the horrendous sounds of Corey fighting for his life.

After several horrifying minutes, the man let go of the cord and dropped it on the seat beside him. Corey slumped forward, his forehead colliding with the steering wheel, causing a brief honk of the horn before he dropped to the side against the driver's door.

An eerie silence filled the car.

The girl remained tucked into the door with her knees up to her face, hands firmly over her ears, her eyes clamped shut. She shuddered when she heard the doors unlock. The back door opened, then soon after, the driver's door, and Corey Tills was dragged out.

Still cowering, the girl opened her eyes and peeped out the passenger window. Corey was positioned on the grass, deep under the nearest tree, so he was out of the way. The man returned to the car and the passenger door opened.

She jolted back, screamed, and tried to scramble away from him, getting her legs tangled on the gear stick and handbrake. The man grabbed her ankle and quickly hauled her back like she weighed nothing.

'Anya,' he said calmly. 'I've been worried sick about you.'

She stifled a short cry and wiped her eyes with trembling hands. The scent of freshly cut grass hung in the air from the gardens nearby.

'You understand why I did that, don't you?'

She considered the question and finally gave him a nod. 'Yes.'

'You're safe now,' he reassured her.

A siren rang out nearby, gradually louder until a fire engine pulled up at the hospital's entrance. The flashing blue lights illuminated the inside of the car. Anya looked over. Three firefighters jumped out and dashed inside. Her head ached. Why had she followed Corey out here so willingly? The building was too far away for her to run back.

'Come on, let's get going.' The man slammed the door closed, ran around the car's rear, and jumped in the driver's seat. He started the Volvo's engine and left the car park.

22

Selena Goldberg sighed deeply when the call went to voice-mail for the fourth time. 'Where the *fuck* is he?'

Annoyed, she slammed her phone onto her desk and turned towards the television on the unit near the window. Usually, she used it as calming background noise, but her irritability prevented her from concentrating on anything. She picked up the remote and turned it off with a heavy sigh, welcoming the silence.

Past 10 p.m.

There had been no sign of Corey or any communication from him since he'd gone to get Anya. During their last con-versation, he'd mentioned the girl was guarded in the chil-dren's ward by a police officer. She'd told him to get the job done — they needed her back, safe under their watch. The last thing they needed was for her to speak to the police. *That* was an absolute no-go. Hell would break loose with the wrong people, and it wouldn't just be her job she'd be losing, that was for sure.

She picked up her phone, tried Corey's number again, and slapped the edge of the desk with a palm when it went to voicemail for the millionth time. 'Corey, for fuck's sake, pick up!'

She paced her office, studying her certificates she'd pinned on the back wall. Her gaze dropped to the unit below. The top shelf housed several photos of her family. She paused at the picture of her and her sister, back when they lived in Trinidad, barely fitting into the tight fluorescent bikinis they'd bought from a market stall, hair tied up in dreadlock ponytails.

Shivering, she moved away from the photos, staring around her spacious office: the dark oak desk, the large windows that, come morning, would fill the room with gentle sunlight, the canvas photos of beaches and sunsets, reminding her of the childhood she missed so much.

God knows what the girls would be getting up to.

But she only had herself to blame.

Shaking her head, she went to the window and stared out into the darkness. During the day, she'd admire the expanse of neatly cut, green gardens, but right now, she could see her plump reflection and half of her dark-skinned face reflecting the nearest lamp against the glass — a lost, confused, and scared version of herself she didn't recognise.

There wasn't much more she could do at the office, so she grabbed her coat from the back of her chair and put it on.

Her phone rang on the desk.

Gasping, she reached for it. 'You got her?'

'Got who?'

'Er . . .' She pulled the phone away from her ear, noticing it was her husband, Alex, calling. *Shit*, she mouthed, then brought the phone back to her ear. 'No one,' she told him.

'Selena,' he said, his voice very serious, 'when are you coming home?'

'Very soon, my love, just tying up a few loose ends here.'

'*What* loose ends?'

'Just work stuff.'

Alex stayed silent.

'I'm coming home now.' She hung up before he could reply.

She turned her desk lamp off, made her way across the dark room to the brightly lit landing, and closed the door on her way out. She descended the quiet stairs and smiled, thinking about the guests in the rooms along the corridor, sleeping soundly and getting better. Along the corridor, she spotted one of the night-shift staff who gave her a gentle wave.

West Manor was an energy and well-being retreat, a place where alternative practitioners worked to heal the guests and make them feel good about themselves, using various techniques such as spiritual guidance, emotional understanding, and yoga.

Selena had managed the place since it had opened in 2011 and had several practitioners working under her. There were eighteen rooms at West Manor, with en-suite facilities and home comforts like televisions, chaise longues, and healing artworks.

Other than her, the caretaker, Reggie Cook, had been there the longest — just over ten years. Selena considered him a close friend and someone she could rely on. But he'd gone for the night, and now just a small team of night staff remained. The guests usually slept soundly, despite their troubles, and it was rare that they encountered any major issues.

She said bye to a passing nurse in the hallway and left through the main entrance. Back in her blue Nissan Juke, she turned the heating on and rubbed her hands before driving down the winding road towards the locked gate. The security guard inside the small hut waved her through. She took a left onto Barnes Road and drove home.

She parked in her driveway in West Park. It was cold tonight, almost wintry. She could hear the television from the living room as she went in.

'That you, Selena?' a voice said from inside the room.

'Yes, Alex,' she replied, taking off her coat.

Alex didn't look up as she entered the living room, his attention on the nightly news. She hovered in the doorway, watching over his shoulder.

On the screen, a reporter held a microphone close to his mouth. The background was dark, but the light from the camera gently illuminated not just his face but the houses behind him. She recognised them as the ones opposite Darlington College, on Haughton Road.

'*Thirty-nine-year-old Mia Mitchell was found dead in the house behind me,*' the reporter said. '*According to local police, Mia suffered a sickening attack in her home. The search for the suspect is ongoing, and we'll update you when we hear any more on the matter.*'

Selena gasped and raised a hand to her mouth. 'Jesus, that's awful.'

'*Mia's nine-year-old daughter, Ella, is still missing. Police are currently searching for her whereabouts, and we ask that if anyone has seen her, please ring the number below immediately.*'

A phone number moved across the bottom of the screen, along with a photo of the missing child.

Selena watched the screen, torn — she wasn't much younger than Anya. If only Selena could go to the police, have the public on her side, searching. But she couldn't. She was on the wrong side of the law now, no better than a common criminal.

As the news rolled on to the next story, Alex looked up at her. 'You feel these things so deeply, don't you?'

'She's just a kid,' Selena said, thinking of Anya. 'All alone.' *And there's nothing I can do to keep her safe.*

23

Tanzy slowly opened his eyes, feeling something nudging him. 'What?' he muttered.

'Ori, your phone's ringing!' he heard a voice say.

'What?' he mumbled again, coming out of a dream. He was standing in town on High Row, helplessly watching a building on fire. The sound of an approaching fire engine siren merged into his ringtone from his bedside table.

'Your phone,' the voice said again, this time clearer to him that it was Pip.

He slowly reached for it. It was PC Andrews.

'Yeah?' he answered as he rolled onto his back.

'Sorry it's late, but we have a serious problem.'

Tanzy heard the worry in his voice and opened his eyes wide. 'What's happened, Josh?'

'Sir, she's gone. The girl at the hospital, Anya. She's disappeared. There was a fire on the ward. I helped put it out. I went back to the room, and she was gone.'

He frowned, still not fully awake. 'Who?'

'The girl we brought to the hospital. Anya.'

'Anya . . .' *Fuck*, thought Tanzy, suddenly sitting up. 'What the hell happened?'

'I — I — There was a fire and—'

'I'm on my way, Josh. Hold tight.'

'You going somewhere?' Pip asked tiredly. 'At this time?'

'I need to. Sorry. Problem at the hospital.' He threw on some jeans, a T-shirt, and a jumper. 'Go back to sleep. I don't know how long I'll be.'

Pip said nothing and rolled away. Being the spouse of a detective was demanding — there was never a day off.

He leaned over and kissed the back of her head. 'Be back when I can.'

She was already asleep.

24

Thursday morning
Darlington Memorial Hospital

The following morning Byrd woke early. He showered, dressed, and was in his car by 7 a.m. He phoned DCI Corbridge on his way, informing him he was going to speak with the pathologist about Mia Mitchell. He knew a full post-mortem would have been completed and wanted to hear if Dr Hemsley had anything of value to add to the investigation.

Surprised to see the car park only half full when he pulled up at the hospital, he headed over to the entrance. Two ambulances were parked outside, both with their rear doors open. Byrd spotted paramedics aiding an older man covered in a blanket, placing a respirator over his mouth.

He headed down the corridor, passing a few nurses and doctors walking in both directions, filling the corridor with idle discussions of recent test results and medicines patients were using. It reminded him of *Grey's Anatomy*, Claire's favourite programme.

An almost overwhelming sadness overcame him as he thought about seeing his parents here after their car crash.

He felt the same sickening stab to his stomach as he did back then. Hospitals were wonderful places that did extraordinary things, but you often only visited when something was wrong in your life or the life of a loved one.

Turning left towards the pathology department, he approached a thick-set guy whose attention was on the computer screen in front of him. He peered up after hearing Byrd's footsteps.

'Can I help you?' he asked in a croaky voice.

'I'm Detective Inspector Max Byrd.' He flashed his credentials. 'Here to see Arnold Hemsley.'

The man lowered his eyes to the screen and slightly squinted as if aiding his concentration. 'Dr Hemsley usually starts at eight o'clock most mornings. I can check if he's here, though. Hang on.'

The man picked up the phone to the right of the keyboard.

Byrd edged away from the desk and looked around to pass the time. There was a small seating area opposite the desk, where the walls were filled with bright-coloured posters. One showed a photo of a pale elderly woman lying on a bed with the sheet pulled up to her chin. There was a quote underneath it: *Struggling with the loss of a loved one? Call this number.* Byrd remembered seeing something similar when he was there for his parents after their crash. Although the posters had been modernised, as if life had moved on, his parents would always be in the back of his mind.

'DI Byrd?' said the man at the desk. 'Go straight through. It's your lucky day — he's in early this morning.'

'Thank you.' Byrd stepped through the automated doors and down the corridor, taking a right. The labs where the pathologists carried out the post-mortems were to the left. He knocked on Hemsley's door.

'Come in,' said Hemsley from the other side.

Byrd did so, slowly.

'DI Byrd. You just can't stay away, can you?'

'It's not out of choice, believe me.'

97

They shared a knowing smile.

Byrd closed the door and took a few steps towards him. The office was neat and tidy, and everything had its own place. The low-level coffee table in the centre of the room had several organised leaflets on it, one titled *Life after Death*, with two leather chairs angling towards it, both positioned close together.

'Please, Inspector, have a seat.' Hemsley motioned to the chair nearest Byrd.

'Thanks.' Byrd lowered himself into one of the leather chairs, which felt softer than it looked.

'So, to what do I owe the pleasure?' Hemsley dropped into the other seat and gracefully crossed his right leg over his left.

'I was hoping to see how the post-mortem of Mia Mitchell went yesterday. Did you find anything unusual or different from what we assumed?'

He gave a slow, measured nod, appreciating Byrd following this up so efficiently. 'Well, apart from the obvious cascade of stab wounds the victim had suffered, nothing in particular, nor out of the ordinary.'

'Anything you've learned about the victim from her wounds?' Byrd shrugged slightly. 'Angle of the knife, that sort of thing.'

Hemsley smiled, again no doubt appreciating Byrd's thoroughness.

'The stab wounds not only indicate whoever did this was deranged, but I'm confident in saying it was an adult of average height, between five feet ten and six feet.' The doctor breathed heavily. 'Also, judging by the damage to the victim, the wounds tell me this was a brutal attack, Detective.'

Byrd nodded slowly.

'The report is done on my end, anyway. I'll email it to you, Max, so you have it in your files.'

'Thanks, appreciate that.'

Byrd stood and firmly shook the pathologist's hand. 'Thanks for seeing me, Dr Hemsley. I promise I won't make a habit of this. Have a good day.' He turned away and headed for the door.

'DI Byrd?' said Dr Hemsley.

Byrd paused at the door, his hand around the handle.

'Whoever did this, they need to be stopped before they do it again. Max, I haven't seen something this violent in a long time.'

25

Thursday morning
Darlington Memorial Hospital

Before every shift, forensic scientist Laura Tilton stood at the edge of the car park to have a cigarette. On her way to work, she usually stopped off at Costa Coffee, buying herself a frappuccino, a drink her colleague Leigh loathed passionately.

Lighting her cigarette, Laura noticed Leigh pull into the car park in her red Vauxhall Astra, the same car Leigh had owned as long as they'd known each other.

'Morning, Leigh,' said Laura, taking a long drag on her cigarette as she approached.

'Thought you were on the vapes now?'

'My mam gave me a pack the other night. Once they're gone, they're gone.'

Leigh rolled her eyes, hearing it all before. She didn't smoke, nor did she vape. She barely drank alcohol either, committing to a very healthy lifestyle, going to the gym several times a week and doing a yoga practice as part of her morning routine. 'Come on,' she said, 'better get to work.'

They headed for the entrance side by side. On the path, they could smell the freshly cut grass in the gardens beyond the bushes and trees. Sometimes, if it was nice on their break, they'd sit in the garden to have their dinner.

Laura stopped to check her bag, swinging it off her shoulder and lowering it to the floor.

'What you lost now — your daft vapes?'

'Just checking I have my phone. Can't remember picking it up.'

Leigh stopped and checked Facebook. She'd recently entered a competition to win a make-up bundle, and this morning, the winner would be announced on the company's social media page.

'What the hell is that?' Laura said, looking at the bush.

'It's a bush, obviously. Come on, we're going to—'

'Leigh, come see!' whispered Laura, struggling to get her words out.

'What is it? We're gonna be late.'

'Someone's shoe, I think.'

Leigh lowered and peered at the base of the bush. 'There's a man lying in there, passed out.'

'Is he drunk?'

They couldn't get through the bush, so they went along the path and through the gate into the garden, then took a left, seeing the top of the man's head on the lawn.

'Jesus, is he okay?'

'God knows,' replied Laura.

Leigh drew close and lowered to the man. His skin looked pale, and he was totally still. She placed two fingers on the side of his neck to find a pulse.

'Is he okay?' Laura asked.

Leigh looked up. 'He's dead.'

* * *

Once they were informed about the man in the garden, three security guards ran out with radios in their hands. They were told during their shift handover what had happened regarding the man who had taken the child from the children's ward last night.

The thinnest of the trio, a man in his late forties with a goatee that made him look like one of the Chuckle brothers, lowered to the man's head. He used two fingers to check for a pulse, but the body was cold.

'Anything, John?' asked one of the other two, watching him with wide eyes.

John shook his head with his fingers lightly pressed on the side of the man's throat. 'Nothing, mate.'

'Recognise him?' asked the guard, peering down at him. The other guard was on the phone to notify the police.

John studied what he could see of his face, then his clothing. 'Is it the same man from last night? The one who took the little girl? I remember watching the CCTV.'

'It could be.'

Minutes later, sirens filled in the air.

26

Although they didn't get much sleep, Byrd and Tanzy were in the meeting room at 8 a.m. sharp, looking shattered and carrying bags under their eyes, darker than usual.

DCI Corbridge stood at the front, waiting for everyone's arrival so he could make a start. His face was grim at the news of Anya's disappearance — the second child to go missing in a day, and the only witness they'd had in the Mia Mitchell murder inquiry.

The rest of the team entered in dribs and drabs, the last being DS Leonard, who apologised with a quick — almost sheepish — palm raise. Punctuality was everything to Corbridge. Something he'd no doubt bring up during appraisals, so they all needed to be mindful not to stretch his tolerance.

'Right, looks like you're all here . . . finally,' he said, his tone sharp and loud. He stared at Leonard for a moment, who was settling into a chair near Tanzy. Using the black remote in his hands, the DCI started the presentation. The first screen was titled *Current Cases*.

There was a list he wanted to go through in a particular order.

Byrd eyed the list: Mia Mitchell, Ella Mitchell, Anya.

'Right, we'll make a start on Mia Mitchell.' He looked around the room. 'What's happening?'

'I went to see the pathologist, Arnold Hemsley, this morning,' said Byrd. 'He counted thirty-one puncture wounds to Mia Mitchell's chest and stomach. He's almost one hundred per cent sure a standard kitchen knife was used.'

'Thirty-one wounds?' The DCI winced.

Byrd nodded confidently. 'So the murder weapon's most likely the knife missing from the rack in the kitchen.'

'Anything else unusual from Mia Mitchell's post-mortem we don't know?'

Byrd shook his head.

The DCI's head was down, his gaze on the grey carpet. 'We'll move on. Ella Mitchell?'

'No sign of Ella Mitchell yet, sir,' answered PC Weaver, who had been liaising with the publicity team. 'No credible tips from the media release. We are holding a press conference tonight to keep attention on it.'

'So, the girl we originally thought was Ella Mitchell, who we found yesterday morning at a house on Haughton Road, turns out not to be Ella Mitchell.'

'That's right,' said Tanzy.

'And we think the killer's a man, judging by the CCTV we've seen and by Anya's story?'

'Well, it's really just Anya's story,' Byrd said. 'The man who entered the house did so hours after Mia was killed. Might have been the same person who killed her, might not have been.'

'We can't just go on *might have*, DI Byrd. We need facts. *Might have* doesn't cut it higher up. You know that, Max.'

Silence filled the room.

'So, who is Anya?' asked the DCI. 'You told me last night that Cheshire police don't have any reports of missing children that match her description. Anything from the council, schools?'

Byrd spoke up again. 'Nothing new from that end. We've asked them to circulate a photograph of Anya to the schools. It's hard when we don't have a surname.'

'Hmmm. And I suppose "Warrington" might just be her nearest town rather than the place she lives.' The DCI started circling the room. 'Okay. Okay. So, we need to dig deeper into her, and we need — and I say we *need* — to find Ella Mitchell. She can't be far. Darlington isn't a huge place, is it?' Corbridge paced about, thinking. 'Do we believe Steve Mitchell's story? Does it check out?'

'I spoke with his manager,' said Tanzy, 'who told me exactly where he was and what he was doing at the time of Mia's murder. We have no reason not to believe him.'

'Do we have anything from the hospital last night?'

'A camera positioned on the road near the car park picked up six cars leaving after Anya was taken. I made the list and contacted the DVLA, who will get back to me ASAP.'

The door opened quickly. Corbridge stopped and faced the door, as did other eyes in the room.

It was PC Degnan. 'I've just been told a body's been found in the hospital grounds.'

Byrd frowned. 'Not Anya? When?'

'No, a man. Turned up less than an hour ago,' she replied. 'It could have been there all night. The security guard thinks the description we gave him matches what the guy who took the girl was wearing. It could be the man we're looking for.'

'I've just been there,' said Byrd, amazed — and slightly embarrassed — at how he'd missed it.

'Well, get back there and find out what the fuck is going on,' said the DCI.

27

Thursday morning
Darlington Memorial Hospital

By the time the police arrived at the hospital, it was a media circus. Several news vans were parked down the side road that ran parallel to the car park, scattered with reporters straining their necks like meerkats, looking for a way in to see what was going on.

'This is the last thing we need.' Byrd pulled into the chaos and parked near the back, in the last available space. They got out, closed their doors, and headed for the area that was being guarded.

'Please, keep back. Let's wait for the police to get here,' said one of the hospital security guards helping to secure the scene, his arms out wide.

'Let me take a photo,' asked some self-centred arsehole trying to manoeuvre past him.

Byrd confidently introduced himself to the guard and thanked him for doing all he could to prevent people from getting too close.

'No worries. Pack of fucking animals, this lot, let me tell you.'

'Hey, what did you call me?' demanded the man trying to take a photo.

Ignoring him, Byrd turned to PC Degnan. 'Louise, could you set up a proper cordon, please?'

The guards had put up yellow tape, which had kept people at bay, but Byrd wanted it widened and the people moved further back.

Degnan grabbed some tape and got PC Weaver's attention. Together, they moved people back, widening the cordoned area.

Byrd and Tanzy made their way into the garden, where they could see the top of the man's head as he lay on his front on the damp grass. Byrd snapped on some latex gloves and lowered to one knee, feeling the moisture soak through his dark grey trousers as he checked for a pulse he knew he wouldn't find. The man's skin was firm and as cold as ice.

'Didn't know you were Forensics now, Max.'

Byrd moved back to make way for Tallow and Hope.

'All yours, guys.'

'What do we know?' asked Hope, putting her gloves on and focusing on the man on the grass.

'Found an hour ago by two lab scientists who work here.'

'Hmmm,' said Hope.

'What?' asked Tallow.

'Just thinking how cool it would be to be called a scientist.'

Tallow frowned at her. 'Forensics are cooler . . .'

Byrd and Tanzy edged away.

'Your thoughts, Max?'

'The CCTV footage wasn't that clear, but it looks like the same clothes as the man we're after. Same build too.'

'Is PC Andrews here yet?' Tanzy peered around.

'Not yet.'

'Be useful to know if he can match the clothes to those the man was wearing last night.'

Byrd was ninety per cent sure this was the same coat the man in the footage was wearing, but he couldn't say one hundred per cent. He couldn't see his legs where he was currently positioned, so identifying his jeans was out of the question for the moment.

Once the scene was secure, Byrd and Tanzy headed inside to find the security office.

* * *

The forensic team went to work. The trainee tech, Amanda Forrest, watched Hope and Tallow closely, learning their craft and methods. The crime scene manager, Tony McCabe, was also there, a rarity nowadays.

'What do we have?' asked McCabe, skipping the pleasantries and getting straight to the point.

Hope leaned over the victim with narrowed eyes. 'He's been strangled.'

'Let me see.' Tallow was in a crouched position under the bush, looking at the victim's legs. He moved to a better position so he could see where Hope was indicating.

'See here, the marks on his skin?'

Although his skin had turned a pasty complexion, his throat showed a slight raise compared to other areas, roughly an inch thick, spanning horizontally across his windpipe.

'I certainly do.' Tallow nodded.

* * *

Byrd and Tanzy returned thirty minutes later having reviewed last night's CCTV footage. Unfortunately, the car park cameras hadn't covered the area where the bush was located. Tanzy recommended they upgrade their system so they could securely monitor the whole site, adding that it would be a pretty basic level of security. The guards appeared embarrassed about that. And so they should.

'How's it going?' Byrd asked Tony McCabe.

McCabe turned and looked at him like he was a piece of dog shit on the bottom of his shoe. 'Going as expected, obviously.'

Yeah, obviously, dickhead, thought Byrd.

PC Degnan wandered over. 'We have officers on the other side of the tape to stop people getting in, sir. The crowd is thinning now, anyway. No one can see anything apart from the shoe. They're getting bored.'

'That's a shame.' Byrd nodded at her. 'Thanks, Louise.'

'Anything on the cameras?'

He shook his head. 'No.'

'They need a bloody upgrade,' said Tanzy, reliving his frustration with security.

'Has the DVLA got back to you yet, Ori?' asked Byrd.

Tanzy pulled his phone from his jeans and checked his emails. 'Nothing yet. The hell's taking them so long? Let me phone.' Backing away, he put the phone to his ear.

Degnan pointed to the body on the grass. 'Is it the man who took the girl?'

Byrd nodded. 'He's wearing the same clothes, and he was here last night. I can't see it being a coincidence.'

Tanzy returned, pushing his phone into his pocket.

'Well?' Byrd asked Tanzy.

'Sending them over now.'

'Taking their time with it?' Byrd frowned.

'Said there was a mix-up with communication at their end. Won't be long.'

Byrd bobbed his head.

'So who's our suspect?' asked Degnan, still close by. 'Not the girl, surely.'

Byrd considered it. It would take a lot of strength to strangle a man, especially a man resisting it at all costs. He wasn't sure if the girl was physically able.

PC Weaver came over to find out what was happening.

'I don't see it, to be honest.'

'What, Max?' asked Tanzy.

'That Anya did this. She's only nine years old. Would she be strong enough?'

'Well . . . someone has.' Tanzy shrugged his muscular shoulders.

They all considered that in silence.

'Someone could have been waiting in the car for them,' suggested Degnan.

Byrd bowed his head. 'It's possible once he was in the driver's seat, whoever was sitting in the back strangled him from behind.'

'Might have done,' said Tanzy.

'Ori, you know what the DCI said about *might have*.'

They grinned.

'Question is, though,' Tanzy went on, 'regardless of who killed him, where is Anya?'

28

Selena Goldberg was in her office, sitting at her desk, replying to the usual string of emails. It was gone 10 a.m. when she'd replied to the last one. She leaned over, picked up her mug, and drained the remainder of her coffee before setting it down on her large desk.

Sunshine illuminated the room, which usually would have brought a smile to her face if other things weren't on her mind. One was the whereabouts of Corey Tills, her assistant manager. She'd phoned him last night, leaving numerous messages. And then again this morning, but there'd been no reply. It was the first morning he hadn't turned up for work in years.

Something was going on.

'Where on earth are you?' she said, worry filling her voice.

There was a knock at her door. It was the caretaker, Reggie Cook.

'Morning,' he said chirpily.

'Morning, Reggie. You haven't seen Corey yet, have you?'

Reggie was in his early fifties, tall and thin with narrow, bony shoulders, a tool belt slung around his waist. His hair was wispy and thinning quickly. His nose was long, his eyes close-set. In reply to her question, he shook his head.

'Not since yesterday.' He frowned. 'Has he not turned up today?'

'No.'

'Well, that's not like Corey.'

She looked down at her desk.

'What's up?' He closed the door to keep the conversation between themselves.

'Oh, nothing. I was just worrying about him, that's all.'

Reggie studied her. 'You sure?'

'Yeah. It's just, he's not answering his phone either. I think something's happened to him.'

'Let me try.' Reggie pulled out his phone, called Corey's number, and shook his head. 'Voicemail. That's strange. He normally answers.'

Selena took a breath. She didn't want to let Reggie know how worried she was about Corey and Anya disappearing, and certainly couldn't tell him why. Only she and Corey knew the real reason she was there. And, if that got out, there was a risk people would find out about the hit-and-run.

'I'll have a look around, Selena. If I see him, I'll let you know. I'll check the car park and see if his Volvo is there.'

'Thanks.'

Reggie opened the door and left her office.

It wasn't just Anya she was worried about either. It was her sisters too. They had escaped with her, but, so far, she and Corey hadn't been able to keep tabs on their locations, despite the ankle monitors they'd made them wear once they'd arrived. Corey had told her tracking Anya had been hit and miss during Tuesday night, but her pin had settled on Haughton Road earlier yesterday morning — what was she doing there?

Using the app, she'd tried tracking Anya's sisters last night and earlier today, but that had proved pointless, their

112

pins bouncing around all over Darlington, not settling in one place. As it stood, the app was showing nothing. Had they found a way to block the signal or turn it off?

Her phone rang.

'Fuck,' she spat, recognising the caller. She let it ring out. There was a short moment of silence before it rang again. 'No, no, no . . .' she whispered.

She had to answer. Otherwise, the phone would keep ringing all day.

'Hello?'

'Selena,' Jarrett Banks replied. 'How are my girls?'

Words clogged in her throat.

'Are you there?'

'I'm here.'

'My girls, how are they?'

'They're good.'

'I hope you're keeping them entertained?'

'Yes.'

'What's wrong, Selena? You're not very talkative today.'

She swallowed hard. 'Everything is fine. The girls are in their rooms. They've been doing some painting.'

'Even Anya? I didn't think she liked painting.'

'Yeah.'

'Can I speak to them?'

Shit, she thought. How could they come to the phone if they weren't there?

'Not right now. They're busy. Can I get them to call you back?'

Silence on the other end.

'Hello?'

'Selena, I feel you're not being honest with me about something. You always let me speak to them. It's the first time you've ever said that. What's happened?'

'No, no, everything is fine. They're just having a nice time painting, that's all. I wouldn't want to interrupt them. They're doing so well.'

113

'Get them to call me as soon as they finish, okay?'

'Yeah, that's fine, will do.'

The line went dead.

Selena knew she needed to find the girls ASAP because he'd be asking serious questions soon. And a man like Jarrett Banks was not the sort of person she needed asking questions.

29

They learned from his driving licence that the deceased's name was Corey Tills. All that was in his pockets were a phone and a wallet.

'No car keys?' Tanzy noted.

'Maybe he walked here,' replied Tallow.

'Or maybe the person responsible for strangling him drove off in his car?' countered Byrd.

Corey's phone was locked with a passcode, so they bagged it, along with the rest of the items, for Forensics to examine back at the lab — it would be interesting to see what was on his phone. The body was sent to the morgue in the hospital's basement.

'Do you think it's the same man we saw in the footage from the Mitchells' back garden yesterday?' asked Tanzy.

Byrd considered it, giving a slow, measured nod. 'He looks very similar. Footage wasn't that clear, but it's possible.'

Byrd had phoned the coroner, Peter Gibbs, to inform him of Corey's death, giving him his name, date of birth, and address. Once the Forensics team were happy they'd collected everything they could, Byrd and Tanzy headed for his address.

Byrd opened the metal front garden gate, knocked on the black door, and stepped back, peering around the street. Tanzy waited on the path for the moment, feeling the faint heat of the bright spring sun in his knee-length parka. Acacia Street was built of terraced houses. One side of the street had its front doors opening onto the path, but the opposite side, where Byrd and Tanzy were waiting, had small gardens. Many were filled with gravel and carefully tended plants, while others had been allowed to fill with moss and weeds.

The door opened, revealing a woman wearing a cautious frown. 'Can I help you?'

Byrd flashed his ID. 'Mrs Tills?'

She nodded, her blonde fringe jolting up and down over the top of worried blue eyes. 'Yes?'

'Are you the spouse of Mr Corey Tills?'

'I am.'

'Would it be okay to come in? We have some unfortunate news to tell you.'

She led them into the living room. Before she sat down, she asked, 'What's happened to Corey? He went out last night but he hasn't come home.'

Byrd sat opposite, but Tanzy decided to stay standing, keeping a little distance so Byrd could do the talking.

'I'm very sorry to tell you that Corey has passed away. He was murdered. His body was found—'

She burst into tears and dropped her face into her trembling hands. Uncontrollable sobbing that seemed to go on for ever filled the room.

'Can I get you some water?' Tanzy offered.

With her hands pressed against her face, she managed a nod. Tanzy disappeared, soon returning with a glass of water in a clear half-pint glass with a faint green pattern.

'There you go,' he said softly, handing it to her.

'Thanks.' Her hands trembled as she took a sip. 'I knew there was something off when he went out last night. I just knew it.'

'How come?'

'We'd sat down to watch television, and then he got up to make a coffee. When he came back, he said someone from work had phoned and he needed to pop out for a little bit.'

Byrd narrowed his eyes. 'Did he say what for?'

She slowly shook her head as more tears came. 'No, he didn't.'

'Where does Corey work?' He asked in the present tense to avoid reigniting her tears.

'West Manor, up on Barnes Road. He's the assistant manager there.'

'What time did your husband leave the house last night?'

'Erm, around half eight, nine, I'd say. Although I can't say for definite.'

'I know this is really hard for you at the moment, Mrs Tills,' said Byrd, keeping his voice as gentle and respectful as he could, 'but could we possibly get your mobile number in case we need to contact you further?'

She sniffed hard and told Byrd her number, which he saved to his phone.

'I'm sorry to ask, but do you have a contact for his manager or someone I can speak to from his work?'

Dabbing her eyes, she pulled her phone from her jeans. 'She's called Selena Goldberg.'

Byrd opened a new contact card and entered the name and number. After saving it, he smiled at her. 'Thank you. Before we go, is there anyone you'd like us to call for you? Anyone that you'd like to be with you? A friend or something?'

She thought hard and settled with a shake of the head. 'Can I see my husband?'

'You can. We'll arrange that for you.'

* * *

117

Byrd and Tanzy arrived at the Darlington Business Centre on Yarm Road at 3 p.m. The police used the building because it was accessible for reporters and members of the public who were in the know about current events.

Byrd and Tanzy entered and were greeted by the media liaison officer, Lucy, who was standing by the open door to the conference room. 'Hello, Max. Hello, Orion.' Her voice was soothing and professional, almost hypnotising. Her long dark hair was as straight as an arrow, reaching halfway down the back of her dark blue suit. She flashed them a smile, showing teeth whiter than snow.

'Hey, Lucy,' said Tanzy. 'Full house in there?'

'Would you expect anything less? Are you guys ready?'

Tanzy drew in a deep breath before they went in, the sounds of dozens of conversations overwhelming as they walked to the table at the centre of the wall nearest the door. They dropped into the two empty seats. Two blinding lamps shone towards them, so bright they could feel the heat on their faces.

'The stage is yours, Detectives,' said Lucy, standing in the doorway with her thumbs up.

Upon hearing her words, the crowd fell silent. Usually, Byrd did these events alone because Tanzy hated public speaking — it terrified him. All those eyes watching, all those ears listening, ready for you to say or do something out of turn that could be captured on camera and last for ever. DCI Corbridge had told Tanzy he needed to get on with it and face his fears. Tanzy knew he was right. He'd told his own kids, Eric and Jasmine, that they needed to be brave and courageous when faced with challenging situations. Right now, he'd have to take his own advice.

He felt his face warming as silence swept over the waiting crowd. He hoped Byrd would take the lead and speak first.

'Thank you for coming here on such short notice,' Byrd started. 'I'm Detective Inspector Max Byrd with Durham and Darlington Constabulary.'

There was a pause. Tanzy realised it was his turn. 'And I'm Detective Inspector Orion Tanzy.'

Byrd looked beyond Tanzy towards the door and nodded at Lucy. 'I've called you here to share some information about the murder of Mia Mitchell and the circumstances around it. Mia was found in her home yesterday morning on Haughton Road in Darlington. Unfortunately, she'd been subject to a vicious attack that resulted in the loss of her life.'

'Is there a suspect?' a man in a green T-shirt asked from the front row.

'We have no one in custody yet, but are working around the clock to find them.'

'What leads do you have?' another man asked from the same row.

Tanzy looked at Lucy, who was standing by a small laptop in the corner of the room, and signalled to her.

'Up on the screen, you'll see two photos,' Tanzy said loud and clear, deciding to face his fears.

The crowd focused on the wall behind them. A photo of Ella Mitchell was projected on the left, an image of Anya on the right.

'You'll recognise the girl on the left from our previous press release. She is Mia Mitchell's daughter, Ella Mitchell. She's currently missing and has been since Tuesday night, the time of Mia's death. If anyone knows her whereabouts, please contact us as soon as possible. The other photo is that of a girl called Anya, who, it seems, was also present in the house at the time of the murder. She claims to be from Warrington. We've been trying to locate her family but are having very little luck in doing so. At the moment, both girls are missing.'

'Is the girl on the right a suspect in the Mia Mitchell murder?'

'No,' said Tanzy. 'Mia was stabbed to death violently — it's unlikely this was done by a nine-year-old child.'

A bombardment of camera flashes blinded the detectives. Reporters in the crowd made notes and nodded.

'If anyone here or watching at home knows Ella Mitchell's or Anya's whereabouts, please get in touch as soon as possible. We need to find them.'

'We've also discovered the body of a male, Corey Tills, earlier this morning at Darlington Memorial Hospital,' Byrd said. 'Very likely a victim of violence, judging by forensic reports. If anyone has any information about Corey Tills or saw anything suspicious on the hospital grounds late last night or early this morning, please come forward as soon as possible. This is potentially linked to the other cases.'

Byrd and Tanzy stood, tucked their chairs in, and headed for the door, ignoring the bullets of questions being fired at them.

30

'Did you get the forensic report on Corey Tills?' asked Byrd, as DCI Corbridge approached his desk.

The DCI nodded. 'I did. It makes it easier when they're carrying their driving licences, doesn't it?' He faced Tanzy. 'What about the info from the DVLA?'

'Just looking over it now, boss.'

The office was louder than usual, most of the desks occupied by officers focused on their computer screens. Others held phones to their ears, deep in conversations and scribbling notes, which was always the case after a press conference when a hotline number had been given out. Unfortunately, most of the callers were jokers wasting valuable police time.

The DCI impatiently expelled air from his nostrils again.

That niggled Tanzy. 'What's up?'

Corbridge stared at him.

'Don't beat around the bush, Mark,' Tanzy said. 'Say what's on your mind. You're pissed off about something.'

He made a 'fair enough' face. 'Eckles is on the warpath. Once he got wind of the girl going missing last night when

121

one of our own was guarding her, it really got his back up. And finding the body this morning at the hospital just added fuel to his fire.'

Tanzy nodded in understanding. Shit always rolled downhill.

'I haven't seen the videos from the hospital, but how sure are you that the man who took the girl from the children's ward is the same man discovered in the garden next to the car park?'

'I'd say ninety-nine per cent sure,' said Byrd. 'Judging by his size, shape, and clothing.'

'I see.'

Tanzy pointed to his left. 'Boss, pull up a chair.'

Corbridge walked across the central aisle, grabbed one unused swivel chair from a vacant desk, wheeled it over, and sat down. 'What have we got?'

'One of the cars leaving the car park last night was a red Volvo XC90. The owner of that car was Corey Tills.'

'Yet we found him face down on the grass,' added Byrd.

'Interesting.' The DCI leaned forward, the scent of his Hugo Boss wafting over. 'So, someone waited for him and drove away with the girl?'

'Ori, we need to speak to your friend Jennifer at the council, to see if we can track the car's movements,' suggested Byrd.

'*Your* friend?' The DCI frowned at Tanzy.

'He has a thing for Miss Lucas down at the town hall. He says he doesn't, but we all know he does.'

Tanzy's face reddened a little, but he didn't comment. 'I'll call her now, boss.'

'Good.' Corbridge glanced down at his watch. 'Let me know where that car is.' He stood and headed into his office.

Tanzy picked up his phone to call Jennifer Lucas, the operator based at the town hall who monitored the security cameras around Darlington. If anyone could track the red Volvo, it would be her — she knew the cameras like the back of her hand.

Byrd's phone rang. It was the forensic tech, Emily Hope.

'Are you in the office, Max?'

'I am.'

'Mind popping along to the lab? We've found something.'

* * *

The forensic lab was on the ground floor of the police station. Three large windows along one wall looked out to the rear car park, closed to prevent the cool spring air getting in.

Emily Hope sat at the far end of the room at her computer, her back to the room. As Byrd passed Amanda Forrest at her microscope, she lifted her head and offered him a brief smile. On the same worktop were tools and equipment Byrd knew very little about. He did recognise the fingerprinting machine that dried items out to show latent fingerprints and the evaporator the Forensics team used to remove liquids from samples that needed to be dried. The rest of it was alien to him.

Tallow was standing in front of a tall evidence-drying cabinet with shelves filled with various objects. He was so focused he didn't even notice Byrd walk past.

Hope stopped typing as he approached.

'Hello, Max. Thanks for popping in.'

'It's no problem.'

'Here, have a seat.' She pushed a chair towards him.

'What have we got?'

'Digital Forensics have managed to get into Corey Tills's phone. Lots of missed calls from last night and this morning, along with text messages and several voicemails.'

'All from the same number?'

'Mostly. One particular number rang eighteen times from ten o'clock until three hours ago. I've made a note of the number.' She leaned over and showed him. 'Familiar?'

'That's his wife's number,' Byrd said, checking his phone. 'What about any other numbers?'

'Another number rang several times last night and this morning too. The caller left two voice messages.'

Byrd checked his phone again. 'That's his manager at work — Selena Goldberg. I got the number off his wife. I haven't spoken to her yet.'

Hope nodded. 'The calls from Selena this morning could be asking why he hasn't turned up for work.'

'Maybe . . . but that wouldn't explain the calls last night.' Byrd tilted his head a fraction. 'How many voicemails were left?'

'There were six voicemails in total. Four from his wife and the other two from his work colleague, Selena.'

'You listened to them?'

Hope nodded. 'His wife was worried about him. Selena asked where he was and asked him to call her back as soon as possible. I heard something in Selena's voice.'

'Like what?'

'She was panicking about something, sounded like.'

'Can we listen to them?'

Hope played the voicemails on speakerphone for Byrd to hear.

'I understand what you mean about Selena,' Byrd said. 'She does seem distressed. I wouldn't have thought it would be all that stressful, working at West Manor.'

'The health and well-being centre? Gives me the creeps, that place.'

Byrd frowned. 'Were there any other calls or text messages from any other number besides those two?'

'No. That's it.'

He thanked her and made his way back to the office. He needed to contact Selena from West Manor because she might not know what had happened to Corey Tills.

Or she just might.

31

Thursday afternoon
Darlington Town Hall

Tanzy parked in the lot under the cinema in town, putting enough money in the machine for at least two hours, and made his way to the town hall. He shivered inside his grey parka, feeling the cold he hoped wouldn't be around for much longer. Entering through the double sliding doors, he saw the familiar face of Tina sitting at the reception desk, focusing on the screen in front of her. The faint glow gently illuminated her face as she looked up and smiled at him. Her cheeks flushed when she recognised him.

'Hello, Ori.'

'Hello, Miss Harrison.'

'Please, Inspector, call me Tina.'

'My apologies, Tina,' said Tanzy. 'I'm here to see Miss Lucas in the control room.'

'I'll sign you in.' Her eyes narrowed in a concentration that seemed a little forced. 'Signed in. Go on up, Inspector.'

'You have a pleasant day,' he said before he headed for the stairs.

'I certainly will.'

He'd been there so many times he felt comfortable enough opening the door and heading straight in. Jennifer was sitting at a large desk, facing the eight monitors that lined the wall, surrounded by grey cabinets and leftover mugs from the morning's meetings. She was wearing a tight-fitting black vest top and smart black trousers. The room was cooler than the corridor and Tanzy wondered if she was cold having so much of her tanned arms on show. She wiggled the mouse, clicked several times, and sighed, leaning back from the computer screen and turning towards him.

Her beautiful tanned face glowed and her long dark hair shone under the room's bright lighting.

'Hey, Jennifer.'

'Well, hello there, Mr Tanzy.'

'How you holding up?'

She sighed. 'It's been a busy one. And I feel you're not here to give me flowers?'

He managed a brief smile in response.

'Come and take a seat, Orion,' she said in her soft northern accent, her eyes glistening under the spotlights. She was born near Durham and had worked at the council for nearly fifteen years.

Tanzy grabbed a chair from the big table behind her and wheeled it over.

'How can I help?'

He told her about the incident at the hospital and the information about the six cars seen leaving the area immediately after Anya was taken.

'You want me to check where all six cars went?' She scowled at the mammoth task he was asking.

'It's your lucky day because I'd only like to know where the red Volvo is for now.' He then explained to her to whom the car was registered.

Her eyes widened with excitement. 'What time?'

Tanzy told her. She navigated through the town's security system and located a camera in the hospital car park. Tanzy recognised it. 'Is there another one that sees the road exiting the car park?'

She switched cameras. 'This one will be better.'

'Yeah.' He looked up at the screen. 'Yeah. That one *is* better.'

He was so close to her he could smell her sweet perfume. It was familiar — Pip may have worn it in the past.

They examined the footage and spotted the Volvo leaving the car park. Jennifer switched to another camera on Hollyhurst Road that showed the car taking a left, heading towards Woodland Road. The next camera, which had the perfect shot of the junction, showed them it went left towards town. They navigated through the town's camera system and tracked the car to Blackwell Lane, just off Carmel Road.

She paused.

'What's up?'

'There are no cameras on Blackwell Lane. Well, there's this one on Carmel Road, but nothing in between. There's one on Grange Road. How long would it take to drive along Blackwell Lane?' she asked. 'It's quite long, isn't it?'

'Two minutes tops, I'd say.'

They watched the camera on Grange Road, with a good view of the opening to Blackwell Lane, but the Volvo didn't appear after five minutes.

'It hasn't come out.' She ran the registration plate through their ANPR system and pressed enter. The last result was on Carmel Road around that time.

Tanzy slowly stood. 'Thanks for looking, Jennifer. Could you tell me if it turns up?'

She smiled, her white teeth shining. 'Orion, you'll be the first to know.' She swivelled towards him, crossing her legs seductively.

Tanzy nodded, walked to the door, and left the room, unsure if she was flirting with him.

32

Thursday afternoon
Mowden area, Darlington

In silence, the man drove around the West End of Darlington, looking for his next potential victim. Luna was sitting in the passenger seat, her legs tucked up with her feet on the edge of the seat, her face buried into her knees. He glanced her way. He liked Luna. She was compliant, unsure of herself, and best of all, quiet.

Hopefully, she'd be more willing than Anya had been last night, but time would tell.

He was taking a big risk here, but there was no reward without risk.

'Why are you doing this?' Luna asked, most of her words lost in her knees.

'Huh? Speak up, child.'

'Why are you making us do this?' she asked louder, lifting her head.

'I'm not making you do anything. You want to do this. You were stuck at West Manor — certainly no life for clever young girls like you. I've heard what you're capable of. And

I know you enjoy it. You told me about your family back in Warrington and what they were like. I need some help, that's all.'

'How long have you been doing this?'

He smiled at her. 'I wish I knew the answer.' Without expanding further, he focused back on the road. The van was crawling along Edinburgh Drive, passing Hummersknott Academy. 'Some nice houses around here. Posh bastards.'

Luna's eyes stayed on the passenger footwell.

'Ahh, here we go,' he said with excitement, suddenly pulling up on the right side of the road. 'You see her?'

Luna peered through the windscreen. 'Who?'

He pointed across the road, a few houses down, to a plump woman tending to her driveway. Dressed in a green jumper and black leggings, she was kneeling on a foam pad, plucking away the drive's weeds.

'Wh-What about her?'

'She's the one. This one will be easy for you.'

Luna spoke quietly. 'I can't.'

'Oh, you can. Remember where your sisters are now?' He turned to study her. 'Huh? Locked in the attic. If you don't go through with this, I'll never let them out. You'll never see your family again.'

Luna said nothing.

'Do you understand me?'

She nodded slowly.

'Good. Now, before you go, put some of this on your face.' He leaned to the right and pulled a bottle of red liquid from the driver's door storage compartment.

'What's that?'

'It looks like blood. Rub a little on your face. Make it look like you've been attacked. She'll let you in, no doubt.'

Luna stared at the fake blood. 'What if she doesn't?'

'She will. And when you're inside, make sure the door is unlocked, and I'll come in.' He scowled. 'Whatever you do, don't think about asking her to phone the police. If I find out you have, your sisters will die. Got it?'

She gulped. 'Yeah.'

* * *

Elaine Thornton pulled the last of the weeds out, proud of another job well done. The driveway looked much better. It was something she should have done during the winter, but with one thing or another, and the horrendous weather, she'd left it. There was no pain without gain, and all this TLC had wreaked havoc with her right knee, the same knee she'd had problems with since breaking it when she was a child. Struggling up, feeling the aches and pains everywhere, she looked around the street she'd lived in for most of her life.

Most of her neighbours' driveways were empty, as they were at work. There was only the guy who'd moved in several houses down on the opposite side. He must be a teacher, she'd decided, given the hours he kept. That messenger bag he carried over his shoulder made her think of school, but then again he could be anything.

The empty driveway reminded her that Tony was still golfing. She didn't mind. It certainly gave her the time to do her own thing. And him being out meant she didn't have to look after him and make him cups of tea while he sat watching golf on the TV. He was bloody golf mad. She bent down, picked up the foam kneeler, and went inside.

In the kitchen, she grabbed the jug full of thick tomato sauce and poured it over the sizzling mince, causing tiny drops of fat to jump out of the pan and land on her forearm. She winced as she stepped back and picked the folded tea towel off the hook to wipe it off.

Her husband, Tony, loved her lasagne, especially when she got creative, adding all sorts of colourful herbs and spices, some of which he hadn't heard of, but it didn't matter because it tasted divine.

While Tony was usually golfing, it gave her time to potter around in the garden or knit clothes for her newborn granddaughter. She sometimes went for coffee with her neighbour, Margaret, but she was currently away in Benidorm with her husband, sunning herself and taking afternoon dips in the sea.

She continued mixing the mince in the hot pan when she heard a knock at the door.

'Who's this?' she muttered to herself.

Her daughter Leanne was coming over but she had a key, so she'd usually walk in, not bother knocking. She peered up at the ancient clock. It was 4 p.m. Turning down the gas on the dial, she padded to the hallway, her new hip causing her an unusual pain she thought she'd seen the last of.

She unlocked the door and gently opened it, seeing a young girl standing on her driveway who appeared no older than eleven or twelve. There was blood around her mouth and smears of mud on her face and throat. Her clothing looked neglected and damaged, as if she'd been fighting.

Elaine stepped forward with a worried scowl. 'Are — are you okay, dear?'

'I need help,' the girl cried.

'What happened to you?'

'I was attacked.'

Elaine frowned. 'What happened to you, dear?' She edged forward a little to get a closer look.

'A group of kids attacked me,' she said.

'Oh God. What's your name?'

'Luna.'

Elaine raised a hand to her mouth and peered around the street, looking for any sign of the group she was speaking of. 'Where do you live? Where are your parents, Luna?'

'I don't live here. I live in Warrington.'

Elaine edged forward, placing a frail hand on her small shoulder. 'Where are your parents, then?'

Luna shrugged. 'I haven't seen them in a while. Please, I just need some help.'

The girl broke down, and tears fell from her face.

'Please, come in,' Elaine told her. 'We'll get you cleaned up and call the police. My husband will be back anytime now. He'll know what to do.'

33

'Mammy?' said the little voice from the back of the car.

Leanne Brook, driving at a steady thirty miles an hour, was wary of the two cyclists up ahead travelling side by side, apparently oblivious to her approach.

'Just a second, sweetie,' she replied to her daughter, angling over to the centre of the road to pass them. 'Yes, Maisy?'

'Grandma house,' Maisy said.

'Yes. We're going there now. We won't be long.'

Several minutes later, Leanne pulled into a parking bay by a detached house on Edinburgh Drive, smiling at the empty driveway, happy her dad was out golfing and enjoying his retirement. She turned to Maisy.

'You excited to see Grandma?'

The two-year-old grinned from ear to ear. Now Leanne's mother had retired, she could visit more often with Maisy, something she'd struggled to do when she was working.

'Come on, then.' Leanne unbuckled her seat belt, opened her door, and climbed out. The sun was bright but it was still chilly. She rounded the back of the car and slowly got Maisy out, careful not to catch her delicate head on the top of the door opening. They padded leisurely up the driveway, Maisy taking her time and telling Leanne all about Grandma's plants. Leanne tried her key in the front door, but it wouldn't go in. She frowned, then realised it was already unlocked. Her parents never left their door open, especially after the recent reports of people doing the rounds in the Mowden area, trying doors, and attempting to access cars during the night — several video clips had been uploaded to various local Facebook groups, and passed on to the police, but no one had been apprehended.

'Grandma,' said Maisy excitedly, patting the front of her thighs with her tiny palms.

'Yeah, we'll see Grandma. It looks like Grandad is out playing golf again, but he'll be back soon.'

Leanne opened the door, stepped into the warmth, and peered down the hallway. There was no sign of her mother from where she stood. Closing the door, she noticed her mother's keys inserted in the lock. Leanne frowned, knowing they never left the keys in the door just in case someone used a magnet to turn the lock — something Tony had told her might happen. To be on the safe side, they always placed them in the small bowl at the base of the stairs.

'Grandma.' Maisy pulled on Leanne's forearm, knowing she'd be getting a treat from her grandmother as soon as she saw her — a small toy or a cake from the local co-op or Cooplands.

'Just wait, Maisy.' Leanne took a few short steps to the nearest open door and peered into the living room. There was no sign of her mam in there. She backed out, stopping at the base of the stairs.

'Mam?'

The house was quiet, but sounds were coming from the kitchen.

'Mam, are you in the kitchen?'

Nothing.

'Are you upstairs?' Her mother's hip was bad. Maybe she was stuck on the toilet and unable to get up. It'd happened before she'd had the hip replacement. 'Do you need any help up there?'

If her mam was cooking something, she wouldn't leave the pan unattended unless it was only briefly. So, she must be out in the garden if she couldn't hear her in the house. It was the only logical answer.

'Come on. We'll try the kitchen and garden, Maisy.'

They walked down the hall and entered the kitchen. The smell of herbs and tomatoes was much more pungent now, but it was different: burnt and sour. Over on the hob, the mince in the pan had turned black. The red sauce that once sizzled with it had evaporated, leaving dark, crispy meat scorching against the boiling pan. Leanne covered her nose and went over, turning the gas off immediately.

'Mam, what are you doing?'

Whatever meal her mother was making, it would have to go in the bin and be started fresh.

'Mam, where on earth are you?' she shouted, her voice filling the house.

She turned to the back door, but it was closed, which was strange too, as it was usually left open to let air in, no matter how cold it was.

'Grandma?' Maisy muttered, looking around in the empty kitchen.

'We'll check upstairs. Come on.' Leanne gently took her hand and led her down the hall. She picked Maisy up at the base of the stairs and carried her up to save time, soon reaching the landing a moment later.

The bathroom door was open, so she looked inside, expecting to see Elaine on the floor or stuck on the toilet, but it was empty, besides a few towels on the floor that had been left, which was also unusual as her mother was a clean freak. Along the wide landing, her parents' bedroom door was closed.

'Mam?'

Nothing.

She cautiously approached the closed door, and raised her hand to edge it open.

'Mam, you in he—'

She froze and let out a blood-curdling scream.

136

34

Thursday late afternoon
West Manor, Darlington

Selena needed answers, and needed them now. It wouldn't be long before Jarrett Banks phoned, demanding to speak with the girls again. So far, she'd done a great job putting him off, but he wasn't the kind of man to give in. She had a strong feeling about that.

She briskly left her office, descended the stairs to the basement level, took a left into the dark corridor, and knocked on Reggie's office door.

No answer.

'Reggie, are you in there?' She knocked again, this time harder. After a long silence, she tried the handle, but it was locked.

Maybe he'd already gone home. Selena pulled out her phone and found his number. After a few rings, he picked up.

'Selena?'

'You still here, Reg?'

'No, I've left.'

'Did you see Corey today?'

'No,' he replied. 'I tried calling him a few times but no answer.'

'I'm getting worried, Reggie. It's not like him.'

'Sure there'll be an explanation for it, Selena. Don't worry.'

She ended the call and stared at Reggie's locked office door. It was an odd place for a caretaker to have an office, but it made sense, as the small office led to a good-sized garage where he could store tools and materials, along with the lawn-mower with which he spent much of his time keeping the gardens presentable. It also worked well because he could open the garage door onto a small concrete area that delivery drivers accessed using a narrow road running down the side of the huge, historic building. Reggie dealt with external suppliers, ranging from new furniture to office equipment to ordering grass seed for the lawns, which were delivered in huge bags. His job was unusual, combining two or three roles that had morphed into one during the years he'd been at West Manor.

She turned and went up the stairwell. Her phone rang. She hoped to see Corey's name, but she didn't recognise the number.

'Is this Selena Goldberg?' the caller asked.

She stopped halfway up the first flight of stairs. 'Who's this?'

'I'm Detective Constable Anne Tiffin from Durham Constabulary. Are you okay to speak for a few moments, Mrs Goldberg?'

She gulped, unsure of the reason for the phone call. 'Erm, yeah. How can I help you, Constable?'

'The call is about Corey Tills. Can you confirm Mr Tills is an employee at West Manor?'

'He is. What's this about?'

'I'm very sorry to inform you, but Mr Tills was found dead earlier this morning at Darlington Memorial Hospital. He was murdered.'

'Oh, goodness.' Selena sat on the nearest step. 'How — How did it happen? Who did it?'

'Our investigation is ongoing.'

Selena couldn't speak.

'We've spoken to his wife, who's confirmed his identity. I thought I'd ring you to let you know what was happening.'

'I . . .'

'I do have a few questions though, Mrs Goldberg.'

Selena gulped, fearing what was coming next. 'Okay.'

'According to his phone records, you phoned him last night and several times today, leaving him multiple text and voice messages.'

Shit, thought Selena, wondering if they'd listened to the voicemails and read the texts, then knew they must have done.

'Are you there, Mrs Goldberg?'

'I am. Have you listened to those messages, Constable?'

'We have. Is there anything you need to tell us?'

Selena thought hard. 'Yes, I need to be honest with you about something.'

35

Thursday late afternoon
Edinburgh Drive, Darlington

Tanzy pulled up outside Elaine Thornton's house, parking half on the path and half on the road. Two police cars and an ambulance were already there in front of the house, along with the forensics van parked over next door's driveway.

'When does this fucking end, Max?'

'I wish I knew,' replied Byrd from the passenger seat. 'There's never a dull day in this town.'

Tanzy rolled his eyes.

'Sorry, that's your phrase, isn't it?'

Through the windscreen, they could see several neighbours standing on their driveways, clearly desperate to see what was happening. Byrd smiled and slowly shook his head. Why was it that when the police were involved, suddenly everyone had all the time in the world to see what was going on?

They got out, feeling the late afternoon warmth on their faces. Tanzy, being Tanzy, grabbed his grey parka from the back seat, closed the back door, and put it on. On their way over, they'd been briefed on what had been found but knew very little detail other than what the victim's daughter, Leanne, had told the police when she'd phoned 999.

'You know, it amazes me how much time some people have,' Tanzy said, settling into his coat and gazing around at the number of eagle-eyed onlookers, echoing Byrd's thoughts of a moment ago.

It was the same everywhere they went.

The house was a huge, dated detached property needing a severe makeover to improve its kerb appeal. Its weathered windows and dark, yellowy nets certainly gave the impression that the house was owned by someone belonging to the older generation, however stereotypical or judgemental that felt.

PC Louise Degnan stood at the cordon with a clipboard in her hand. Her hair was tied up again, and Tanzy wondered what she'd look like if she wore it differently. She watched Byrd and Tanzy approach and smiled at them.

'You got here fast,' said Tanzy.

'Me and Eric were first here, sir,' she replied. 'You going in?'

'Of course.' Tanzy stopped before her and looked around, unable to see anyone else. He assumed PC Degnan had been the first responder and took charge of signing personnel in and out of the house. 'Where is everyone?'

'Amy and Josh are inside, sir.'

'Forensics inside too?' asked Byrd.

She nodded. 'They cleared us to enter the premises five minutes ago.'

'You been inside?' Tanzy asked.

She shook her head. 'Based on what I've heard, I'll stay out here and leave the dirty work to you guys. You might need these.' Degnan tucked the clipboard under her arm and pulled out some plastic gloves and overshoes from one of her stab vest's pockets. 'Here you go.'

They both nodded thanks and put them on once they reached the open front door, Byrd using the house's brickwork to aid his balance.

141

Tanzy went in first and slowly moved down the hall. Byrd followed him cautiously, peering around the hallway, taking it all in the way he usually did. An unmissable smell of something they couldn't distinguish, similar to food but with something added, lingered in the stale air.

'Hello?' shouted Tanzy.

'Up here,' they heard Emily Hope say.

Byrd and Tanzy slowly climbed the stairs and turned left, finding PC Amy Weaver and PC Josh Andrews further down the landing, outside the door to the main bedroom at the front of the house. Both were wearing face masks and overshoes. Weaver glanced their way. The look in her eyes informed them that she'd already seen what was inside the bedroom. PC Andrews remained silent, standing side on to them, staring down into the room with his arms crossed.

Weaver and Andrews stepped aside to make space for Byrd and Tanzy. The landing was spacious but contained very little other than a waist-high, narrow unit with a lamp and a photograph of an elderly couple sitting together on a beach, smiling into the camera. The pungent smell hit their noses afresh as they reached the doorway to the bedroom. Byrd moved in front of Tanzy to get a closer look.

Emily Hope was dressed in her white coveralls with her mask pulled tightly over her face. Her fabric hood was drawn securely over her head so the detectives couldn't see any of her short blonde hair. She was crouched inside the room, close to the open door, studying something on the victim's back.

Byrd remained in the doorway. The victim appeared in her late sixties or early seventies, but it was hard to tell as they couldn't fully see her face. They distinguished the body as female by the clothing and slightness of the frame. She was awkwardly positioned on her front — almost like a common sleeping position with her legs slightly bent — but there was something about the way her body was twisted. The way her arms were reaching for the doorway indicated there had been a panic and a desperation to escape this room.

Tanzy stepped level with Byrd to see into the room.

'Jesus,' he said. 'Max, what's happening in this town?'

He shook his head, but his focus never left the victim on the carpet. 'Never a dull day, Ori.'

The woman was bare-footed and wore black leggings, with big white pants that had been pulled down to reveal her wrinkly bottom and the top of her veiny thighs. Her clothes had either been pulled down by whoever was responsible for this, or they'd caught on the carpet when she'd frantically attempted to escape the room.

Judging by the horrendous knife wounds on her back, it was probably the latter.

Byrd took a small step forward to count the marks. 'How many times was she stabbed?'

'Looks like five or six, Max,' replied Hope.

'Who the hell would do this to her?' Tanzy shook his head in disgust. 'She's what — in her seventies?' He stared in silence. 'Defenceless.'

Hope didn't reply. Instead, she continued taking photos.

'Any signs of a break-in?' asked Tanzy.

Hope shook her head. 'No. No damage to the front or back door. The locks are intact. We've taken fingerprints, so we'll check that too. Whoever was in here either had a key or was invited in.' She shook her head once again. 'Bet she was fucking terrified.'

'You're not kidding.' Byrd edged the door further open so he could inspect the knife wounds closer. He stepped over the victim and had a look around, playing the scene over in his head. 'I think the fact her trousers are halfway down tells us she attempted to crawl away in a panic.'

'The killer could have had a sexual motive,' Hope pointed out. 'You'll have to wait for the post-mortem to be sure.'

'Have you checked under her fingernails yet?' asked Tanzy. 'If she was crawling away there'll no doubt be pieces of the carpet under there.'

'Yeah, there were carpet strands. That doesn't rule much out.'

Byrd studied the victim's head. 'Judging by the blood, the killer slammed the door into her head, crushing it against the wall until she was dead.' He took a short, sharp breath. 'Such a horrendous way to go.'

Tanzy sighed deeply, still standing on the landing.

The victim's stoved-in head and the thick pool of blood on the carpet wasn't a sight for the faint-hearted, that's for sure. Whoever had done this had been ruthless, and cruel.

'How many blows must that have taken, Ori?' Byrd whispered, struggling to get his words out.

Tanzy stared in amazement, a palm pressed against his mouth and chin. 'Doesn't bear thinking about.'

36

Thursday late afternoon
Edinburgh Drive, Darlington

Once they'd had a feel for the scene in the bedroom, the detectives returned downstairs to speak with the victim's daughter, Leanne, who was sitting on the long sofa in the living room, staring sightlessly at the marble fire surround as she rocked back and forth, her chin resting on both clenched fists. A toddler was sitting beside her, captivated by the cartoons on the television. Like the rest of the house, the decor was old-fashioned but not shabby: the television was in the farthest corner, just left of the wide, flat window, resting on an ancient wooden unit that was probably older than Tanzy. There was a faint scent of lavender from incense sticks on the windowsill and a strong smell of clean fabric, but there were no signs of clothes drying on the radiator under the window.

PC Amy Weaver was sitting on a smaller sofa closer to the door, watching Leanne closely. She said very little but was keeping them company in case the woman or her daughter needed anything. Weaver had told Byrd and Tanzy she'd already taken a statement from Leanne, accounting for the period from when she turned up to the point of discovering her mother in her bedroom.

Tanzy introduced himself awkwardly. The room felt enormous with the lack of furniture. He didn't want to speak down at her, so he went over to the sofa she was sitting on. 'Is it okay if I sit?'

Leanne bowed her head.

'I'm very sorry to have to go through this again with you, Leanne, but could you tell me and DI Byrd here what happened when you arrived?'

She closed her eyes, the thought of repeating what happened seemingly too much to bear. The detectives gave her a moment to collect herself.

Over the next few minutes, she told them her version of events.

'Who did this to her? My mother wouldn't harm anyone. She's the sweetest . . .' She trailed off, unable to finish her sentence, and welled up again.

'Well, that's our job to find out,' Byrd said softly from the doorway.

She looked his way, studying him for a moment. 'What will my dad do now?'

Byrd and Tanzy couldn't answer that. No words could justify what had happened here.

'Please find out who did this,' she begged.

'We will,' Tanzy told her. 'We'll do everything in our power.'

* * *

Byrd and Tanzy looked around the house, diligently studying each room, wearing gloves to ensure they didn't contaminate anything. Because of the size of the property and the number of rooms, it took a little while, so they covered half each. Tanzy concentrated on upstairs, and Byrd focused on downstairs.

Nothing stood out as unusual. Judging by the number of photos of Leanne and Maisy, it was a fair assumption they were a small family.

Byrd entered the kitchen and perused the flower-filled calendar attached to the fridge. Today's date included *Tony golfing*. He smiled sadly — they hadn't seen Tony yet. Leanne had called him to let him know he needed to come home immediately, so they were expecting him back very soon.

He had a look around the dated kitchen. The once-white cupboards had now faded to magnolia. In the centre of the room, he noticed one of the table chairs had been pulled out, as if someone had been sitting on it. He went over to the chair, turned, and looked at the cooker. It was clear from the pans on the hob Elaine had been in the middle of cooking. Had she come over to sit down for breaks in between stirring?

Surely there'd be a magazine of some sort?

It was also strange that the angled chair wasn't the closest chair to the cooker. Had someone else been sitting there, watching her as she cooked?

He moved away from the table and peered down the hall for a moment, then looked back at the cooker, remembering that Leanne had said she'd turned off the gas hob when she arrived.

'Someone knocked on the door,' he whispered to himself, going back in his mind. He walked down the hallway, hearing chatter from Hope and Tallow upstairs. He could hear Tanzy moving around somewhere directly above him as he stopped at the front door, frowning at the welcome mat before his feet. Spotting a small amount of mud, he stepped back, turning to see if any trails or patterns were on the dark grey carpet, although the colour made it difficult. He squinted, sure he could see something.

He found Hope standing on the landing upstairs.

'Emily, would you mind having a look at something for me?'

She nodded, followed him downstairs, and looked at the small area near the doormat.

'Could be a footprint of some sort there?'

She smiled at him.

'What?'

'Already lifted those prints.'

He returned the grin, then frowned at her. '*Those* prints?'

She nodded. 'Two partials.'

'I only saw one,' he said, squinting in search of the second.

She grinned. 'Leave that to us, Max.'

He opened the door and looked out at the ground and the driveway. A strip of soil separated the grass from the driveway's concrete.

'What size are they? Do they belong to the victim? Or it could be Leanne and Maisy, or the husband — Tony?'

'No, doesn't look like it.' She pushed out her bottom lip, now visible after pulling her mask under her chin, revealing thin red marks where it had been tight against her face. 'The bigger one is size ten — a man's shoe, looks like, bigger than the men's shoes I've compared it to in the house. The second print is either a petite woman or an older child — women's size five. Both Elaine and Leanne's shoes are too large. Maisy's way too small.'

He scowled. 'There were two other people here?'

'I can't say for certain, but I'd say so. I'll know more back at the lab.'

He followed her up the stairs looking for Tanzy, whom he found in the back bedroom, beside the bathroom.

'Ori,' he said from the doorway.

'What is it, Max?'

Tanzy was inspecting inside the wardrobes, his gloved hands holding the edge of the open doors.

'Anything?'

'Just old, musty clothes. What you got?'

'Footprints near the front door. Emily thinks she's found a men's size ten and a women's size five. They don't belong to anyone in the family, victim included.'

Tanzy lowered his arms and slowly turned to him with a frown on his tanned face. 'So there were two other people here?'

'Seems that way. Keep looking up here. I'll see if the others have anything from the neighbours yet.'

Once through the front door, he looked around the street. PC Degnan stood at the cordon just beyond the end of the driveway, holding a clipboard. The cordon had been set up from the side of the house, across the garden, around the forensics van, and back up the other side. The small crowd had thinned, but a handful remained, interested to see how the investigation was developing.

'Any sign of Andrews and Weaver?' he asked Degnan.

'Still knocking on doors.'

Byrd heard footsteps to their right. PC Weaver approached with an elderly gent, who was wearing a chequered shirt and beige trousers held up with flexible braces that looped over his narrow shoulders. He moved with uncertainty from his hips, as if they'd caused him issues in the past, and wore glasses that magnified his blue eyes.

'Sir, this gentleman spotted something earlier.'

'I'm Donald.' He turned and pointed at a large detached house across the road with a red MG on the driveway. 'I live just there. I went out earlier, Inspector, and saw someone at their door.'

'How long ago was this?'

He flicked his wrist to check the time. 'Maybe an hour ago, maybe more. I can't say for certain.'

'Who did you see at the door?'

'As I pulled off my drive, I saw Elaine talking with a girl. No taller than this.' He raised a flat palm, indicating a height around his chest.

'Can you recall her description or what she was wearing?'

'She had long dark hair, maybe to her shoulders. She was wearing blue jeans and a light-coloured T-shirt. Might have been white.'

'How old would you say she was?'

He curled his lip. 'Hard to say. I only caught half of her face. Early teens, maybe. But she looked dirty — you know, grubby. I remember Elaine speaking to her like she was concerned about something the girl was telling her.'

'You didn't stop to check?'

The man smiled, showing several missing teeth. 'Why would I check? What business of mine is it who knocks on my neighbours' doors?'

'Did she go inside the house?'

'I don't know. I saw her only briefly.'

'Okay. Thank you for your time.'

The man nodded and slowly shuffled off towards his house. Byrd sighed lightly. 'One of those days, Amy.' He panned the street. 'Any sign of Josh?'

'Right here, boss.' PC Andrews ducked under the cordon and stopped when he reached Byrd. 'Nothing so far. Most neighbours aren't in. The ones who are in claim they haven't seen a thing.'

'Have you—'

'Checked to see if they have CCTV?' said Andrews, finishing his sentence.

Byrd smiled.

'Of course. Not everyone answered but so far the only cameras in this street are six doors down on the opposite side of the road.'

'Damn it.' Byrd dropped his head a little. 'Keep checking, Josh.'

PC Andrews nodded and ducked back under the cordon in search of more information.

'Excuse me, but what's going on?' asked a woman in a red coat nearby. 'I'm Neighbourhood Watch, you know,' she added when she got no reply.

A car approached, followed by a sudden shriek of brakes, then a door slammed. 'Where is she? Where's my wife?' a disgruntled voice said.

Byrd looked up sharply. 'Mr Thornton?'

Tony stopped at the cordon when he saw the look on Byrd's face and burst into tears.

37

Thursday early evening
Darlington

'I'm so disappointed in you, Luna,' the man said, momentarily turning to look at her.

She cowered in the front of the van, her knees up near her chin, her face half hidden, her body facing the passenger door. The further away she was, the safer she felt.

'I did as you asked. I left the door open.'

He scowled. 'After I came into the house, you told her I was there to hurt her.'

'I didn't, I—'

'Don't lie! You were up in the bathroom with her. I heard you whispering. Why were you up there anyway?'

'She was getting a towel to clean my face.'

He looked away, focusing back on the road. 'I'm disappointed.'

'Please, just let us go.' Her voice was muffled in the small space between her knees.

'You know I can't do that, Luna.' He sighed heavily, noticing the traffic up ahead on Coniscliffe Road as they approached the roundabout at Elm Ridge. He dabbed the brakes, slowing the van. 'Always busy, this bloody town.' He looked her way. 'If anything, I'm helping you.'

'It doesn't feel like it,' she whispered.

'Hmmm?'

She stayed silent.

'What did you say?'

'I said it doesn't feel like it.'

'Selena was keeping you prisoner at West Manor. You're free of that now.'

'But you're keeping us prisoner at your house. We can't leave.'

He considered this with narrowed eyes as 'Club Tropicana' by Wham played on the local radio station.

'I'll let you go soon. I just want to help you.'

He put the car in gear and went straight over the round-about, continuing towards the town centre.

'We don't need help,' she said, building up the courage. 'We want to go home.'

'Listen, whatever arrangement is in place for you girls being here has nothing to do with me. You were prisoners at the house. Like I said, I'm helping you. So I don't want to hear any more on the matter, okay?' He leaned over, extending his left arm, and gently squeezed the outside of her thigh.

She winced, compressing herself closer to the door. His touch made her skin crawl.

She knew what he was capable of, but she hadn't seen such violence before. It terrified her like nothing ever had.

'When the time is right, I'll let you girls go.'

38

Selena Goldberg wearily looked up at the office clock. It had been a long, draining day. She'd been doing Corey's work as well as her own, and breaking the news of his death to their colleagues and the guests.

Where was Anya?

Did someone know Corey was going after Anya?

And if so, why would they kill him?

Or was Anya the one who had done it? She didn't have it in her, did she?

Since her phone call with DC Anne Tiffin, she'd thought long and hard about the story she planned to tell her. Obviously, the truth would open a can of worms she wanted to keep closed, but she needed to tell her something. With the police listening to the voice messages she'd left for Corey, it was apparent she knew something that they didn't.

The knock at the door made her snap out of her thoughts. It was Elisha, the receptionist.

'Surprised you're still here, Elisha.'

'I'm going soon.' Elisha padded into the room. 'There's someone here to see you, Selena.' The receptionist was in her early twenties and had worked at West Manor for three years now. She was pleasant, kind, and soft of voice, the ideal receptionist.

'Come in.' Selena's heart rate rose.

The detective entered the room wearing a dark suit and a white blouse underneath. She wore large, square glasses, had a blonde bob, and slightly larger teeth that made her top lip more prominent than usual.

She extended a hand. 'I'm Detective Constable Anne Tiffin.'

Selena stood and courteously shook it, then looked beyond the detective at Elisha, who nodded and understood it was her cue to give them some privacy.

'Please, have a seat.' Selena motioned to the spare chair beside DC Tiffin.

'Thanks.' Tiffin sank into it and pulled it closer to the table. 'So, as you're aware, we found the body of Corey Tills earlier today.'

Selena nodded sadly, waiting for the next part.

'And we checked his phone.'

Another nod from Selena.

'We listened to the voice messages you'd left for him. It appears you knew why he was at the hospital.'

She nodded.

'Care to expand on what happened, Mrs Goldberg?'

She took a deep, silent breath and mentally collected herself. 'Corey was looking for someone.'

DC Tiffin took out a notepad. 'Who?'

'A girl called Anya Deacon.'

Tiffin was aware of the Mitchell murders and that Anya was found at the house. 'And who is Anya?'

Think, Selena told herself before she spoke. 'She's a guest here at West Manor.'

'A guest?'

'Yeah, she was here for treatment for anxiety.'

'And how are *guests* here at West Manor cared for? I didn't actually know this place existed until very recently.'

'We've been here for some years. We have guests who stay here and some who come for day visits. We teach them techniques to cope with anxiety — for example, breathing, mindfulness. It's a safe space for people who need a retreat, somewhere to get better.'

DC Tiffin frowned. 'And Anya was being treated for anxiety?'

'Severe anxiety.'

'How long has Anya been here?' asked the detective.

'Just over one month.' That part was true, at least, so Selena didn't need to worry about whether her body language gave any indications that she was lying.

'And is she getting better?'

'We're trying hard with her, but . . .' Selena trailed away.

DC Tiffin nodded. 'So, where is she? As far as we know, she's been at scenes where two people have been killed. We need to speak with her immediately.'

'I don't know.' Selena shrugged hopelessly, wishing she did.

'When did Anya leave West Manor?'

'Tuesday. I have CCTV footage of her in the garden first thing with some other guests, then she was seen in a corridor near her room, but after that nobody saw her again.'

'So she didn't go out of the main gate?'

'She must have done. It's the only way out,' Selena explained. 'But nobody saw her. And it wasn't on the footage.'

'Why didn't you report her missing when she first went?'

'We just assumed she would turn up.'

'So, let me get this straight. You're treating a nine-year-old child for anxiety, but you don't appear to be a paediatric facility. The child goes missing, but you don't report that to the police. You discovered she was at the hospital and sent Corey Timms, one of your employees, to abduct her from police custody.' DC Tiffin scowled. 'What's going on here? I've listened to the voice messages. There's something you're not telling me.'

She shrugged. 'Nothing is going on here, Constable. I knew she'd be at the hospital and sent—'

'How?'

'How what?'

'How did you know she'd be at the hospital?'

'All our guests wear a health monitoring anklet. It measures their well-being, but also allows us to track their location using an app.'

'Seems excessive from someone who runs an energy and well-being centre,' countered Tiffin, narrowing her eyes. 'Is it standard practice to monitor the location of your patients?'

'Guests.'

'I'm sorry?'

'We call them guests, not patients.' Selena's voice faltered under Tiffin's stare. 'When the guests are full-time, it's our policy during their stay here that we are able to track their location.'

'You may have to show me that policy sometime.'

Selena felt her face grow warm.

'So, if you can track Anya, where is she now?'

'We can't track her right now. The monitor could be broken.'

'How does this app work?'

'I don't know much about it, to be honest. Corey dealt with the tech stuff. He told me last night that her location had been highlighted on the app he was using and that she was at the hospital. That's all I know, Constable.'

Tiffin nodded, but Selena could see she had her suspicions.

'So, what are your thoughts on Corey's murder?' the PC went on. 'There must be a reason behind it. It isn't every day something like that happens.'

Selena shrugged once more. 'I honestly don't know.'

'Do you think Anya was involved?'

'She's only nine years old. I highly doubt it.'

'Is there a name and phone number for her parents? We must speak to them immediately as they might know her whereabouts.' Tiffin scowled. 'I'm assuming you've informed them she's gone missing?'

She nodded. 'Jackie and Martin Deacon. You want their number?'

Tiffin took out her phone and waited patiently. 'When you're ready.'

Selena told her a made-up number she pretended to read from the screen the detective couldn't see.

Tiffin noted it down. 'I'll call them,' she said. 'If you hear anything, let the police know ASAP.' She leaned forward. 'Here's my card. We'll be in touch very, very soon.'

39

Thursday evening
Darlington Business Centre

With most of the team still at Edinburgh Drive investigating Elaine Thornton's murder, Tanzy pulled up at Darlington Business Park on Yarm Road just after 6 p.m. Once parked, he inhaled deeply, readying himself for what was about to come.

He picked up his phone and informed DCI Corbridge he'd arrived.

The phone beeped immediately. *Good luck, Orion.*

Smiling nervously, he got out and made his way over to the entrance, remembering a technique he used for speaking in public, a way to trick the mind into turning the anxious, nervous energy into something positive and exciting — something to do with the body feeling the same way when it was scared and when it was excited. It sounded easy.

He stepped into the main entrance dressed in tight black jeans, brown shoes, and an open, thin grey jacket instead of his parka, passing a couple of reporters standing nearby, speaking between themselves. They recognised him and went silent.

Down the corridor, he spotted Lucy near the open door of the conference room. She was peering down at an iPad, her finger moving elegantly across the screen. Her straight hair shined beautifully under the white spotlights above her.

'Hey, Lucy,' he said before reaching her.

She pulled her attention from the screen and smiled widely at him. 'Hello, Orion. Thanks for making this on such short notice. I know the police must be very busy today.'

'They are.' He took a lungful of cool, air-conditioned air. 'News travels fast around this town.'

'And it's your job to give the public the answers,' she said, her hair falling to one side as she tilted her head.

'I've got something with me.' He pulled out a memory stick. 'Could you play this when I ask — is that okay?'

'Of course. Just let me know when. Are you ready to go?'

He nodded.

'Then the stage is yours, DI Tanzy.'

'Brilliant.' The sarcasm in his voice made her smile for a second too long, showing her perfect teeth and the shape of her lips. It made him feel good about himself; there was nothing wrong with mild, harmless, flirtatious eye contact.

He entered the busy room and headed straight for the desk, focusing on the jug of water and empty glass on the table as a distraction from the crowd of eager reporters and members of the public to his left. He could feel his heart pumping inside his chest, but he took slow, measured breaths, remembering the techniques he'd watched earlier to calm him.

Lucy took a few steps into the room. The room fell silent apart from the occasional movement of people trying to get comfortable on the hard plastic chairs that were never designed for comfort.

'This evening, we have Darlington's own Detective Inspector Orion Tanzy here to update us on the recent police cases, and hopefully, he can answer any questions you may have.' She turned to Tanzy and nodded, indicating it was his time to speak up.

He leaned an inch closer to the microphone attached to the stand on the tabletop. 'Hello, everyone. It hasn't been very long since the last update, so I'll keep it as direct and informative as possible.' His voice was loud but soft and clear without sounding too imperious. 'In our last update, we mentioned the murder of Mia Mitchell, who was found in her kitchen at her home on Haughton Road here in Darlington. At the time, we had footage of a man we believed was heavily involved, seen at their property by a close neighbour. Since then, we have learned the man's identity is Corey Tills, whose body was found earlier this morning, within the grounds of Darlington Memorial Hospital.'

A wave of gasps and whispers swept the room.

Tanzy raised a hand to silence them and nodded to Lucy, who understood what she needed to do. She inserted the memory stick into the side of the laptop.

'We have footage from the hospital which I'd like to show you.' He fell silent and waited for the screen to appear. Lucy pressed play. The footage showed Corey walking with a little girl towards the exit of the children's ward. 'This man, whom we now know is Corey Tills, entered the children's ward without any authorisation, started a fire, and left with this girl, Anya.' Tanzy gazed over to Lucy. 'Could you pause it there, please?'

He stood and moved closer to the screen.

'We don't know what happened after they left, but Corey's body was found in a garden outside the hospital. His car, a red Volvo, was seen leaving the car park, so we believe someone drove it away after they'd attacked him with the girl inside. We don't know who that individual is or their connection with Anya, but we assumed, looking at CCTV, they ditched the car somewhere around Blackwell Lane and walked the rest of their way to wherever they were going.'

A hand went up in the crowd. Tanzy ignored it and continued.

'So, we have a team currently working with the council to look through the town's CCTV to see if we can pinpoint where they went.'

Another hand went up. A woman in her late forties. Red fleece, a phone in her hand, her arm outstretched. This time, Tanzy was open to a question.

'Yes?'

'Have the police found Ella Mitchell yet?'

Further whispers filled the room.

'Not yet.'

'Don't they say once someone has gone missing for longer than twenty-four hours, the chance of finding them alive is dramatically reduced?'

Talk about putting a negative spin on things, thought Tanzy. 'No, that's untrue,' he told her. 'But it is unusual for someone to be missing for longer than twenty-four hours, and it is especially concerning when the missing person is a child. The sooner we find Ella, and the sooner we find Anya, the better.

'I can also now confirm that Anya's full name is Anya Deacon. We're searching for her family, and ask that if anyone recognises her or knows her family, please do come forward.'

More whispers circulated the room, making Tanzy more uncomfortable than he was already feeling. He figured he'd got off to a good start but the people in the room were there to ask difficult questions.

A hand went up, this time at the back of the room. A man this time, quite young, possibly mid-twenties, a trendy-looking dude with short hair and a thin goatee.

Tanzy nodded at him.

'So what's happened today, then? I heard there was another body found in the Mowden area?'

News travels fast, indeed. 'We discovered the body of Elaine Thornton earlier this afternoon on Edinburgh Drive. Unfortunately, Mrs Thornton endured a very violent death in her own home.'

'Any leads on that one, Inspector?'

Tanzy scowled. 'A neighbour informed us he witnessed a small girl knocking on Mrs Thornton's door as he left his house. We also have footage from one of the neighbours of her walking in the direction of Mrs Thornton's property.'

'Any idea who the girl is?'

'We aren't certain of her identity yet — here is the CCTV footage.' He paused as it played. 'We are appealing for any members of the public to come forward if they have any CCTV or doorbell footage of the area.' He raised a finger. 'We have reason to believe a man with size-ten trainers was also in the house today.'

'You think two people murdered Elaine Thornton?'

'We can't say for certain,' replied Tanzy, keeping his cards close to his chest.

A different hand went up. 'Do you think this girl is Anya Deacon?' asked the man. 'I know the footage is poor, but she looks quite similar.'

Tanzy thought about the question and shook his head. 'No, our witness suggested this girl is in her early teens. So probably three or four years older than Anya.'

He scanned the crowd. Another man raised his hand.

'Yes?'

'Are the police under the impression that these murders are connected in some way? There are obvious similarities here.'

'Based on what we know so far, that's definitely something we're considering at this stage, yes.'

On the wall behind him were three images: one of Ella Mitchell, one of Anya Deacon, the other a distant still shot of the girl who'd knocked at Elaine Thornton's door taken from a neighbour's CCTV, which didn't show much detail but was better than nothing.

'We don't believe that Anya Deacon is involved in the murder of Mia Mitchell, the victim we found at Haughton Road, but there's nothing to say this girl here—' he pointed at the third image, furthest right — 'whoever she may be, isn't involved with Elaine Thornton's savage murder. We can't rule it out. If anyone out there knows anything, please get in touch immediately.'

40

Byrd stood on Elaine Thornton's doorstep, observing Peter Gibbs's team placing her body into the back of the van parked at the end of the driveway. Once secured in the vehicle, Gibbs returned to Byrd, wearing a long, black coat that made him appear even more serious than he already did. He stood a few inches taller than Byrd, looking tired, dark bags under his dull eyes.

'We'll take her to the hospital. Let Dr Hemsley take it from there,' said Gibbs.

'You spoken with him?'

The serious-mannered coroner nodded. 'I've updated him.' He turned his wrist to check the time. 'It's getting on, so I don't know if he'll make a start today.'

Byrd nodded. 'Hopefully we'll get something back by tomorrow either way.'

'Yes, I'd like to think so.' Gibbs looked at the house, almost as if studying it. 'Forensics still in there?'

'Yeah. They're clearing things up before they move on.'

163

'They put in some hours, don't they?'

Byrd shrugged. 'We all do. You know what it's like.'

'I've booked a clean-up team for tomorrow, so make sure your guys have everything they need.'

Byrd bowed his head. 'No worries. I'll make sure we have everything sorted.'

'What's your verdict, then?' asked the coroner. 'Think the girl was capable of doing this?'

Byrd shook his head. 'No, I don't think so. I don't think a girl of that size would have what it took, strength-wise, to do that. Certainly not to crush the victim's head with the door.'

'Elaine Thornton looked quite frail, though, Max.'

Byrd pushed out his bottom lip. There was no denying the victim was petite, almost birdlike in appearance. But if anyone had undergone such horrific torture and endured that much pain, they'd do anything to get away from it.

'The second set of footprints indicates someone else was here,' he pointed out. 'But the question is: was the girl involved?'

'Teamwork? She gets entry to the house, and a man comes in after?' Gibbs lifted his chin, considering that. 'Why, though? Robbery?'

'We don't know yet.' Byrd paused, then added, 'I don't like this at all. What happened with the door . . .'

Gibbs winced. 'Yeah, to crush her head like that must have taken some effort. I feel for the husband. No doubt left the house earlier, assuming he'd return like it was any other day.' A certain sadness was in his eyes.

'Not like you to show your emotions, Peter,' said Byrd, seeing the coroner in a different light for the first time since he'd known him.

'I know . . . but going for a nice game of golf and expecting to come home to tea with his daughter and granddaughter.' Gibbs shrugged his narrow, bony shoulders under his coat.

He's getting soft, thought Byrd. *But how we all take these simple things for granted.*

'I'll get going,' Gibbs said. 'Thanks for the update today. I'll contact the department and Dr Hemsley over the next twenty-four hours. See where we are on this.'

Byrd nodded and watched the coroner stride away down the drive.

Minutes later, DC Tiffin drove up and bounded over.

'Going in?' asked PC Degnan, ready to sign her in.

'No. I need to speak with DI Byrd for a minute.'

Byrd heard her and took a few steps from the house, meeting her halfway down the drive. 'How did it go with Selena Goldberg?'

'Selena says Anya is a patient — a "guest", as she put it — at the West Manor facility, being treated for severe anxiety. She ran away a few days ago.'

'Anya did?'

'Yeah. She claims Anya wore an anklet that allows them to track her, hence why they knew she was at the hospital. She says it isn't working now.'

Byrd bobbed his head. 'The hospital took it off her. What about her parents?'

'Selena gave me a phone number for them, but the phone seems to be off. I've left several messages. I'll keep trying.'

Byrd pressed his lips together, unsure he was buying the story. 'Theory?'

'She knows much more than she's letting on.'

41

Byrd turned into Low Coniscliffe and followed the narrow road towards his house, the BMW's dazzling headlights illuminating a way through the awkwardly parked cars and building supplies stacked up from the recent housing development. Two years ago, it was a tranquil little village. The odd car would drive through and park down at the river. Traffic was light. However, due to the local housing development, the village had grown, which, in Byrd's mind, was not why he'd chosen to live here all those years ago. He liked it quiet and peaceful.

He slowed and parked in his usual spot by the kerb. Claire's Volkswagen Tiguan had taken priority on the driveway, as it usually did, the bonnet several feet from the garage door. Byrd spotted one of Alan's blankets in the rear window resting on the parcel shelf and smiled to himself. He had told Claire it was safer to reverse in — that way, when she left the house, she wouldn't have to reverse out, something she had done a few weeks ago and nearly crashed into an oncoming

166

car filled with teenagers excited about spending their day at the river, presumably drinking, judging by the contents of the carrier bags in the back. Byrd had told them to be careful down there and behave themselves.

They'd purchased the Tiguan last month because the previous car wasn't big enough for Alan's pushchair and God knows what else you needed being a parent to a baby nowadays. Everywhere you went, it was a military operation, and it certainly was more complex and time-consuming than Byrd had ever imagined it would be.

After switching off his engine, he sat and enjoyed the silence, feeling almost too exhausted to move. He sluggishly opened the door and stepped down onto the road.

A neighbour who'd moved into a nearby house several months ago was on the other side of the road, walking the Alsatian everyone seemed to be wary of. It hadn't given Byrd any reason to question whether it was a well-behaved dog, but he certainly wouldn't risk it anywhere near Alan, that's for sure.

The dog-walker waved half-heartedly as he passed, the nearest streetlight casting light on top of him, creating a huge moving shadow. Byrd returned the wave before he closed the front door, happy to block out the outside world for the evening.

The warmth and cosy lighting in the hallway were welcoming. Soft light shone from the lamp to his right, and heat emitted from the radiator to his left. He lowered his bag and slipped off his shoes, leaving them at the bottom of the stairs while he quietly climbed them two at a time until he reached the top and took a left. He quietly opened Alan's door and padded over to his cot to watch him sleep. His little chest slowly rose and fell, his face gently lit by the lamp on the landing. His room smelled of baby shampoo and the fabric conditioner they used to wash his sleepsuits.

Byrd was in such a trance he hadn't heard Claire approach from behind and slip her arms around his waist.

'Jesus.' He grabbed her hands but quickly realised he wasn't being mugged by a stranger in his son's bedroom.

She stood on her tiptoes and kissed his cheek. 'You're back late,' she whispered.

He sighed. 'It's been a long day.'

She rose on her tiptoes to kiss his cheek again. 'You coming downstairs?'

'Let me have a quick shower. I stink.'

'You do,' she said, playfully tickling his side with her fingertips. 'There's tea in the microwave.'

Byrd stole another glimpse of his son before backing out of the room and closing the door, leaving a small gap for a bit of light for him. Once showered, he went downstairs in thin blue shorts, which he usually wore for football, and a faded red T-shirt.

He warmed his tea and sat down next to Claire. They rarely spent time together in front of the television; Byrd was often in the kitchen on his laptop if he wasn't playing football, using the time away from work to research things about work. It was never-ending for him due to his inability to let things go. Although his work ethic and focus were things that Claire really admired about him, it was something she was starting to worry about. Once Byrd got his teeth into something, he tinkered on the edge of obsession.

'What are we watching?' he asked her.

She picked up the remote from the arm of the sofa and sat up. 'Here. Your choice. I've been watching it all week.'

Grinning, he held up a palm. 'I'm not willing to get between you and your TV remote. Honestly, you can choose. I won't be up that long anyway. I'm exhausted.'

The bags under his eyes were darker than usual, and his skin was drier than normal. Although he was tired and could fall asleep on the sofa right there, he knew he'd be up half the night, tossing and turning. After the day the police had had, not many of them would be sleeping — there was too much on their minds.

Claire dropped back onto the sofa and chose something to watch on Netflix. Byrd didn't recognise it but had noticed Claire watching it before. The women in bikinis on a South American beach certainly made it easier for Byrd to sink further into the sofa next to her.

'How are Ori and Pip?' she asked. 'I haven't seen them in a while. Maybe we can go out together again soon?'

'Sounds good.'

'I can ask my mam to come round to watch Alan?'

'I'll speak to Ori and see if they're up for it.'

She reached over and gently patted his thigh, smiling, looking forward to a child-free night.

Byrd mentally calculated his diary for the next month, thinking of a good date to suggest to Tanzy and Pip, but he knew, as well as Tanzy did, they had more important things to work on — the same things that would keep him up half the night, along with wondering what delights were in store for them tomorrow.

42

One month ago
Warrington

Jarrett Banks waited in his Range Rover opposite the primary school, watching the entrance. Two women stood outside the school gate, giggling between themselves, absorbed in their own little story. Hendo, who worked for the Molnar brothers, was parked two cars ahead of him. He did the school run daily. Jarrett looked around and, when the coast was clear, got out and made his way along the path, knocking on the passenger window of the BMW that Hendo was sitting in. He unlocked the door, and Jarrett climbed in.

'What you doing here?' asked Hendo, frowning at him.

Jarrett settled into the seat, his left hand inside his leather jacket pocket, and scanned the outside of the car to see if anyone was looking their way.

'Tomas asked me to say . . .' Jarrett whipped the knife out and drove it into Hendo's throat, then removed it, quickly opening the passenger door and climbing out. Hendo coughed and gagged, his hands immediately clutching at his bleeding throat. His death was quick. Jarrett manhandled the body into the back of the car and drove the BMW into the next street, so that it would be hidden from Anya's view when she came out of the school gates. He knew Anya was allowed to come out by herself — he'd overheard the Molnars discussing it with Hendo. He returned to his Range Rover like nothing had happened and waited in the driver's seat, watching through the windscreen. The time was 3.07 p.m.

When more parents turned up to collect their children, Jarrett knew it wouldn't be much longer. Soon, a flood of pupils and parents came through the gate. It wasn't long before he spotted Anya. He opened the door and crossed the road.

'Anya,' he said. 'Hendo's not here today. I'm picking you up.'

'Uncle Jarrett?'

'Yeah, he's on a job. Your dad sent me to get you instead.'

They got into the car and closed the doors. This was easy.

'Uncle Jarrett, what's happened?'

He turned to the back of the car. 'Something's come up, that's all.'

That seemed sufficient enough for her not to ask any further questions.

The time on the dash was 3.22 p.m. Luna and Nina both finished at 3.30 p.m. Their secondary school was less than half a mile away.

'Why are we getting my sisters too?' Anya asked once they'd parked just along from the school.

Jarrett focused through the front windscreen, watching for signs of students leaving. He glanced at the watch. *Anytime now*, he thought.

'Uncle Jarrett?'

'Something bad's happening at home — I need to get you three to safety.'

Students started spilling out of the school gates. Some of the boys were as big as grown men and had stubble, and others were half the size and fresh-faced, wearing blazers far too big for them with square block shoulders. Amid smiling students happy to finish the school day, Jarrett spotted Luna walking through the gates. It looked like she was arguing with someone across the road. The other girl said something, and Luna quickly gave her bag to a friend, ran over the road, and punched the girl in the face. The girl fell to the path and covered her bloody nose with a hand.

'Fuck's sake,' Jarrett muttered, getting out of the car.

'Go on, Luna!' chanted Anya from the back seat.

'Luna!' he shouted, walking over to her. 'What are you doing? Get in the fucking car.'

'Uncle Jarrett . . . Wh-What are you doing here?' Her cheeks reddened. She pointed at the bloody-nosed girl on the floor. 'She asked for it. She had it coming.'

He leaned in and whispered in her ear, 'We can't go around doing things like that.'

Luna silently nodded and scowled at the girl, who was now surrounded by timid friends helping her up.

'What's going on here?' a loud voice said.

Luna turned back through the school gates and noticed the headmaster storming out.

'Shit, let's go!' She ran over to the Range Rover and got in.

Jarrett casually returned to the car. 'Where's Nina?'

'She's already set off — she's gone down there.' She pointed straight ahead at the street that veered off to the right.

Jarrett started the car and pulled out, slowly making his way up to thirty, keeping his eyes on the students. Anya and Luna were in the back, discussing why Luna had punched the girl. Jarrett wasn't really interested. His primary focus was getting all the girls into the car, so the first part of the plan was almost a success.

He followed the road and saw Nina walking, wearing the red coat he'd seen her in before, bobbing her head to the music playing in her earbuds. Jarrett slowed, beeped the horn, and lowered the window. 'Nina, get in!'

She frowned as she walked over the road, checking for cars before she crossed. 'Uncle Jarrett, what's going on?'

'I'm picking you up today.'

Nina was old enough to know what that meant and rounded the front of the car before opening the door and climbing in. 'What's happened?'

'Business has taken a turn for the worse. Your mum and dad have asked me to take you somewhere for a while until things blow over.'

'What things?' asked Luna from the back of the car.

'I can't get into it right now. All I've been told is I must take you somewhere safe.' He hoped that would convince them. The girls knew their family and the people they associated with, along with the trouble that came with it.

'Remember our conversation last week when I was at your house?' Jarrett reminded them.

They all nodded.

'Well, it's happened. Your dad told me that Warrington isn't a safe place right now.'

'What about you, Uncle Jarrett?' asked Anya. 'Are you in danger?'

He made a show of looking upset. 'Afraid so. I'm going to have to help your dad on this one.'

'Where are you taking us?' asked Nina.

'It's a place a few hours away. Don't worry, you'll be safe from harm. But I'll need you to trust me on this next part.'

'What is it?' Anya queried.

'I'll need to look after your phones for now and keep them with me. If the families coming for us find your location, they'll come for you too.'

Anya pulled hers from her pocket and handed it over without asking questions. Seeing her do this, Luna followed suit.

'Thank you. We need to turn them off so they can't be tracked.' He leaned over Nina, put them in the glove box, and sat back straight. 'I'm going to need yours too, Nina.'

She frowned. 'How long are we going for? What about school?'

'It's only a few days. We'll ring them, say you're all sick or something. It'll be fine.'

'How will we make calls if we need to?'

'The place we're going to has a phone.'

Nina sighed and looked away, shaking her head, unsure if she'd cope without her social media for longer than ten minutes.

'Listen, I know the next few days will be difficult, but it's better than being dead, isn't it?'

They sighed collectively.

Jarrett had packed things for the girls: toiletries, spare clothes, and accessories. He had done this after meeting with their father and other gang members at their house. The meeting itself hadn't gone how Jarrett had wanted it to go, so he'd had to take action.

'Ready, girls?'

'Just get us there, Uncle Jarrett,' said Luna.

He nodded and set off towards Darlington.

43

Thursday evening
Warrington

Jarrett Banks sat at the grand circular table in the huge kitchen of Tomas Molnar's house. Tomas's brother, Matej, was there, as were several other men who worked for Jarrett and the Molnar brothers. Tomas's wife, Maria, came in to fetch something from the sink. She was slender, with long dark hair almost to the curve of her lower back. In normal circumstances she would have caught the attention of most men, but the Molnar brothers' gang never allowed their eyes to wander. Jarrett noticed tears in her eyes as she turned and left the kitchen.

'What does the note say?' asked Jarrett.

'Here, fucking read it!' Tomas stabbed his chunky fingers on the paper and slid it across.

Jarrett calmly picked it up and read it. The letter was short and straight to the point. 'So, they want us to stop selling drugs in Warrington. And . . . if we don't, the girls will die?'

Tomas couldn't speak, he was so furious. His face turned red, bordering on purple. His thick, boulder-like shoulders swiftly rose and dipped with his quick breathing.

'These stupid notes, every few days there's a new one. "Stop selling on the east side, do this deal — or else." Is it ever going to end? This has been going on for a month.' Matej stood up and sighed heavily. 'They killed Hendo, kidnapped the girls . . . and it's all been leading to this. Stop selling in Warrington? I can't wait to find these fuckers!' He pressed his palms on the table. He was thinner than Tomas, with short-cropped hair, whereas Tomas was bald. If anything, Matej was more dangerous than his brother, often acting under rage-fuelled impulses rather than being methodical. 'Whoever the fuck this is wants Warrington for themselves.'

'I promise you, whoever is responsible for this will suffer an excruciating death.' Tomas spoke with quiet fury. They all knew what the Molnar brothers could do.

'Has it really been a month?' Jarrett put the letter down. 'And still no witnesses to the kidnapping, Hendo's killing?'

Tomas scowled. 'If anyone *had* seen anything, I would have beaten it out of them.'

Jarrett edged back, curling his lip. 'No CCTV anywhere?'

The scowl on Tomas's face deepened. 'I've checked everything.'

Jarrett made a 'fair enough' face. 'Do we know if the girls are still okay?'

Tomas slowly pulled a photo from his pocket and showed Jarrett. It was of Nina, Luna, and Anya, standing in a field, unaware the photo had been taken. The sun was shining on their faces.

'When was this taken?' asked Jarrett.

'It came with that letter in the post.'

'What's the plan, then?'

Matej moved back a few inches from the table and crossed his thick, muscular arms. 'I love making money, but I love my nieces more.' He turned to Tomas. 'We have to stop selling in Warrington.'

Tomas considered this. Jarrett knew he was thinking about the astronomical profits from the drug game, the flashy lifestyle they funded. He dropped his face into his palms. 'Okay. Text the number, tell them we've knocked the Warrington game on the head and pulled our lads back.'

'It's a big call, Tomas,' said Jarrett.

'It's our only play,' Tomas said into his hands.

Matej was already typing the message. 'There, it's done.' He lowered the phone to the table and sat. 'If Warrington's out, we'll have to branch out further.'

'And risk stepping on someone else's toes,' muttered Tomas, his face still buried in his hands.

Jarrett checked his watch. 'Listen, I need to go.' He stood up. 'I'll see you boys tomorrow. I need to make a call about something.'

'Watch how you go,' Matej told him. Tomas said nothing and sighed heavily.

Jarrett left the house, closing the front door on his way out, and almost walked into one of the Molnars' henchmen standing by the door.

'Oops, sorry,' the man said to Jarrett.

'Watch it!' scolded Jarrett.

The man scowled at him and finished a cigarette before flicking it onto the gravel and heading back inside. Jarrett walked over to his Range Rover parked in the row of expensive cars, his feet crunching on the gravel.

He climbed in, coughed at the sharp smell of the air freshener fixed to the rear-view mirror, and lowered the window an inch. Looking around to make sure he couldn't be overheard, he plucked his phone out and made a call straight away.

'Jarrett?'

'Selena, listen to me. I'm getting fucking fed up with calling you and asking to speak to the girls. Where are they? I don't have to send that video to the police, do I?'

'No — no, you don't. You don't need to do that.'

'Well, put the girls on. I need to speak to them. This thing is almost over.'

'I — I can't,' she whispered.

'I'm sorry, say that again.'

'I can't.'

'Put them on the fucking phone, or there'll be—'

'They're not here, Jarrett.' She fell silent for a beat. 'They've escaped. All three of them.'

'How?'

'I don't know. They were here on Tuesday morning, but they managed to get out. We can't find them anywhere.'

'Tuesday morning and you didn't tell me till now? Your place is meant to be secure.' He sighed heavily. 'That's why I asked you to look after them and keep them safe.'

'Jarrett, there's something you should know.'

'What!'

'There's been murders in Darlington. From what the police are saying on the news, it could be the girls. Too many bad things have happened since they've escaped the house.'

'I don't fucking believe this! There's no chance they would do that. They're decent kids.'

'I'm sorry, I—'

'I asked you to keep them safe. You said you would take care of them. I'm coming to Darlington tomorrow to fix this fucking mess.'

Jarrett hung up and drove away quickly, propelling stones up as he sped off.

As the Range Rover vanished, the Molnar henchman who had been fixing a leak under the Alfa Romeo parked next to it wriggled out from under the car, frowning.

He had heard the whole conversation.

44

Nina waited just inside the gates of St Cuthbert's church grounds, hidden in darkness by one of the thick stone pillars. She stared out onto the open area of concrete where the outdoor market used to be, watching people pass over the cobbles on their way to the next pub and hearing their loud conversations. She peered up at the town clock — it was just after 9 p.m. The town was busy for a Thursday evening.

Nina waited patiently, letting the conversations of passers-by wash over her. She knew someone suitable would come along very soon but didn't want to catch their attention. She wasn't keen on completing the task she'd been given.

She gulped hard, dropping her head, wishing there was another way out of this. She'd been away from West Manor for two days and missed her family in Warrington very much. Uncle Jarrett had promised it would only be for a few days until things settled at home, but the days with Selena at West Manor had turned into weeks, and eventually a month. The girls had decided they'd had enough of it. For the past two weeks, during their free time away from their room, they'd studied the relaxed security of West Manor, trying to figure a way out. Nina had been the one to work out their escape route, but she'd soon realised their current situation was no better. If anything, it was worse. She needed help.

Shaking as she thought about the task she'd been asked to carry out, she reminded herself of what was at stake if she didn't: Anya and Luna's safety. It was obvious what the man was capable of, and it would be wise not to cross him. If only she'd known this before their escape.

A group of men dressed in dark colours were idly chatting, speaking so quietly that Nina only heard the odd word. They seemed to be discussing the weekend's racing.

Moments later, a large, overweight man appeared to her left. He was walking alone and looked somewhere between fifty and sixty. His yellow shirt was half tucked into his dark jeans, and he tripped on the cobbles as he walked. *Drunk*, thought Nina, but maybe he could help her.

'Hey,' said Nina, loud enough for him to hear but quiet enough so others wouldn't.

The man frowned, his thick eyebrows arching like slugs. He pulled up to an unsteady stop and frowned her way. 'Who zat?' he mumbled, swaying slightly.

Nina slowly stepped out from behind the concrete pillar. 'I need some help.' She kept her voice low.

'Wazzat?' He took a few paces towards the open gates of the church grounds, occasionally picking up pace and then slowing.

'Come here.' She waved him towards her. 'Please.'

'Waz your name?' he asked as he staggered.

'My name is Nina. Listen, I need your help. I've been kidnapped.'

'Kidnapped?' He frowned. 'You don't look like you've been kidnapped.'

'Where's the nearest police station?'

His drunken, glazed eyes narrowed suddenly. 'I don't know. I . . .' He trailed off, patting his stomach before he belched loudly. 'Actually, the police station is over there.' He half found his bearings and pointed across the church grounds somewhere behind her. 'I can take you.'

Nina thought of using the knife on him, but no matter the threat to her sisters, she didn't have it in her to kill someone. She needed to be smart about this and use this strange situation to her advantage. She followed the drunk man as he made his slow way across the cobbles.

* * *

The man peered through the windscreen of the van he'd parked almost out of sight and smiled to himself. 'I knew she couldn't be trusted.'

He watched Nina and the man slowly make their way along the cobbles, further into the church grounds. Not knowing what their conversation had been about in the last minute, he needed to intervene. The police station was just beyond the church and over the bridge. If they reached the station, it was game over. Nina would take them to his house and tell them everything she knew. He couldn't allow that.

* * *

'Please, we need to go now. Hurry up,' she said to the man in the yellow shirt.

'It's just through here.' He pointed across the church grounds. The church was lit up beautifully, lights fixed at the base, angling upwards, illuminating the building's exterior in all its glory.

To their right, Nina spotted the man from the van speeding over the grass towards them.

'Shit, he's here. Please help me,' she begged him.

'You'll be fine,' he said, waving her concern away. 'We just need to get across these cobbles and across the river. The police will help you. I'll make sure you get there.'

Through the fug of alcohol, the man hadn't seen the van, nor was he aware of the figure approaching them, silhouetted against the town's lights.

'There you are, dear!' the man from the van shouted towards them, throwing his hands to his mouth in concern. 'I've been looking all over for you. Thank God you're safe.'

The drunk man stopped abruptly, squinting in the darkness of the quiet church grounds. 'Who's that?'

'Please help me,' she gasped, grabbing his arm.

'You're hurting me.' Her fingernails were digging into his skin through the fabric of his yellow sleeve.

The man from the van strolled across the grass until he reached the cobbled path. 'Where have you been?'

'Who are you?' the drunk man asked him.

'I'm her father. I've been looking all over for her. I'm so happy I've found you, Nina.'

Nina didn't let go of the drunk man. 'Please, help me,' she begged him. She clung to him so tightly that she almost knocked him off balance. 'He's not my dad. Don't listen to him.'

The stranger stepped closer. 'Nina, dear, come on.'

'I'm taking this girl to the police,' the man told him. 'She says she's been kidnapped.'

'Oh, please.' The stranger held up his hands. 'There really is no need for that. She's my daughter. She's on medication. We have a tough time with her, and sometimes, like tonight, she gets out, and I have to come looking for her.' He took another step forward, closing the gap to roughly a metre. 'Thank you for taking care of her, it means so much to me. I'll get her home. Her mother is worried sick.'

The man scowled and looked down at Nina, weighing up who was really telling the truth here. 'He says he's your father. You're okay now.'

'He isn't my father!' she screamed. 'He's a mur—'

'Shhhh, dear, there's no need for this,' the stranger said softly, as if soothing her. 'She gets like this. We just need her home, where she's safe.'

The drunk man thought about it briefly. 'How do I know you're her father?'

'Listen.' He stepped forward, now less than a foot from the other man. 'I—' And with that, he covered the ground between them and drove a knife straight into the man's thick gut.

Nina screamed and jumped to the side to get away from the blade, but he lunged across and grabbed her neck. His grip was so tight it froze her to the core.

'Get back in the fucking van now. I give you one simple task, and you couldn't even do it.'

The man's yellow shirt was covered with blood, and he stumbled a few steps until he tripped and collapsed to the ground. The blood filled the dark crevices of the cobblestones, shining in the church lights.

Where had all the people gone? Nina eyes darted about as he dragged her to the van — nobody was around now. He opened the passenger door, threw her in, and slammed it closed.

She sat shaking in the passenger seat as the other door opened and slammed shut with some force. He started the van and sped away, leaving the man in the yellow shirt to bleed out on the cobbles.

45

Tomas and Matej were still at the table, quietly discussing their future, when they spotted one of their men standing in the doorway.

'Hi, Joe,' Tomas said. 'Fix the leak on the Alfa Romeo?'

Joe stopped still, nervous about what he was going to say. Everyone in the room was looking at him now.

'Joe, what's up?' asked Matej.

'I — I overheard something,' he said. 'Jarrett was on the phone in his car. He — He didn't know I was listening, I'm — I'm sure of it.'

'Stop fucking stammering and tell us what Jarrett said,' demanded Tomas.

'He was talking about the girls. He said he wanted to speak to them. He sounded panicked.'

'Who was he talking to?'

Joe shrugged. 'Someone called Selena. I don't know if Jarrett spotted me, but then he sped away.'

184

Tomas leaned back and turned to Matej. 'I guess we know who's responsible for our girls going missing, then.'

'Certainly would explain why he's been acting weird this last month. Let's go and find out, eh?'

46

Thursday evening
Haughton Road, Darlington

Emma Slater had had a shit day. She'd been knee-deep in meetings and was glad to clock off and get herself home, even though she'd have to continue pushing through her workload at some point later this evening. The solicitor's firm she worked for demanded a lot from their workforce, not really delivering on that work–life balance they'd promised her when she'd joined.

After she finished eating her pasta, she placed the empty bowl in the sink. She had her routine: making her tea and filling the washing-up bowl with hot, soapy water before she ate so it was ready when she finished. It made sense in her head and was something she'd always done.

She plodded over to the French doors of her kitchen diner and flicked the latch open. She stepped out on the decking and felt the cold evening air against her. She considered grabbing her coat to go over the top of her smart work attire, but she'd only be out there a few minutes.

It was her time to stand and stare at the sky, to wonder what life could have been like if her husband hadn't died last year. She couldn't help but play the car crash over in her head, the way the car had flipped and landed on its roof; the way her husband, Jerry, had looked when she saw past the blood covering her own face. *Bastard drunk drivers*, she thought, shaking her head. It had happened on the A66 near the Sadberge turn-off on their way to Stockton to watch a comedian. A Friday night she'd never forget, back in July. She knew exactly what she was wearing and could vividly recall it in her mind to the exact point when Jerry had frowned, peered in his rear-view mirror, and said, 'They're coming fast.' She'd turned and looked through the rear windscreen, seeing two cars racing, quickly approaching. Before they knew it, one of the cars, a blue Vauxhall Corsa, had ploughed into the back of them. Jerry had gripped the wheel but couldn't control the car well enough to avoid the kerb, which consequently flipped them, sending them hurtling into the undergrowth at the side of the carriageway, landing on the roof. Jerry had died instantly.

'Emma,' said a voice, pulling her back to the present.

She turned her head to the left, seeing her neighbour's face over the top of the five-foot fence. 'Oh, hello, Susan. Didn't see you there.'

'I've just come out. My charming husband left his muddy boots in the kitchen again. I keep telling him to put them outside, but he doesn't listen to me.' Something in her tone told Emma they'd been arguing, though she already knew that. She heard many conversations through the wall separating the house, although it was old brick.

She smiled. 'Jerry was the same.'

'I know he was, love.' Susan disappeared momentarily behind the fence as if putting something down before reappearing. 'How are you holding up?'

'Ahh, you know, I'm okay.'

Susan looked the cloudless sky. 'Lovely night for stargazing, eh? Much planned for the weekend?'

It was an unusual question from Susan, one she'd never asked before, although they'd been neighbours for as long as she could remember.

'Nothing much, really. I have my niece staying over, so I'll probably do something with her. Might go to Teesside Park maybe, heard there are some good films on.'

'Sounds good. Anyway, I'm heading in. Enjoy it.'

Emma turned her attention back to the sky.

* * *

'Did you ask her?' asked Jeff, as Susan came into the living room.

'Not directly, no.' She sat down on the sofa opposite her husband and settled herself in. 'I'm not rude.' She rubbed the outside of her arms with her hands. 'Cold in here. Did you put the heating on?'

'It's on, I've already told you.'

'Well, it's cold in here. I'll give Matt a call. He'll sort the radiator.'

'Listen, you don't need your son to travel from Newcastle to fix a bloody radiator. I'm more than capable, you know.'

She rolled her eyes at him. 'Okay, then, Mr DIY.'

Jeff's eyes were on TV in the corner of the room. 'Just strange, that's all. I've heard her talking to someone for a few days now.'

'She did say her niece was staying, so it's probably that.'

'Yeah, I suppose so. You know what these walls are like. We used to hear everything when Jerry was here. All the arguing. The action in the bedroom.' He pushed out a lip. 'Kinda forgot what that was like . . .'

'For God's sake, Jeff, stop going on about sex. It's all you talk about.'

He frowned, looking at her sharply. 'Susan, it isn't all I talk about, I—'

She held up a quick palm. 'It's the last I'll hear about it, thank you.'

'I'm only sixty-three, you know, men still have their—'

'Jeff!' she shouted. 'I'm trying to watch this.'

Jeff fell silent immediately, knowing better than to argue.

They watched TV in silence for a little until Jeff said, 'Is she okay?'

'Who?' asked Susan, pulling herself away from the TV.

'Emma, obviously.'

'Yeah, she's okay. Just think what you'd be like if I died. You'd probably lose your marbles a bit.'

It would be more peaceful, he thought.

47

Friday morning
Darlington police station

Byrd pulled into the car park just after 7 a.m., seeing from their empty spots that he had beaten both Tanzy and DCI Corbridge to the station. He hadn't slept very well. Alan hadn't settled due to his teething and had been up more than usual, so Byrd had caught less than three hours of broken sleep.

He made his way to the rear entrance, feeling the faint morning sun on the back of his neck. *More of that, please*, he thought, looking up at the clear sky, excited for the summer to arrive. Although it was fresh, the temperatures were predicted to be in the double digits today, which would be warmer than yesterday.

Before going to the office, he went to the canteen to make a strong coffee, hoping it would pull him around before the day started and the team arrived. It was quiet. A few night-shift PCs were finishing their reports at their desks, looking exhausted.

Reaching his desk, he placed his coffee down, removed his coat, and put it on the back of his chair. He sat and turned his computer on, picked up his coffee and sipped it while he waited, planning to use this time to go over his report from yesterday — the death of Elaine Thornton on Edinburgh Drive — before sending it to the DCI. Even if Alan had slept well, Byrd would have been awake most of the night, the weight of the current cases playing on his mind. He always envied Tanzy in that way, who seemed to be able to switch off as soon as he walked out the door.

His phone beeped in his pocket. It was a text message.

Fancy 5-a-side tonight?

It was the last thing he could think about, so he put it away, intending to reply to his friend later.

'Morning, Max,' said DCI Corbridge, walking down the central aisle with a coffee in his hand. He stopped at the row of computers where Byrd sat. 'I'm going to start calling you Early Bird.'

Byrd turned and smiled.

'Get it?' Corbridge said, grinning.

'I get it, boss.' He rolled his eyes. 'Great joke . . . first time I've heard that one.'

'Did you sleep standing up, Max? You look terrible.'

'Appreciate the compliment. I might as well have done.' He sighed. 'My son Alan wasn't very considerate last night.'

The DCI nodded in understanding. 'Know the feeling. My two never slept when they were young.'

Byrd swivelled towards him. 'Don't think I've ever asked, but how old are they?'

'Oh, they're grown up now. Both in university back in Birmingham. Cara, who's nineteen, is doing criminology, and Eleanor, who's twenty-one, is in her third year of her psychology degree.'

'You must miss them?'

The DCI nodded, then smiled. 'Sometimes. I don't miss them rolling in in the early hours full of drink and waking me up playing music and falling around, though.'

Byrd laughed.

Corbridge took a few steps towards him. 'How come you're in so early?'

'Like you said . . . early bird. I thought I'd start the day as soon as possible. Claire was up anyway, so I left Alan with her.'

'Tanzy not here yet?'

'Haven't seen him.'

The DCI checked his watch. 'Meeting soon. You got some notes ready?'

'We do. Orion thought of some great points we need to cover last night.'

'I'll leave you to it. See you in there.'

Byrd went back to yesterday's report as Corbridge entered his office. He read some notes that Hope and Tallow had sent over. The door handles around the house were free of any intruder's prints. The only ones found belonged to Elaine, her husband Tony, and daughter Leanne.

Byrd took a lungful of air and exhaled.

Three murders within three days, each one with suspicions of teenage girls being involved in some way.

'Who's the early bird?'

Byrd looked up at Tanzy, his tanned head reflecting the bright office light.

'Good afternoon, Ori. Nice of you to finally show up.'

Tanzy screwed his face up.

'Early bird gets the worm.'

'Yeah, but the second mouse gets the cheese, Max.' Tanzy lifted the laptop bag strap off his shoulder and opened the flap.

'Such a feeble excuse for being late.'

Tanzy smiled, not rising to the bait, and removed his laptop, placing it on his desk and opening it.

Byrd studied him. 'You seem in a chirpy mood.'

'I've been to the gym for an hour.'

'Go on, Orion Van Damme.'

Tanzy grinned as he sat down. 'Just cardio this morning, nothing too strenuous.' He turned to Byrd. 'And I'm just so happy to see your lovely, handsome face, Max.'

'You must have got some last night.'

Tanzy pushed air through his closed lips as if to say, *No chance.*

'What time you get here?'

'Been here hours, slaving away,' replied Byrd, focusing back on his computer screen. He picked up his coffee and took a sip.

'Judging by how shattered you look, you could have been.'

'Alan was up half the bloody night.'

Tanzy logged on to his computer. 'That coffee smells nice.'

'I'd have got you one, if you were here on time . . .'

'You know, I don't think it's because of Alan that you're tired,' said Tanzy.

'What is it then?'

'It's because you're old and out of shape.'

'I'm literally four years older than you, and I'm in the best shape I have been for years.'

Tanzy raised his eyebrows. 'Be getting your pension soon.' He stood. 'Want a top-up?'

Byrd shook his head. 'I'm fine, Ori.'

Tanzy went to the canteen and returned a few minutes later with a coffee.

'I've put together some material for the meeting,' Byrd told him. 'I told Corbridge we both did it.'

'To be fair, I did the conference last night, so it's about time you did something around here.'

* * *

DCI Corbridge stood at the front of the room, waiting for everyone to arrive. PC Louise Degnan was the last one to enter and sheepishly made her way to a free chair, knowing Corbridge was watching her.

'Morning, everyone. Thanks for coming and turning up on time.'

He briefly smiled at PC Degnan, who looked down for a moment and missed the humour he seemed to be developing in his new role.

'Well, what a day for Darlington yesterday,' he went on.

The room was packed. All the PCs involved in the case with CID were present, along with Hope and Tallow from Forensics.

'Max. Orion. Can one of you lead, please?'

Byrd stood up and walked to the front, picking up the small black remote off the table like he'd done many times before. He'd already set up the PowerPoint presentation and had wheeled in the investigation board before anyone arrived, so everything was ready to go. There were dozens of yellow notes stuck to the board, mixed in with the photographs they had of the recent victims.

'Morning, all. I'll take this point by point, so we don't get all bogged down with information. Number one: Mia Mitchell. Mia was murdered on Tuesday night around teatime. She was stabbed by a man who was chasing Anya Deacon, a bad man who wanted Anya "to kill people", according to her. But we should perhaps take Anya's statement with a pinch of salt — DC Tiffin will tell us more about why shortly.

'Anya herself didn't tell us why it took her a whole night to call the police. She ran out of the house with Ella, realised she had lost her necklace, and went back to get it — she didn't know where Ella went. She called the murder in on Wednesday morning from a cupboard in the Mitchell house. Not long after the phone call began, Corey Tills entered and left the house very quickly. In the brief amount of time we had to question Anya, she didn't tell us much at all, and unfortunately, Anya left the hospital with Corey and went missing before we could get more information from her. Corey is now dead, so we can't shed any more light on this particular point. However, the evidence backs up what Anya has told us — that a man killed Mia. Both of these murders were carried out with extreme force — a nine-year-old girl would have been incapable of carrying out these killings.'

A hand went up from PC Andrews.

'Josh?'

'Are we one hundred per cent sure the man on the CCTV at the Mitchell house is the same man we found strangled at the hospital?'

'We're sure, yes.' He briefly scanned the investigation board, mentally collecting a few notes he planned to mention. 'Secondly, Mia's daughter, Ella, is still missing. Does anyone have any information on the leads they've been pursuing?'

'Nothing new from the tipline, sir,' said Timms. 'Nothing from her schoolfriends or family. We've been knocking door to door with photos of her and Anya. Not a word. It's like they've vanished into thin air.'

'Any further information from Cheshire on locating her parents?'

Again, the room remained quiet. Over to Byrd's left, DCI Corbridge let out an almost unnoticeable sigh. He decided to move on.

'Next, we come to the killing of Elaine Thornton in her home on Edinburgh Drive — found by her daughter. The Thorntons were very security conscious but there was no forced entry to the house. A neighbour saw her talking to a girl of twelve or thirteen. We have a short clip of the same girl walking away from the house. We know the nature of the murder, and it wasn't a sight I'd be keen on seeing every day. Again, it would have required some strength to inflict such injuries. A men's size-ten shoeprint was found in the house — we can consider that the footprint of her killer.' He found Hope's gaze. 'Emily, any update on the print?'

She nodded. 'Shoe belongs to an Adidas Samba.'

'Well, that shouldn't be too hard to find, then,' Corbridge commented, his tone filled with sarcasm.

'Early 2010 model Samba, according to a source I've spoken to. The issue is that the print itself isn't crisp, which tells me the trainers were worn and not new, which is obvious based on the year it was produced.'

'When did the next model of the Samba come in?'

'Good question,' said Hope. 'I'm glad you asked. The next model came in 2019, and slightly differed.'

'So we have a shoeprint belonging to a man who bought the trainers between 2010 and 2019, from possibly anywhere in the world?'

Hope shrugged. 'It isn't much to go on, I know.'

'Well, we have a lead on Anya Deacon.' Byrd turned to DC Tiffin. 'Anne, you went to West Manor. Fill us in.'

Tiffin cleared her throat. 'I did. The manager, Selena Goldberg, told me Anya had been staying at West Manor for the last month.'

'What's West Manor?' asked DS Leonard.

'A facility for "emotional well-being", apparently.'

'Why was Anya there?' asked DCI Corbridge.

'Mrs Goldberg says she had anxiety. Came from Warrington.'

'Long way to come to treat anxiety.'

Byrd nodded, agreeing with him.

'Has anyone spoken to Anya's parents?' Tanzy asked Tiffin.

'They are Jackie and Martin Deacon. Selena gave me a contact number. I've called and left several messages, but nothing back yet.'

Tanzy sighed lightly and turned back to Byrd.

'Keep trying,' pushed DCI Corbridge, leaning forward to get more comfortable in the chair. 'If nothing comes back today, we'll contact Warrington police again and try to get a location for them. Has Selena got any more information on her, such as an address?'

'All she had was a contact number for her parents. She said the systems were down, and she couldn't access them.'

Byrd reviewed the notes from the scene at Edinburgh Drive before he looked over at Hope and Tallow. 'Either of you got anything to add about the scene yesterday?'

Tallow shook his head. 'Other than the footprint at the front door, no, we don't.'

Byrd did his best to hide his disappointment, maintaining an even expression. 'So, at the moment, we need to press Selena Goldberg about Anya. It sounds like she knows more than she's letting on.' He looked at PC Degnan. 'Louise, have we got Digital Forensics to check over the CCTV from the neighbour on Edinburgh Drive?'

She nodded. 'Yeah. Did it yesterday before they finished. No matches, unfortunately.'

An invisible cloud of doom and gloom hung over them. DCI Corbridge looked fed up. Byrd knew he had to come up with something quickly.

Before he had the chance to, his phone rang. He checked the caller. It was PC Weaver, the only PC involved with the current cases who was absent. She was attending a call about youths breaking a window yesterday.

'Excuse me a second,' he told everyone. 'Amy?'

'Boss, just been notified by Dispatch there's a body in the town centre.'

'Where?'

'St Cuthbert's Church. Right near the marketplace.'

'Jesus.'

'I'm there now.' She paused a moment. 'If you're with Forensics, tell them to get their kit.'

48

Friday morning
St Cuthbert's Church, Darlington

Tanzy pulled off the roundabout and headed towards the market square. Up ahead, several police cars were parked diagonally, blocking access to the area where the body had been discovered. He slowed and pulled up on the right at a bus stop, knowing buses weren't coming down anytime soon — not until the scene had been worked on, everything was wrapped up, and the road was clear.

Tanzy and Byrd made their way up the path towards the cordon. A small crowd had gathered already, which wasn't surprising considering the prime location for nosy rubber-neckers with nothing better to do. There was a smell of cannabis in the air.

Byrd gritted his teeth. 'This is all we fucking need, Ori.'

'Never a dull day, mate.'

They carried on towards the cordon, fixed to the side of the Boot and Shoe pub, across a number of bollards, until it reached the wall that made up the edge of the church grounds.

'Wish I was in the Boot and Shoe having a quick pint,' Byrd muttered, feeling a jolt of pain in his left knee.

Tanzy smiled thinly. 'A night out sounds like something we should definitely organise soon.'

'Once this has all blown over,' Byrd agreed.

PC Weaver signed them into the scene and the detectives ducked under the cordon.

'And they said the town centre was dead,' Byrd said to Weaver, shaking his head at the number of people watching.

'Funny what brings the crowds out,' muttered Tanzy, just loud enough for Byrd and Weaver to hear.

'Got everything under control, Amy?' asked Byrd.

She nodded. 'Yeah. What's up with your knee?'

He frowned.

'I noticed you limping on your way up,' she added.

'You'll be a great detective one day.' Byrd looked down at his leg. 'I'm not sure — it'll wear off soon.'

The detectives walked through the open gates of the churchyard. Over to the right, another cordon had been set up, much larger in size due to the position of the lamp posts. A few people were standing, peering into the scene, but they couldn't get close because PC Andrews was keeping his eyes on them.

The forensic team had already set up a tent to protect the scene and prevent anyone getting a look — they'd only need a few seconds to snap a photo good enough for world circulation via social media.

Byrd and Tanzy made for the tent's opening, which had no floor and was roughly ten feet long, five feet wide, and six feet tall, meaning Tallow would need to spend most of his time crouched or on his knees.

'Looks like he didn't quite get the night he hoped for,' commented Tanzy, seeing the body on the cobbles. The victim lay on his side, almost as if he was sleeping, but the blood surrounding him told the detectives another story.

'Thoughts?' asked Byrd.

Crouching on one knee, Tallow studied the man's blood-stained yellow shirt. There was so much blood that only a tiny amount of yellow could be seen to indicate the colour of it.

'Looks like a knife wound to me,' he said.

Hope took a short video and snapped some photos before they moved him to get a better look at his face and the front of his body.

'How long's he been here?' asked Byrd.

Hope had already studied the man's skin and how the blood had settled due to gravity. 'Ten hours, I reckon.' She looked at Tallow. 'Jacob?'

'Yeah, ten hours wouldn't be far away. Sometime late last night.'

Tanzy remained over the body, just beside Tallow, observing him study the man before he and Byrd moved away to allow the forensic techs to work alone. They'd seen all they needed to and were happy to be out of there. They peered up, searching for nearby cameras.

'It's the middle of town. Surely one of the cameras has something here, Max?'

Tanzy took further steps, looking up with a flat hand pressed against his forehead to block the faint sun. Several cameras were dotted around the market square that might cover the entrance to the grounds, but there were two other access points to the church to consider.

Byrd noticed a camera on the side of the Boot and Shoe. Its focus would be the outdoor seating space, but it would be worth following up if they didn't get much joy from the others.

'I'll go and speak to Jennifer. She'll be able to help.'

Byrd said nothing.

'What?'

Byrd shook his head. 'Nothing, Ori.'

Tanzy pulled his phone from his pocket and found Jennifer's number. When she answered, he said, 'Hey, it's DI Tanzy.'

'Hello, Ori.' As usual, her voice was soft, gentle.

'You working today? I need some help with something urgent.'

'I am.'

'I'll be there in two minutes.'

49

Friday morning
St Cuthbert's Church, Darlington

As the morning passed, most of the onlookers dispersed. The occasional newcomer turned up, curious about the road closure and all the police cars. The sight of a forensics tent and a crime scene cordon always caused a stir in any town, never mind Darlington.

The man who'd found the body was waiting to speak to Byrd on the cobbles just outside the cordon, closer to the church.

'Sorry for keeping you here, sir,' said Byrd. 'I'm sure you have other things you could be doing.'

He raised a soft hand. 'I'm retired, Inspector. I would only be doing sudokus at home. It's really no problem.'

'Well, we appreciate that. I know you've informed our colleagues what happened earlier, but could you recap for me, please?'

The witness was in his seventies. He was small and thin, and judging by his faded blue bomber jacket hanging off his narrow shoulders, he'd probably lost weight during his retirement. He wore large glasses that magnified his brown eyes, and what was left of his thinning hair was brushed back and fixed to his scalp with too much gel. His teeth were so perfectly white Byrd would have put his mortgage on them being false.

He coughed to clear his throat of phlegm and turned away from Byrd for a moment. 'I walked up this way. I always do every morning. It's nice to get out, you know. I used to work in the town, did for years. I kind of miss it, you know.' He smiled, as if remembering his whole career in a matter of seconds. There was a touch of Yorkshire in him, the way he finished his sentences.

Byrd wasn't interested in where he used to work and moved the conversation on. 'So, then what happened?'

'I saw something on the path. I assumed it was a drunk, unable to make it home after having a skinful, but I thought it could be someone who needed some help, so I went over to see. And that's when I saw the blood on the cobbles.'

'What time was this exactly?'

'About eight o'clock.'

Byrd nodded. 'See anyone else around or anything unusual?'

'Not really. Just me around at that time.'

'Okay. Thank you for the witness statement you've already given. You're more than welcome to go.'

The witness hesitated. 'Any idea who's done this to him?'

'It's our job to find out.'

Byrd returned to the cordon, swooping under it. The pain in his knee had vanished, at least. He wondered what progress Tanzy was making. If there was anything to find, Jennifer Lucas would be more than capable of finding it.

Peter Gibbs was kneeling at the tent's entrance, inspecting the body. The victim now fully lay on his back, and it was clear to see, although the front of his shirt was covered in blood, there was a tiny slit where the knife had penetrated through the material.

'Hey, Peter,' said Byrd.

'Hi, Max.' Gibbs knew Byrd's voice without looking his way. Gibbs seemed calm, collected, his usual self. 'Interesting scene you have here, Detective.'

The warm stench inside the tent hadn't eased since Byrd had last stepped inside it. It smelled like the victim had soiled himself.

'Let's get the body to Pathology,' Gibbs said. 'I'll call Dr Hemsley right now and ask him to prioritise this one.' He slowly found his feet and left the tent. Byrd followed him. 'Any idea what happened, Max?'

Byrd shook his head. 'Nothing yet. DI Tanzy is checking local CCTV. See what comes back.'

'Been a tough week for you lot, eh?'

Byrd pressed his lips together in agreement.

Behind him, he could hear quick footsteps. DC Anne Tiffin dashed over to him. Judging by her narrowed eyes and stern expression, she had something important to tell him.

'Anne.'

'Sir, I've had Selena Goldberg on the phone.'

'From West Manor?'

She nodded. 'She needs to speak to us immediately. Says she wasn't honest with me yesterday.'

'Let's go then. We'll take PC Degnan's car. You can drive.'

50

Selena lived in a new-looking semi-detached house with a pale
green door and tidy PVC windows in the West Park area of
the town. Byrd walked up the short path, knocked three times,
and stepped back beside Tiffin, who was peering at the flowers
in the garden to their left. He turned and scanned the driveway and front of the house, seeing no other cars there.

It wasn't long before the door opened. Selena looked rather
shy for the manager of a place like West Manor, Byrd thought.
As Tiffin introduced him to Selena, she peered out onto the
street like she was worried about something, before she invited
them in.

They followed Selena through the first door on the right,
leading to the living room, and all sat down. A sweet cit-
rus smell lingered from somewhere. Byrd scanned the room,
absorbing everything in it. A few photo frames were fixed to
the wall behind him, which he'd studied as he entered. The
television was over in the corner on a wooden unit. Beside the
screen, a yellow candle flickered with a flame likely responsible

for the room's scent. Besides that, the room was tidy, clean, and airy.

The sofa that Byrd and Tiffin were sitting on faced the rectangular window. Selena moved to the single chair in the corner opposite the television, settling into it and biting her nail.

'My name is Detective Inspector Max Byrd.' He motioned towards Tiffin. 'I believe you already know Detective Constable Anne Tiffin.'

Byrd noted Selena appeared uncomfortable. 'Is everything okay?' he asked.

She slowly shook her head. 'No.'

'You said on the phone you needed to be honest with us?'

Selena dropped her head, focusing on the grey carpet. 'Yes.'

Byrd studied the top of her tightly braided hair as he waited.

'I lied to you yesterday, Constable Tiffin. I'm sorry.'

'Okay, take your time,' Byrd reassured her.

'So, I'd told you that I was looking after Anya and that she'd run away.'

Tiffin nodded. 'You did.'

'Well, it wasn't just Anya that ran off.' Selena inhaled heavily, keeping her eyes on the carpet. 'Her two sisters were staying there with her. They've both disappeared too.'

'Three sisters in total?' asked Tiffin.

'Yes. I should have said yesterday.'

'Then why didn't you, Mrs Goldberg?' asked Byrd.

'I — I was embarrassed. I run a professional establishment. Three of our guests getting out is not something I want to shout from the rooftops. But I saw the news that there had been more murders in Darlington and saw the footage. It looks like the girls. The killings must stop because this town isn't safe with those girls wandering around.'

'Who are they?'

'Their names are Anya, Luna, and Nina.'

'During their stay at West Manor,' said Byrd, 'was there any evidence to suggest they were violent in any way?'

Selena narrowed her eyes, thinking carefully. 'Not that I noticed. We had people working with them, but nothing in their reports flagged up anything other than being anxious and not quite fitting in with society.'

Byrd studied how she looked to the left and fiddled with her hands. She wasn't entirely telling the truth here either.

'Something seems off to me,' Byrd said.

She silently frowned at him.

'Well, it just seems strange to me why a family would allow their children to stay in a place like yours for so long without missing them so much that they'd want them home.'

Selena shrugged. 'Unless they had other issues going on at home. Maybe it was dangerous for them in Warrington?'

'The father said that?' asked Tiffin.

'He didn't say much, to be honest. All I know is that they're my responsibility while they're here, and not only have I let the girls down by not keeping them safe, I've let him down.'

'But why West Manor?' asked Byrd. 'It's a facility for adults' emotional well-being, not children's. There are no paediatric facilities for children at West Manor. I don't understand.'

Selena carefully considered an answer. 'I was approached by a man about the facility, querying what we do. I told him. He asked if I'd consider taking in the three girls. We're here to help people. How could I say no?'

'Are the staff qualified to look after children?'

'Of course,' she said. 'Otherwise I'd have said no.'

'Is he aware the girls ran away? I tried contacting the number you gave me, but it went straight to voicemail.'

Selena frowned. 'I'm sure I gave you the correct contact details. Yeah, I spoke with him yesterday. He said he was coming to Darlington this morning to help find them. He didn't sound happy with me.'

Byrd raised his eyebrows to suggest he couldn't blame him. 'What time's he coming?'

'He didn't say. Just said he'd set off first thing from Warrington.'

'Is that why you seemed anxious when you opened the door to us?' asked Byrd.

'No, he would come to West Manor rather than my home.'

'Warrington's a good few hours away,' said Tiffin. 'Could be arriving anytime now.'

Byrd pushed his tongue into the inside of his cheek and watched Tiffin make some notes on the small pad she pulled from her pocket.

'Is there anything else you can suggest that might help us find them?' he asked.

'No, Inspector. I just wanted to let you know there were three of them, not one. And from seeing the news last night and what the police are saying, it must have something to do with those girls.' She fell silent for a moment. 'I'm sorry I wasn't honest with you yesterday,' she told Tiffin.

'We need all your information on those girls,' Tiffin added. 'Are your systems back up and running at West Manor?'

'I hope so. I'm heading there now anyway — I can check when I'm there.'

She looked away from them towards the window and Byrd saw something in her face — she seemed frightened. He turned his head, seeing the rear of a black 4 x 4 moving past the house.

'Is everything okay?' asked Byrd.

She checked her watch, breathing light and fast. 'I'm waiting for my husband to come back. He's got the car.'

'We can take you,' said Byrd. 'It's really no trouble.'

She offered a reluctant nod.

'Anne, please drop me off in town and go with Selena to West Manor to get the necessary information.'

51

Friday late morning
West Park, Darlington

Jarrett Banks followed the satnav and turned into Collingsway on the West Park estate, eyeing the house numbers on the left. He was angry. He'd called Selena multiple times on his way from Warrington, but the calls had always gone to voicemail.

He had stayed away from the Molnar brothers since their meeting yesterday. It was obvious they were livid about their daughters being taken, and who could blame them? They were convinced it was a new local gang or family wanting to take over the drug scene in Warrington. After all, who else would dare challenge them, let alone kill one of their men and kidnap their daughters from the school gate?

The Molnar brothers had arrived in Warrington ten years ago, and had spent the first three years fighting other gangs until they'd killed enough people to instil fear in everyone else. But in the last seven years, no one had bothered them, and it had been plain sailing.

Jarrett had been Tomas's right-hand man since day one, helping to build their empire. Trusted. Hell, Tomas's kids called him uncle. But he knew he'd never be one of the family really, not when it came to financial rewards. He'd put as much into building the business as the brothers had, and what did he have to show for it? One day soon they would have to part ways — and he wasn't going to go without a fight.

Jarrett knew what they were capable of. If he was ever caught, they'd slowly torture him, the same way he and the Molnars had done with other people in the past. But he was willing to risk it all because he wanted the Warrington trade to himself. He had put his plan in place and gathered a team, people who would do the work for him so he didn't have to. Once the Molnar brothers had pulled their gangs out of Warrington, he'd execute his second plan, setting up a meeting with them to arrange something that would work for both parties. Then he'd take them out together to ensure the job was done properly. It would also give him enough time to know which men were on his side and not the Molnars'. But he'd never hurt the girls or their mother. He felt a twinge of guilt at the thought of Maria's tear-stained face.

He saw the police car parked outside Selena's house. 'Shit,' he muttered. 'What are they doing here?'

He slowed and crawled by, peering into the living room window. He could see a few figures sitting on sofas, but the sunlight cast shadows, hiding their finer details. He drove to the end of the street and smoothly carried out a gradual three-point turn, then pulled up against the kerb a few houses down to think for a moment. He needed to be patient and find out what was happening.

A few minutes later, he watched Selena walk out of the house, followed by a man and a woman. They were dressed well but weren't in uniform, which told Jarrett they were possibly CID.

'Why are you getting them involved?' he whispered.

He slouched further down in his seat, peering over the top of his steering wheel to hide. Selena turned back to the house to lock the door, then looked towards his car.

'Shit,' he whispered, hoping she hadn't seen him.

* * *

Selena couldn't see anyone in the driver's seat of the Range Rover.

'Are you coming, Mrs Goldberg?' Tiffin asked.

She froze on the path, halfway between her front gate and the road, staring down the street.

'What are you looking at?'

'Nothing.' She blinked several times and nodded at Tiffin, who was in the driver's seat with the window half down, watching her.

She climbed into the back and closed the door.

* * *

Once DI Byrd got out of the car near the Dolphin Centre, DC Tiffin made a three-point turn because the road was still blocked off, and took a right at the roundabout, powering up Victoria Road. It took less than five minutes to reach West Manor on Barnes Road. After she had lowered her window and explained to the security officer at the gate who she was, the barrier was raised, and they went straight through.

Tiffin found a space at the front, the same spot Selena usually parked in.

'Will this take long?' asked Selena as she opened her door.

'I hope not.' Tiffin got out and closed hers, then looked around, studying the security of the place, wondering how it would be possible for three children to leave without being seen, especially with twenty-four-seven security.

Selena headed for the entrance. 'What is it you need, Constable?'

'We need all the records you have on them, any pictures too. It's important we know exactly who they are.'

They passed the receptionist, Elisha, who smiled at them. The reception area was clean and light, and the floor was made up of large white tiles reflecting the spotlights shining down from above. The walls were white with not a single blemish or smudge anywhere. There were six chairs and a small coffee table with an elegant pile of magazines and another pile of smaller brochures about mental health and energy. As they walked through the small space, Tiffin heard quiet, soothing piano music playing from somewhere, but she couldn't see a speaker, or a piano.

They walked the flight of stairs up to Selena's office on the first floor. Selena unlocked it and entered, and Tiffin followed her in. Something stale lingered in the air, but Tiffin couldn't put her finger on it.

'Gosh, let me open a window.' Selena opened two windows facing the extensive gardens and dropped her small bag on her desk before she sat down and pulled herself into her computer.

Tiffin studied the office while she waited. Impressive but vague certificates that West Manor and Selena had earned filled the wall, ranging from a diploma in something called 'Mental Well-Being' to more questionable topics such as 'Functions of the Brain' and 'Working with Energy'. Tiffin was unsure what to make of the place, but it didn't really matter what she thought — snake oil was a real money spinner, from the look of West Manor. Tiffin went over to the window and looked out onto the gardens.

'This really is a beautiful place.'

'It is, isn't it?' agreed Selena. 'This shouldn't take long.'

'I'm trying to work this out,' said Tiffin.

'Hmm?'

'How the girls left without anyone knowing about it.' Tiffin turned, moving away from the window. 'It seems a pretty secure facility to me.'

Selena nodded in agreement. 'I know.'

'And the fact the cameras picked them up earlier on Tuesday morning proved they were here then. But then it's as if they just vanished.'

'Oh, no. I — I can't find their files.' Selena scowled. 'I don't understand.'

Tiffin frowned and walked around the desk, stopping beside her. 'Where are they?'

'Look.' She pointed to the screen. 'This is where we keep all the guests' information.'

Tiffin followed her finger at the vast list of names on the programme she'd opened. Judging by the scroll bar at the right side of the page, there was a substantial number of guests. There was a column on the right titled 'Inactive' with a red square next to each name, meaning they were no longer at West Manor.

'I don't understand,' she said again. 'The active ones aren't here. They were here yesterday. I was reading them myself.'

Tiffin placed her hands on the desk for support as she checked for any options to search for the active ones. 'Go through the list again, please.'

Selena slowly scrolled through the names and sighed heavily when she reached the bottom of it.

'They're not here. These are only the previous guests.'

'What can you tell me about the girls?'

'Only their names and where they're from.'

'Is there anyone here who knows about your computer system?'

'Reggie Cook knows.'

'The caretaker?'

She nodded. 'He helped the IT firm set everything up when they were here, including positioning the cameras for our security system.'

'Is *he* here?'

'He might be. Let me call him.' She pulled out her phone, found his number, and put it to her ear. After a while, she ended the call and tried again.

'Not picking up?'

Selena shook her head. 'He might be downstairs already. We'll check.'

It took them several minutes to walk along the clinical white corridors and descend the two flights of stairs to the basement level, which was much smaller than ground level.

Tiffin observed the dark, narrow corridor to the left, then panned a complete one-eighty, seeing a couple of doors in front of them and two doors to the right. They were all painted brown and were closed.

'It's this way.' Selena guided Tiffin down the narrow corridor to the left.

Tiffin squinted as she moved further into the darkness. 'Is there not a light down here?'

Selena raised a hand and turned on the light switch next to the nearest door. The short hallway lit up with a dim bulb that flickered every few seconds as if trying its best to stay on. Up ahead was a brown door with a sign fixed to it saying *Caretaker*.

Selena knocked twice. 'Reggie, you in here?'

Tiffin stopped beside her. 'Try the handle.'

Selena did. Locked.

Tiffin sniffed the warm, stagnant air. 'What's that smell?'

'I'm not sure.' It had smelled the same the last time she was down here looking for Reggie. She tried knocking again, and after waiting a few minutes, they returned upstairs.

'Where is he?'

Selena shrugged. 'I'll try the IT firm. Hopefully, they can help.'

52

Most of the team was in the meeting room. DCI Corbridge was at the front, wearing a tightly fitting dark blue suit. He appeared agitated and couldn't seem to keep still. The room's spotlights reflected off the thin coating of sweat that lined his forehead. His tie was neat but too tight, his collar almost constricting his throat and slowing the blood flow to his head.

Byrd and Tanzy were seated on the table to the left, the one closest to the door. PC Weaver was at the next table, sitting beside DS Leonard. Tanzy observed them momentarily, wondering if they'd rekindled their romance. Beyond them, PC Grearer and PC Timms were both looking hot and bothered in their uniforms, their faces tinged pink. DC Tiffin sat beside them, recently back from West Manor.

'Right, come on then,' Corbridge said. 'Hit me with what we have today.'

'We went to see Selena Goldberg,' Byrd said. 'She's made Anne and me aware that Anya wasn't the only minor in her care at West Manor.'

215

The DCI frowned.

'Anya and two of her sisters were staying there,' explained Byrd. 'All three went missing on Tuesday morning. We have some CCTV images from Tuesday — I think you'll recognise one of them from another case.'

A couple of the officers gasped when the image appeared.

'That's the girl from the Edinburgh Drive crime scene, isn't it?' Corbridge said, pointing.

'The resemblance is undeniable. That's Luna Deacon, Anya's older sister.'

'So let me get this straight.' Corbridge had a look of horror on his face. 'Selena Goldberg is treating children at her quack clinic. She realises three children have gone missing and doesn't report this to the police for three days. And she hasn't told the parents?'

'She has. The father is on his way.'

'On his way. Three days later. Sounds like she's having you on.'

Corbridge looked at Tiffin. 'Please tell me that Selena Goldberg is in custody?'

Tiffin opened and closed her mouth.

'Sir, might I suggest we leave Selena in the wild for now?' Byrd looked thoughtful. 'She's a consummate liar, as we've found out, and I think she'll run rings around us in the interview room.'

'You think she'll lead us to the girls?'

'I think she's scared, and she'll give us more information if she thinks she can trust us.'

'Very well. Can't say I like it much. So, why are two of these children pictured at or near horrific murders? We know they can't have physically carried out the killings.' Corbridge turned side on and inhaled a lungful of warm air. 'Can someone please open that goddamn window?' He dug two fingers into the knot of his tie and wriggled his wrist, loosening its grip around his throat.

'What are Forensics saying?'

'Forensics are still at the church,' answered Byrd. 'Peter Gibbs turned up and sent the body to the hospital for a post-mortem with Dr Hemsley.'

'Have we identified him? Is he local?'

'Yes. Lives in Darlington. Name is Josh Carter. Aged fifty-eight. Got this from a driving licence in his wallet.' Byrd paused before continuing. 'I've been to his house to deliver the sad news to his wife, asking what he was doing last night. She said he'd been out with friends in Newcastle and had spoken to him when he was on the train coming home. According to her, he always walked through town before heading towards the Denes, where he lived.' How different things would have been for Josh Carter if he'd decided to get a taxi home instead of choosing to walk.

'What did the pathologist have to say about Mr Carter?'

'Just spoke to him on the phone: a single stab to the stomach.'

Corbridge winced as he imagined the scene. 'Do we have any footage of the attack?'

'We do.' Tanzy stood up, pulling a memory stick from his dark jeans and slotted it into the meeting room laptop. Moments later, the video started, a view from the camera positioned just above The Pennyweight and overlooking the outdoor market area. 'See, Josh approaches from the side of the Dolphin Centre and crosses the road. Might have been heading for the Boot and Shoe maybe.' They watched Carter stumble drunkenly along the path. 'We see him here walk past the entrance to the church grounds, but then he stops. He then turns and stares towards the church.'

'Someone is talking to him there?' suggested Byrd.

'Looks that way.'

Moments later, Mr Carter stumbled into the church grounds, out of the view of the camera.

'Do we see anything else on this camera?'

'Well, this is where it gets interesting . . .'

Corbridge frowned. 'Go on.'

Tanzy shifted the time bar along a little. 'Notice this van come out here.'

The footage was murky and low-definition, but it was clear enough to see what was going on. A grey van drove up the ramp along the side of the town hall.

'This happens five minutes after we lose sight of Mr Carter,' Tanzy said.

'Can we see who's in the van?'

'It isn't clear enough,' replied Tanzy. 'I'll hand it to DFU to see if they can enhance it.'

The van reached the end of the short road and took a left. They could see the registration plate.

'Pause that and zoom in. I assume we've ran that plate,' said the DCI.

'Fake,' said Tanzy. 'It belongs to a written-off Renault Clio.'

'Did the town cameras track the van?' asked DC Tiffin.

'We've followed it up Yarm Road before it took a right at Neasham Road. A camera picks it up halfway down Neasham Road, but then we lose it.'

'No more cameras along Neasham Road?'

Tanzy shook his head. 'There is, but much further down. After the Geneva Road roundabout.'

The room absorbed that information.

'So, there's a good chance it's on Neasham Road or Geneva Road, then,' noted Byrd.

'There are dozens of streets around there.'

'Well then, I guess we should get a move on and start looking,' the DCI replied. He focused on Byrd and Tanzy. 'Get a team to search that area, please.'

'You got it,' said Tanzy.

'Right, get to work. Let's find that van.' Corbridge sighed very heavily. 'This week is a dark stain on our force. Four vulnerable children missing and no leads, and four murders in one week. We need a win.'

53

Selena Goldberg had received a text message late morning from Reggie Cook saying he wouldn't be in today due to feeling unwell, but he reassured her it was nothing too serious and that he'd be in on Monday. She'd spent most of the day worrying about whether Jarrett Banks would turn up after she'd received several calls from him but decided to ignore them. She'd expected a call from security at some point, but the time ticked on, and there was no sign of Jarrett at West Manor, thank God.

At 5 p.m., she decided it was home time.

Traffic was a blessing considering it was a Friday afternoon, and West Auckland Road was almost empty for the first time Selena could remember. She reversed into the parking space outside her house, scanned the street looking for Jarrett's Range Rover, and was relieved when she couldn't see it. As she got out, she noticed a blue Mondeo parked thirty metres down the street with two men inside. They weren't familiar but seemed to be watching her. She freaked out and dashed to the door, relieved when she'd made it inside and the door was locked.

Kicking her shoes off and feeling something was amiss, she scowled down the hall. 'Alex?'

She waited.

'Alex,' she repeated, louder. She frowned and crept down the hall, expecting to see him at the kitchen table, where he spent most of his time at home reading or on his laptop.

But he wasn't there.

One of the patio doors was half open. She went over, opened it fully, and peered out.

'Alex, are you here?'

She edged back, closed the door, and pulled her phone out to call him. It rang but went to voicemail. She tried again with the same result. He mustn't be here as she would've heard his stupid football ringtone, the same one she'd become sick of hearing for the last three years.

Was he doing something today that she'd forgotten about? She couldn't remember.

'Alex?' she called again, leaving the kitchen and returning to the hallway. His trainers were still there.

'Huh?' He went everywhere in them.

At the base of the stairs, she peered up.

Maybe he was asleep? He didn't usually sleep if he was at home, but perhaps he was tired and needed a nap. She slowly climbed the stairs and quietly opened the bedroom door.

'Hey, sleepyhead,' she whispered.

The room was bright, the sun shining through the wide window. The bed was empty and made just how she'd left it earlier that morning.

Maybe he'd gone to the shop or needed something from Aldi or Lidl. It's not as if he'd never done that before. She left the room and decided to run herself a bath, assuming he'd be home soon. The hot water would make her feel better.

Before she reached the bathroom, she froze. Something had creaked in the back bedroom. She scowled, looking at the closed door, the one she always left open.

Another creak.

'Alex?'

She slowly opened the door. 'Al, you in—'

'Alex isn't here, Selena.'

Jarrett was standing in the middle of the room, smiling at her. A gun was nestled in his hand.

'Nice to see you again,' he said to her.

'I — I — What's going on?'

'Where the fuck are my girls?'

'I don't know.' She raised her hands. 'Please, don't do anything. Don't hurt me.'

Jarrett took a step closer towards her and raised the gun.

'No!' she screamed, edging away from him. 'Please . . .' she begged.

'Where are the girls?' he asked calmly.

'Please, I don't know, Jarrett!' she blurted out. 'God, if I knew, I would tell you. Even the police can't find them. They're causing havoc around this town.'

'I wanted you to protect them at West Manor.'

'I'm — I'm sorry. I—'

'You have until tomorrow to find them, Selena. Don't think about talking to the police. They were here earlier. I saw them. Find the fucking girls. Otherwise, I'm coming back to kill you. And your husband.'

54

'What the fuck is going on in there?' Tomas Molnar asked his brother, Matej, pointing through the front windscreen towards the house. They were parked in a blue Mondeo forty metres away and had just watched a woman park on the drive and run inside.

'Who the hell is she?'

An hour ago, Jarrett Banks had appeared on foot and disappeared down the side of the house. He hadn't come out during that time.

Last night, after one of their men had heard Jarrett on the phone, the Molnar brothers had put a plan in place. Knowing he wouldn't succumb to torture — Jarrett Banks was one of the most brutal bastards they knew — they needed to be more intelligent, putting a tracker on his Range Rover during the night while he slept. They had followed him to Darlington, and it was the second time they'd followed him to this particular house. Based on the conversation their man had heard last night, there was a good chance it was regarding the girls — *their* girls.

222

'We should go in and kill him and whoever else is there.'

Tomas calmly raised a hand to silence the impulsive thoughts in Matej's head. 'It's obvious he's deceived us. But if he has the girls, killing him won't help us find them. And you know what Jarrett is like. Even if he admits it, we won't be able to get it from him. He'd rather die than give us that — the man's a rock.'

That was true. Jarrett Banks had been stabbed, shot, and almost beaten to death — the man didn't give up. The Molnars were hard men but Jarrett was something else.

'I just don't understand why he'd do it though, Tomas?' Matej said, turning to his big brother. 'We have a good thing going in Warrington . . .'

'Obviously not good enough for him.'

'What are we going to do?'

'We need to bide our time. The most important thing to me is the girls. Once we see him with the girls, then we make our move.'

Matej slowly pulled a gun from the inside of his leather jacket. 'Then we kill him?'

Tomas nodded. '*Then* we kill him.'

55

55

Friday evening
Low Coniscliffe, Darlington

Byrd wasn't feeling particularly healthy and swung by McDonalds before pulling up on his driveway just after 9 p.m. He'd asked Claire if she wanted anything, and to his surprise, she requested a Big Mac with a strawberry milkshake and a caramel McFlurry.

After he turned the engine off, he grabbed the bag of food and cardboard tray of milkshakes and got out, feeling the cold around him as he made his way to the door. Light shone through the closed curtains in the living room, and Byrd could hear the dull sound of the television.

He slipped his shoes off and went straight into the living room to find Claire on the sofa to the left, with Alan asleep in her arms.

'What's he still doing up?' he asked quietly, trying not to disturb him.

'He wakes up every time I put him down. He's sleeping now.'

'Well, he looks nice and snug. Kind of jealous of him, lying there like that on your chest.'

'I'll give you a snuggle later, Max,' she said, smiling.

As Byrd put the food and drinks down on the coffee table, Claire's eyes widened at the brown bag with the large yellow 'M' on it. 'That smells unbelievable,' she whispered.

'Here, let me take him — see if I can put him down.' Byrd leaned over, gently picked up Alan, lovingly snuggling him into his chest, and made his way to the door. That had been the third time this week he'd come home to find Alan asleep on Claire. Byrd worried about his wife, stuck under the baby for hours on end without adult company. Was she lonely? He wasn't sure.

Byrd opened Alan's bedroom door and lowered him into the cot. 'Sleep well, Alan. Love you,' he whispered before he backed out. Success.

He returned downstairs to find Claire halfway through her burger, half of it around her lips and on her chin.

'Making a meal of that, aren't you?' He grabbed his own food and settled in next to her.

'Good day?' she mumbled through a mouthful of food.

'I've had better.'

They ate their food in silence. Byrd felt sick, wishing he hadn't ordered a large meal, and regretted adding the McFlurry to his order, although it definitely hit the spot.

'What have you been doing today?' he asked.

She told him about seeing a friend she'd recently met at one of the baby groups, but didn't really expand on why she'd had better days, just that she hadn't felt her happiest. Since having Alan, she'd often told him about feeling this way. Byrd understood it could be hormonal and wanted to support her any way he could.

'Any closer to finding those girls?' she asked.

He shook his head. 'Progress is very slow.'

Her programme finished, and she grabbed the remote. 'Want to watch anything?'

Byrd considered it, knowing he should really get back to the laptop to do more work.

'Max?' she said after no response.

'You watch what you like. I'm gonna get a shower.' He stood, picked up the food wrappers, and disposed of them in the kitchen, then went upstairs, switched on the shower, and removed his clothes, putting them in the washing basket. In case someone urgently called, he placed his phone on the vanity unit and studied his naked body in the mirror, thinking he needed to tighten his chest and build his shoulders up.

'Maybe I do need to do judo,' he told himself, then smiled, shaking his head.

He stepped into the shower and let the hot water wash away his day. Once he was dried, his phone rang. He scowled at the caller. PC Weaver. At this time?

'Amy?' he answered.

'Boss. I've been looking around Darlington for the grey van. Found one on Geneva Road parked on a driveway.'

Byrd finished getting dressed as he spoke. 'You checked the registration?'

'Yes. It's all legit. But we know the reg on the CCTV footage was fake, so it could have easily been taken off by now. It's the only van we've seen that matches the one on the CCTV.'

Byrd nodded to himself. 'Who are you with?'

'On lates with PC Grearer, sir.'

Byrd considered asking them to knock on the door the van was parked at, but it had gone 10 p.m.

'Sir?'

'Where are you now?'

'We're parked a few houses down, on the opposite side of the house on Geneva Road.'

'See anything unusual? Anything you can use as an excuse to knock?'

'Nothing that stands out.'

'Knock on the door and say you're responding to a noise complaint. If they ask who made the complaint, say you can't disclose that information. Ask questions about where he or she was last night, see what they say.'

'Okay. I'll ring you back soon.'

'Thanks, Amy.'

* * *

Once he'd put the girls up in the attic and locked the hatch with the tower bolt, he went back downstairs. He didn't know what to do with them now. Things hadn't turned out like he'd planned at all. He'd originally seen potential in them, something dark that he now realised maybe didn't exist. And he'd shown them a side to him that they definitely didn't warm to.

Could it be simple enough to let them go? Would they say anything to anyone about him?

He couldn't risk it now. Things had gone too far.

Just as he entered the kitchen, there was a knock at the door. 'Who the fuck is that now?'

Opening the door with a frown, he saw two uniformed police officers. 'Can I help you?'

'Hello, sir, my name is PC Amy Weaver of Durham Constabulary, and this is my partner, PC Donald Grearer. We're here regarding a noise complaint.'

His frown deepened, his eyebrows knotting to the top of his nose. 'Noise complaint? From who?'

'I can't disclose that information, sir.'

He studied them both and suddenly remembered the girls upstairs. He moved forward onto the step and edged his door almost closed in case they made any noise the police officers could hear.

'Well, I want to know,' he demanded.

'Can I ask your name, please?'

'No, not really. I don't have to give you it by law, do I?'

The PC partly smiled, partly frowned, knowing he was right. 'No, you don't. But as there's been a noise complaint, we would have the right to search the property to make sure everything is okay here.'

Fuck's sake, he thought. 'My name is Jonathon Bedlam.'

227

'How do you spell that, please?' asked PC Grearer. He spelled it for him.

'Have you got any ID to prove you are who you say you are?'

'Not on me, no. I'm in the process of renewing my driving licence, so I can't provide that right now.'

'Passport?'

He shook his head. 'Ran out last year. Need a new one.'

He watched the male PC write something down and wondered why they were really there.

PC Weaver nodded. 'Is this your van?'

He shook his head. 'No, it's not mine. The guy who owns the house uses it.'

'Does this guy have a name?'

'Matthew.'

'Matthew?'

'Matthew Allen.'

'And where is Matthew? Can we speak to him?'

'He's working tonight, I'm afraid.'

'Strange, because the van itself is registered to Reginald Cook at this address.'

'I'm not sure if Matthew is just using it for the time being — you know, borrowing it from a friend.' He shrugged.

'But the van is registered here,' replied Weaver.

'I haven't been here long myself. Maybe this Reginald moved out and left the van behind with Matthew.'

'Where does Matthew work? We need to speak to him.'

'I'm not sure what he does, to be honest. He works shifts, out all hours of the night sometimes.'

PC Weaver grinned, her perfectly white teeth visible even in the darkness. 'So, Matthew owns the house — but not the van — and you just live here?'

He nodded. 'That's right. Moved in only last month. I don't even get any bills here yet — I've just changed my address.' He sighed, figuring he needed to expand. 'My wife still gets them and rips them up. Awful woman, if you ask me.'

'How long have you known Matthew?'

'Years now, can't say how many for certain. My *lovely* wife and I decided to take a break a month ago, and Matthew kindly offered me a room here for a while until I find my feet again.'

'That's kind of him,' said Weaver. 'Can you tell me what Matthew was up to last night?'

He scratched his head and made a 'hmmm' sound through his closed lips. 'He was working nights.'

'And was he using this van?' asked Weaver.

He nodded. 'As far as I know, yeah.'

'So, if he's on nights tonight, why is the van here now?'

Good question, he thought. 'He lift shares with a guy who lives on Neasham Road, just around the corner. They take turns, I think. Not sure why the van's here.'

'You're home alone?' PC Grearer asked.

'Yeah,' he replied.

'Can we come in to check what that sound was?'

He studied them a moment. 'There's no one here, I can assure you of that.'

'Then you won't mind us coming in to confirm that,' pressed Weaver.

'Fine, but don't take long. I'm in the middle of something.'

Weaver followed him inside the house. Grearer trailed, closing the door once he was inside. From the tiny hallway, the living room was to the left, with a lamp on in the left corner and the television in the other, on the other side of the front window. Weaver looked around, eyeing the sofas, fireplace, and bookshelves in the alcoves.

'See, no one here,' he said, shaking his head.

'We'll know for certain when we check the house, sir,' countered PC Grearer, inspecting the living room.

They passed the closed front door and entered the dining room, both PCs glancing up the narrow, steep staircase as they did so. The dining room was messier than the living room, clearly used as a dumping ground for many things. Piles of paperwork were resting on the table pushed against the nearest wall. A pile of coats hung on a mounted trio of hooks to the right, threatening to pull them off the wall. Beyond the tall, narrow window, a chair was tucked into the corner with a lamp beside it — a nice place to sit and spend time reading.

They walked through the dining room into the kitchen. Weaver sniffed.

'What's that smell?' she asked, looking around. The kitchen was immaculate.

'That's strong.' Grearer raised a hand and squeezed his nostrils for a moment.

'It's bleach. I've just cleaned.'

The brilliant spotlights shone on the damp, drying floor, the worktops on both sides, and the table in the centre of the kitchen.

'Did you clean the table with bleach too?' she asked. 'That's unusual.'

'Yes. I've always done it. Mix it with some Cif — it works wonders. You should try it sometime.'

'Maybe I just might.' She walked over the wet floor and inspected the kitchen.

There was a sound from upstairs. Both PCs looked in the direction of the dining room and then gave each other a knowing look.

'On your own, are you?' Grearer asked.

'That's right. Matthew's gone to work.'

'Let's check upstairs, shall we?' suggested Weaver.

'Be my guest.' He motioned them forward.

The PCs cautiously moved through the dining room and turned at the base of the stairs. Weaver went first, holding the handrail to steady herself on the steep incline.

Watching the back of PC Grearer, he pushed his hand into his pocket to check his penknife was still there. His fingers closed around the handle.

Grearer stopped at the bottom of the stairs and watched Weaver reach the top.

'After you.' He waved him on.

Grearer turned to face him. 'I'm okay here, thanks.'

Weaver took a left at the top towards the bathroom and front bedroom.

He peered at the locked attic hatch, praying the girls didn't make a sound up there.

'Go upstairs if you'd like,' he told PC Grearer.

'I'll stay right here, thank you.'

He shook his head and climbed the stairs two at a time. He found Weaver in the bathroom, looking around. The door to the bedroom on the right before the bathroom was nearly closed, and the room was in darkness.

'What's in here?'

'Just a bedroom. Have a perusal if you want.'

She entered and found the light to her immediate right. The room erupted in harsh light from an old, faded cream lampshade. A wide wardrobe to the left covered most of the wall. One of the doors had a mirror fixed to it, which she used to briefly examine the other side of the room through the reflection. Boxes and black bags were stuffed on top, reducing the gap between the wardrobe and ceiling. She went in further. A double bed stood to the right, dressed with a pale, faded yellow bed cover. She stopped at the foot of the bed and looked around, seeing the end of a phone charger loosely on top of a bedside unit next to a small lamp. She went over to the loose wire.

'Is this the room you're using?'

He nodded.

'What phone do you have?'

'A Samsung.'

'Show me.'

He plucked his phone from his pocket and showed her. She plugged the phone into the charger to see if it matched up. The phone pinged, and the charging icon appeared on the screen. He sighed lightly, wondering how much longer this would last.

'It smells sweet in here,' she said. 'Like cheap perfume.'

'Sounds like I need a better aftershave, then.' He smiled and held it for a few seconds too long, which seemed to annoy her, if her scowl was anything to go by.

She moved to the door and wandered across the landing to the rear bedroom. He followed her.

'Everything okay?' PC Grearer was still standing at the base of the stairs.

'Yes,' she replied, peering down at him.

Entering the rear bedroom, she found this room was much bigger and more liveable.

'Is this Matthew's room?'

'It is, yes,' he said, stepping inside.

Studying the bed, wardrobe, bedside unit, and boxes piled up on the right, she asked, 'What's in those?'

'I have no idea. They're not mine,' he told her.

'Okay.' Satisfied no one was there, she returned back downstairs and opened the front door. Before they left, she said, 'Let Matthew know we'll be back at some point to speak with him.'

He nodded but said nothing.

'You have a good evening, sir.'

Smiling, he closed the door, locked it, and breathed deeply, backing up and sitting on the stairs for a moment to catch his breath.

'Jesus,' he whispered.

He desperately needed to do something with the girls. He had to come up with a plan.

56

Saturday morning
West Manor, Darlington

Selena woke up before it was light outside, quietly got out of bed so she didn't wake her husband, and went into the en-suite, closing the door silently. She hadn't slept well, waking every hour, her body covered with sweat and her head filled with worry. Jarrett's visit yesterday had terrified her. How was she supposed to get the girls back? She didn't know where to start.

Maybe it was worth phoning DI Byrd and telling him about Jarrett? She would have to tell him how she knew Jarrett, meaning she'd have to come clean about the hit-and-run incident in Warrington last month. But going to prison was better than being killed.

She got dressed in the dark bedroom, the closed curtains blocking the majority of the morning light trying to seep in, and listened to her husband snoring lightly as he faced away from her. His back and arm rose and fell as he slept. Descending the stairs, she put on her trainers, opened the front door, and peered outside to check for any signs of Jarrett or his Range Rover. The street was quiet. Only the familiar cars belonging to her neighbours were parked there. She dashed to her car, got in, and set off for West Manor.

On her drive down West Auckland Road, her mind raced. Phoning the police was a last resort — she knew that. She needed to figure out where the girls were and get them back to Jarrett immediately.

She'd already spent enough time in the last three days driving around the town looking for them. And now Anya's picture was in the papers, the whole of Darlington was on the lookout. No, the best thing she could do was go back to the place they'd escaped from. Perhaps if she figured out how they'd left without being seen on the CCTV, she'd work out where they'd gone.

The security guard at the gatehouse looked surprised as she pulled in.

'What you doing here today, Selena?' he said, grinning.

'Morning, Tim,' she said. 'I need to check something, that's all. Hope you're keeping the place safe?'

Still showing his crooked teeth, Tim nodded twice. He was tall and thin, but his posture was arched, his back slightly bent, the effects of his desk job before he joined their security team, Selena guessed.

'Is Dr Ellis coming in too?'

She frowned. 'Why would Dr Ellis be in? Dr Jacobs covers the weekend shifts.'

Tim shrugged, slightly losing the smile. 'Well, I just thought with Reggie coming in earlier, you all might be in.'

Selena's eyes narrowed. 'Reggie's here?'

'Turned up less than half an hour ago.'

The dashboard clock said 7.13. She put the car into first gear. 'Looks like just me and Reggie, then.'

'Well, be sure to have a good day.' He leaned to the right and pressed the button to open the metal gates.

'Thanks, Tim. See you when I come out.'

She drove up the winding drive and parked in her usual space. Within a few minutes, she was up in her office, sitting at her desk. She planned to review Tuesday's CCTV footage, hoping to find a trace of the girls. They had already done it, but it was the only thing she could think of before contacting DI Byrd.

She spent the next twenty minutes reviewing various clips, but they were the same as before. First thing Tuesday morning, the girls had been out in the garden, and then in the hallway on their way to their rooms. Then nothing.

'Where did they go?' she whispered.

Slamming the desk with a palm, she stood and went to the window, desperate for inspiration. Her gaze dropped down to Reggie's garage, and she noticed his grey van parked outside. *Why are you here?* she wondered.

Leaving the office, she descended the two flights of stairs to the basement, taking a left and turning on the light before walking briskly to the door labelled *Caretaker*.

She frowned and tried the handle. Locked. She knocked several times.

'Reggie, are you in there?'

Pushing down on the handle, she barged a shoulder into the door.

'Reggie!'

A rattling sound came from inside, followed by a door closing.

'Who is it?' he asked from the other side of the door.

'It's Selena. Let me in, please.'

She had to wait a few moments until the door was unlocked and opened. Reggie stood there, dressed in dark, grubby jeans and a black T-shirt. The smell of sweat seeped out into the corridor.

'What are you doing in today? I thought you were ill yesterday?'

'I was, I feel better now,' he explained. 'I need some tools for some home DIY.'

She frowned at him curiously. 'DIY?'

'I'm doing some decking at home. Needed the chop saw.'

She stepped inside the room, and the smell of sweat changed to something unfamiliar.

'What's that awful smell?'

'What do you want?' he asked, ignoring her.

She studied the small room. Reggie's desk was over to the right with a lamp on. Paperwork and two empty mugs took up the area to the left of the keyboard. To the right was a shelving unit with boxes containing purchase orders from years gone by from various suppliers they'd used. She looked at the locked door in front of her, which led to the garage. The rattling sound she'd heard must have been those doors closing.

'What's that smell, Reggie?'

He shrugged. 'Probably the grass in there. Cut it this week, didn't I? The recycling hasn't been collected yet. It should be on Monday, hopefully. It's starting to stink.'

'You should put it outside, then.'

He pushed his lips out. 'That's a good idea. Right, I'm gonna get off, get my jobs done.'

She held up a hand, stopping him in his tracks for the door. 'Can I look in the garage, Reggie?' she said calmly. 'I need to check something. We're getting a delivery next week, and I want to see what space you have down here.'

'A delivery?'

She nodded. 'Yeah.'

He stared at her silently and shook his head.

'Reggie, let me in there.'

'No.'

'Reggie, why are you being funny about this?'

He took a lungful of the warm, stuffy air around them. 'Okay, I'll show you in there. Come on.' He placed his hand on her back and guided her to the door.

Behind her, she heard him remove his keys from his pocket. Waiting for him to pass her to open it, she turned.

An explosive, bright flash sparked her vision, and her legs buckled under her. She dropped to the floor, and her world went black.

* * *

236

She woke to a throbbing headache. She slowly opened her eyes. One side of her face was cold against the wooden floor, and the other was hot and swollen. In front of her, she saw the closed door that led to the garage and took a moment to remember what had happened.

'What the hell?' she muttered, pushing herself into a sitting position, suddenly realising she'd been attacked. Why would Reggie do that? The pain in her head intensified. She raised her hand and touched her face, feeling the tender bruise forming.

'Why would . . . Why . . . ?' Climbing slowly to her feet, struggling to balance, she used Reggie's desk to steady herself.

The door that led to the corridor was closed. Trying the handle, she screamed when it wouldn't open. Turning, she tried the other door leading to the garage, which was also locked.

'For fuck's sake!' she shouted, her anger filling the small room.

She felt in her pocket, found her phone, and dialled the gatehouse.

'West Manor gatehouse, how can I help?' answered Tim.

'Tim! Tim, it's Selena. Has Reggie left yet?'

'Yeah, he left in his van about half an hour ago.'

Jesus, she thought, realising she'd been unconscious for some time. 'I need help. I'm stuck in his office. He locked me in.'

'He — He locked you in?' asked Tim, sounding unsure that he'd heard her correctly.

'Yes. I'm locked in his office. I know you have a spare set of master keys in the hutch. Can you come and let me out?'

'I can't really leave the front, I—'

'Tim, get your arse down here now and unlock this goddamn door!'

'Of course,' he replied sheepishly. 'I'll be right down.'

Soon after, she heard a patter of feet and a rattle of keys, followed by a short ping and a key being inserted into the lock. The door opened to reveal Tim standing there, peering nervously inside with the keys in his hand.

'Selena, what happened to your head?'

'Never mind that.' She put her hand out. 'Give me the keys.'

He stepped inside, ducking to miss the top of the doorframe, and handed them to her.

'Thank you.' She turned to the locked door leading to the garage and rifled through the keys.

'Selena, what's going on?'

'Shush a second, let me figure this out.'

After trying the eighth key on a bunch of at least twenty, the lock shifted, and she pushed down the handle to open the door.

Entering the dark garage, the smell worsened, forcing her to cover her nose and mouth. A tiny sliver of light crept in under the closed garage roller door, giving them a sense of the size of the garage. She hadn't been in there for a while.

'Oh, God, what's that?' Tim asked, following her inside the dark space and cupping his mouth with a hand.

She flicked a switch and a bright, harsh light came on, illuminating the garage. She peered around. A metal shelving unit stood to the right, filled with various tools and organised boxes for smaller devices and fittings. To the left was a worktop with several cupboards below it. Towards the front of the garage was a sit-on lawnmower and a dozen black binbags with tiny knots at the top of them.

'That smells awful,' Tim said.

The smell grew stronger as she went towards the binbags. She remembered watching Reggie cut the grass a few days earlier, but the smell wasn't just of damp grass. It was something else. Down on the concrete, she spotted a red stain on the ground, like something had been spilled and cleaned up.

She grabbed one of the binbags and pulled it towards her, moving it to the centre of the garage away from the other bags. She untied the knot and opened the bag cautiously, then peered inside.

'Oh, Jesus,' she muttered, then gagged uncontrollably, taking a few steps back. 'Tim, call the police, now!'

57

Saturday morning
West Manor, Darlington

Byrd was downstairs in the kitchen when his phone rang. He answered it while Claire held Alan with a hand on his back, getting his wind up after his milk bottle.

'Sir, we have a situation at West Manor,' explained DS Leonard.

'The place the three girls went missing from?' He sat straighter, his eyebrows knotting as he concentrated on the call.

'Yes.'

'Okay, I'll head over now.'

Byrd hung up and placed his phone on the table. He sighed, looking over at Claire. 'I'm sorry, love.'

She stood and offered him a smile that never reached her eyes. 'You go do your thing, Max.' Turning, she disappeared into the hallway. A moment later, Byrd heard the living room door slam, an obvious sign that she was fuming he was giving up another Saturday.

Once he'd dressed in something a little smarter than jogging bottoms and an old T-shirt, he left the house, not bothering to say bye to Claire and Alan. It would only be rubbing salt into the wound. The sun was already up, shining its light on the weekend morning, the promise of a warm day ahead — shame he couldn't spend it with his family.

* * *

The metal gates next to the security hutch were already open. A tall man dressed in a dark grey uniform stood inside and put his hand through the hatch, signalling Byrd to stop, who slowed and showed his badge.

Byrd followed the winding road until he pulled next to PC Weaver's Astra. Beside it was DS Leonard's Vauxhall Insignia. There were more parked cars he didn't recognise, presumably belonging to staff and patients. As he got out of his car the Forensics team arrived, followed by DC Anne Tiffin. None of them looked pleased to be here on this fine Saturday morning.

'You guys don't waste any time,' Byrd said to Tallow and Hope.

Tallow smiled. 'What else are we going to be doing on the weekend anyway?' The tone he used suggested he'd had things planned.

Byrd knew how he felt.

'Well, exactly, mate,' he said, trying to keep the mood lighter than he felt inside. 'We can't be having too much fun outside of the job, can we?'

Tallow grinned again. His white coveralls were lowered, the arms wrapped around his waist. Considering they had the day off, they'd certainly arrived quickly. Hope had her coveralls fully zipped and went straight to the van's side door with a scowl, wasting no time getting on with it. The bags under her eyes were darker than usual. Byrd wondered if she'd been drinking last night, not that it mattered or was any of his business. As she leaned in to grab their forensic kit, Tallow pulled his coveralls up, pushed his arms into the sleeves, and zipped himself up.

'Nice to see you, Anne,' Byrd called to Tiffin.

'Likewise. No place I'd rather be,' she said, stopping by his side.

'Snap!' Hope joined them with the cube-shaped black case, shortly followed by Tallow.

'Right, let's see what delights we have in store this morning.' Byrd turned for the entrance.

'No Orion today?' asked Tallow.

'He's on his way.'

* * *

Jarrett was parked round the corner from Selena's house. On his phone, he observed the small flashing dot indicating the position of Selena's car from the tracker he'd fixed to the underside of her wheel arch in the early hours. Frowning, he looked up at the time on his dashboard: 6.45.

The Molnar brothers had left several messages on his voicemail. One of them was Tomas Molnar telling him he had a plan to get his daughters back. Jarrett frowned, unsure how that was possible, but he hadn't returned the call just yet. He'd need to answer soon, though. Ignoring them would only arouse suspicion.

Jarrett peered up from the phone nestled in his hand and stared through his windscreen at Edward Pease Way. He had a good view of the main access road into West Park: if Selena was going anywhere, she'd use this one.

Although it was chillier this morning, the sun was up, casting faint shadows across the quiet road before him. Several dog walkers had passed, but none had seemed to notice him.

It wasn't long before the dot on the app started moving slowly across the digital map until she joined Edward Pease Way, heading towards him.

'Where are you going?' he whispered.

Through the front windscreen, he watched Selena drive by just after 7 a.m.

He slowly pulled away from the kerb, making sure to keep a reasonable distance. He trailed her along West Auckland Road and turned left onto Woodland Road, until he took a right onto Staindrop Road. The traffic was very light at this time, so he needed to stay back. The risk of her seeing him was too high, and he knew he could always track her with the app.

As he drove down Staindrop Road, he watched the flashing dot take a left onto Barnes Road. It appeared she was heading for West Manor. He pulled up on the opposite side of the road as her car disappeared down the driveway.

'Working on a Saturday, Selena?'

He decided to wait, knowing he wouldn't get past security. More than an hour passed before a police car approached, slowed, and turned into West Manor.

'What the fuck?'

Soon a BMW X5 went by and turned in, shortly followed by a dark blue Volkswagen van and another police car.

'What's going on here?'

He tried calling Selena's number. It went to voicemail.

'Fuck this.' He turned on the engine and made a rash three-point turn. He'd had enough of waiting — it was time to punish her.

He powered the Range Rover into second gear and went down the hill. A Volkswagen Golf approached him and the driver, a tanned-looking man, frowned at him as he passed.

'Fuck you staring at?' he said.

Minutes later he parked just along from Selena's house so his car was out of sight. He took the path down the side of the house and slipped through the unlocked back gate, patting his waistband to check his gun was still there. He rounded the back corner of the house, scanning nearby windows, staying low, and peeked through the kitchen window. Selena's husband was standing by the kettle wearing a black dressing gown. He dropped down, looked along the rear of the house, and saw a set of French doors and another window further along.

The door slid open less than a minute later with a dull *whoosh*. Jarrett moved back to the corner to stay hidden but kept his eyes on the door. Selena's husband appeared, holding a cup of tea, and stepped down onto the patio, moving as if his joints were in pain. He placed his mug on the table, then pulled a pack of cigarettes out of one of the pockets, removed one, and lit it, inhaling deeply and blowing smoke into the air.

It would be easy to attack him here, but any shouting would draw attention, and the garden was overlooked by the neighbouring houses. No, better to surprise him inside. Jarrett watched him pull his phone out and make a call, facing away from the house. Jarrett kept low, shifting along the back of the house, and sneaked inside the open patio door without being seen.

A few minutes later, he heard him enter with a deep sigh. Jarrett stood straight and watched him with dark eyes. When the man finally saw him, he stopped and gasped.

'Jesus! Wh-What are you doing here?'

Jarrett pulled the gun from his waistband and pointed it at his face.

'Sit down.' He indicated the kitchen table.

Selena's husband showed no resilience, immediately raising his hands in surrender, and moving towards the table.

'Sit down and stay silent.'

He dropped into a seat, shaking as he did so, eyeing the gun in Jarrett's hand with terrified eyes.

'Keep still,' Jarrett told him. He pulled out his phone and took a picture. He sent it to Selena, waited a minute, then called her.

'Hello?' she answered, her voice nearly breaking.

'You've received my photo?'

'Yes.'

'Where are my girls?'

'You said I had a day.'

'I changed my mind. Tell me where they are, and I won't have to kill this man.'

'God, please don't hurt Alex, please—'

'Selena, where the fuck are they?'

'Okay. Reggie Cook has them. He works here at West Manor. I've just found out he had something to do with them going missing.'

'Where can I find him?'

'He lives on Geneva Road.'

'What number?'

She told him.

'If this is false information, your husband dies. Do you understand?'

'He has them. Reggie has them!'

Jarrett hung up and pushed his phone into his jeans but kept the gun pointed at Alex.

'Looks like it's your lucky day,' Jarrett told him.

'But not yours, Jarrett,' said a familiar voice behind him.

Frowning, Jarrett spun around quickly.

Tomas and Matej Molnar were standing on the threshold of the double doors, pointing a gun at him.

58

Saturday morning
West Manor, Darlington

Tanzy drove up Barnes Road and slowed, waiting for an approaching black Range Rover to pass him before veering around the parked car. The Range Rover driver scowled at Tanzy for some reason as he drove past. He continued up the road and took a right into West Manor, quickly waved through by the security guard.

He wasn't his usual chirpy self this morning because he'd taken a knock last night at judo, and his shoulder was in agony. Not only that, but telling Pip he had to go to work had not only upset her, but Eric and Jasmine had had tears in their eyes as he left. He'd promised to take them to the seaside for the day, but yet again, he was putting work before anything else — something he was becoming frustrated with.

He parked next to Byrd's car, recognising the forensics van and two of the police cars as he made his way into the building. He spotted the back of a PC in what he assumed was a reception area — one of the new recruits talking with a member of staff, a middle-aged woman with a lanyard hanging around her neck and a clipboard in her hand. The young twenty-something PC heard his approach and turned away from the woman, offering a courteous nod. He'd probably been asked to wait here to make sure they knew who was coming in and out of the building.

'Where's the action?' asked Tanzy, wasting no time with pleasantries.

'Hello, DI Tanzy.' The PC stepped back and pointed towards the open doorway. 'Go down the stairs and you'll see.'

Once he'd descended the stairs, he heard a conversation coming from the left, but stopped in the narrow corridor when he received a text message.

You need to start putting the kids first. They're so upset. You'd better make it back in time to go to the beach.

Shaking his head and deciding not to let it bother him more than it already had, he put his phone away and took a deep, sharp breath. He walked down the short corridor until he reached an open door. 'Hello?'

'In here, boss.'

He pulled out a pair of blue overshoes and put them on, then snapped some latex gloves on before entering the small room. PC Degnan was shuffling through paperwork on the desk with gloved hands. She half turned towards him with a thin smile. Her skin appeared paler than usual.

'You okay?'

She shook her head silently, telling him everything he needed to know.

He briefly studied the small room before moving to the threshold of a garage or workshop area. Two bright yellow strip lights illuminated the space, roughly eight metres deep and twelve metres wide. There was a workbench, a large shelving unit to the right, and a row of cupboards under a long worktop to the left. He sniffed the air, smelling something unpleasant close by. The floor was concrete, and the area felt colder than the room before, probably because the garage door was raised and coiled up at the top, allowing daylight and fresh air to enter.

Byrd and Tiffin, wearing gloves and blue overshoes, were concentrating on the surface of the workbench to the right. He turned to the left and saw Tallow and Hope dressed in their whites. Tallow was standing a few feet behind Hope, an iPad in his hand, his finger dragging something across the screen, which dimly illuminated his eyes and nose. Hope was crouched down, her arm extended, touching something inside a black binbag. Tanzy had no idea what to expect but counted at least six bags, all looking rather full, positioned in front of the worktop and cupboard.

He angled over to Byrd. 'Hey, Max.'

Byrd turned his way. 'Welcome to paradise,' he said before he returned to Tiffin, pointing at something on the workbench. 'Interesting one, this.'

Tanzy approached Hope and Tallow. 'Morning, you two. Thanks for coming.'

Tallow grinned. 'We live for this stuff, Ori. We wouldn't want to be anywhere else in the world. Isn't that right, Emily?'

'Yeah, sitting on a warm beach in Spain with a vodka and Coke in my hand sounds like my idea of hell,' replied Hope, still crouched on the ground, focusing on something with serious eyes.

Tanzy admired their humour, momentarily forgetting about his upset family at home. 'What do we have, guys?' He shifted over a few feet for a better view.

'The manager, Selena Goldberg, came here this morning,' Byrd said. 'She was attacked by one of her colleagues, Reggie Cook.'

Tanzy frowned.

'Reckons he was acting weird and punched her in the face.' Byrd raised a hand to make the blow's location clearer. 'She thinks he has something to do with taking the girls we're looking for too, because she can't think of any other way they'd have got out. After she was attacked, she found herself locked in that room. The guy at the security gate let her out, and that's when she came in and found this.'

248

'What is this?'

Byrd motioned him forward. 'See for yourself.'

'Whatever it is, it bloody reeks!' Tanzy peered inside the nearest binbag. He knew already from the familiar smell of decomposition that it wasn't going to be pretty. 'Is that someone's fucking hand?'

'Certainly looks like it,' said Hope. 'Severed at the wrist.'

'You checked all the bags?'

'Just two so far. Found a hand, a forearm, an ear, and a few fingers.'

'Jesus.'

'Mind out the way, Ori.' Tallow stepped forward.

Tanzy shifted to the left. Tallow pulled a plastic sheet from the forensic kit, then he and Hope unfolded it and positioned it in an open space.

'We'll put everything on here.'

'Reckon there's more in the others?'

'I wouldn't bet against it, Ori,' replied Hope.

Tanzy shook his head and wandered over to Byrd. 'Jesus, Max.'

'I know.'

'Where is Selena right now?'

'Up in her office with DS Leonard, giving a statement.'

'And she thinks her colleague is responsible for this?'

'Reggie Cook, his name is.'

Tanzy scowled. 'That the place Donny and Amy were last night on Geneva Road, the house the van was registered to?'

Byrd nodded twice. 'Maybe Jonathon Bedlam wasn't Jonathon Bedlam after all.'

'Well, let's go find him.'

59

Saturday morning
Haughton Road, Darlington

Steve Mitchell stepped out and locked his door. The sound of the traffic behind him on Haughton Road was already testing the headache he'd had since waking at 4 a.m. He'd lain awake, trying to sleep, but the image of Mia on the kitchen floor peppered with stab wounds had played over and over in his mind, even though he hadn't physically seen her there.

Where the hell was his daughter?

Images of her wandering aimlessly around Darlington in the darkness reached the far corners of his mind. Something must have happened to her. He couldn't help but assume the worst.

Since being allowed back into his home late Thursday after the Forensics team had deemed the house fully checked out, he'd spent most of his time in the kitchen and Ella's bedroom, the two places he felt most connected to his wife and daughter. He couldn't keep still, spending much of his time walking in small circles, shaking, his mind in overdrive thinking about where Ella could be. He'd thought about all the places she loved

— her friend's houses, places around the town where the family lived — and had checked literally everywhere he could think of. But he wouldn't give up. There must be something.

He'd spoken with DI Byrd yesterday, who'd informed him they hadn't got any leads yet and that he'd be the first to know if the police found anything of value. But he couldn't just sit and wait.

He turned to face the morning traffic. He'd had a shower yesterday morning but had no intention of making an effort with his appearance, now dressed in faded shorts and an old black T-shirt and trainers he'd had for as long as he could remember. His brown hair looked the same as when he'd woken up, tousled and off to one side. His only goal was finding Ella. He had no intention of driving either and walked past his car on the driveway. Just ahead, Susan Brown, his neighbour four doors down, pulled her car into the small, set-back road in front of the row of houses. She stopped suddenly and lowered her window.

He slowly wandered over. 'Morning, Susan.'

'Steve, how've you been? I've been worried sick about you. I've knocked several times but assumed you weren't in.'

'The — The police have had access to the house for a few days, only got back on Thursday night.' He stopped, unsure what else to say.

'Listen, I'm so sorry about what's happened.'

'Thanks,' he replied.

'I was talking to the detectives the other day, you know, the day when . . .'

He nodded. He knew the day she meant.

'I showed them my CCTV from the garden. Maybe it might upset you, Steve, but Ella is on there. Do you want to see it?'

Without a second's hesitation, he shouted, 'Yes! Where is it?'

'Pop down for a coffee, I'll show you.' She looked forward through her windscreen. 'Let me park first.'

She drew up outside her house and he walked along the road while she unclipped her seat belt and got out.

'So, how've you been?' she asked, stepping around her car and immediately shaking her head. 'I'm sorry, I—'

'It's okay,' he said, more excited about seeing a clip of his daughter. At this moment, it was the closest thing he had to her. 'I've been staying at my sister's across town. Police said I could come back Thursday evening. Been difficult.'

'I can only imagine.'

Susan opened her front door, stepped inside, and held the door for him, then led him to the kitchen.

'Can I get you a coffee, Steve?'

He shook his head. He had no interest in the coffee. All he needed was to see another clip of his daughter, a different angle, a real-life video of the one person in the world he was so desperate to see right now.

'Have a seat.' She grabbed an iPad from the worktop and came over to the table, pulling out a chair. He did the same with the one beside it. 'So, let me find it.'

He shook as he waited nervously to see Ella. He sat close to Susan, smelling her faint perfume, which reminded him of the lavender plant in his own garden, the one Mia spent so much time tending to in the summer months.

'When the police were here, I showed them this video.'

The clip showed Ella running from the back door towards the right of the screen towards the garden. A moment later, she came back with another girl.

'She's the one from the hospital!' Steve stabbed the air in front of the screen.

'Who is she?'

'We don't know. Social services got involved. During the night, someone came and took her.'

They continued watching the clip, and then she showed him the one of the man entering the house. As Steve watched it, he rocked back, hand to his mouth, anger and sadness filling his body. He was speechless.

'Do police know who this is yet?' she asked.

'They think he's the man they found at the hospital. The one who took her from the ward. Did you hear about him?'

She nodded. 'I did.'

'Have you watched all of the footage from then until now?'

'No, I haven't. I . . .' She trailed off. 'Should we?'

He nodded. 'Please. You never know. I just have no idea where Ella is, that's all. And there might be something we've missed here. I just can't work it out.'

Steve felt her gaze on him for a few seconds before she said, 'Okay, we'll have a look — ahh, bastard!'

'What?'

'Bloody thing needs charging. Where's the charger at?' She stood up and searched for it. 'Bet he's bloody taken it upstairs last night. Hate it when he does that.'

Steve smiled to himself, wishing Mia was still at home and he could have a moan about her too. 'Listen, I need to go,' he heard himself say, suddenly feeling like he needed some air. Seeing Ella on the CCTV had excited him, but it hadn't made him feel any better at all. If anything, it had annoyed him, seeing the strange man walk in then come back out ten minutes later. Standing, he thanked her.

'It's okay, Steve. Just to let you know, I'm here if you want a chat. I've been watching Emma next door with her niece playing, and I've been thinking about you, that's all. I can't imagine how it feels.'

He smiled weakly, looking away, hoping the feeling of emptiness inside of him would leave soon. 'Thanks for your time, Susan.'

He followed her back through the house and walked through the door she held open for him. Once outside, he turned right and walked up Haughton Road with no destination in mind. He was just walking in search of Ella Mitchell.

253

60

Jarrett Banks stared at Tomas and Matej Molnar with wide, cautious eyes. He couldn't move. 'Wh-What are you doing here?'

Tomas beamed at him and looked away momentarily, clearly not impressed at Jarrett's false innocence. 'You're the one who took our girls.'

Jarrett frowned and made a theatrical show of shaking his head, doing his best to be convincing. 'No, it's not me, I—'

'Cut the bullshit!' screamed Tomas. 'You're the fucker who killed Hendo too when he was waiting for the girls, aren't you?'

Jarrett stared at the barrel of the gun in his partner's hand. 'Listen, Tomas, I don't know where you have that from, but it's not me.'

Matej left Tomas's side and slowly walked past the sink to grab a knife from the block. He studied the blade in the daylight coming through the window.

'This knife is sharp,' said Matej softly, then he hummed an unfamiliar tune. 'I bet it could do some serious damage.'

'Drop the gun, Jarrett,' said Tomas, his voice even.

Knowing it was two against one, Jarrett placed the gun on the kitchen table close to Selena's husband.

'Where are my girls?'

Jarrett raised his hands innocently. 'Listen, I don't—'

The ear-piercing noise of a gunshot bounced off every kitchen wall and echoed throughout the house.

Jarrett had subconsciously turned side on and automatically curled up to protect himself, his arms pressed against his own body to protect his vital organs. As the seconds ticked by, he realised he couldn't feel any pain. He squinted at Tomas. The scent of gunfire filled the air. Tomas was lowering his weapon, smiling. Jarrett turned to the left and saw Selena's husband leaning back at an unnatural angle. The bullet had hit him in the centre of the forehead. Behind him, on the table, was a thick spray of blood and brain matter.

Jarrett was speechless.

'Please, Jarrett . . . take a seat.'

Without hesitation, Jarrett sat down.

'The next bullet is for you, Jarrett. As you can see, I'm not playing around here.'

Jarrett took deep breaths to settle his racing heart, thumping against the inside of his chest.

'Where are the girls?'

Silence.

'Jarrett, fucking answer me now.' Tomas sighed and tilted his head slightly. 'You have three seconds. One. Two. Th—'

'Okay, okay!' he shouted, bringing his hand up to protect himself from the potential bullet coming his way, not that it would help. 'The girls are with someone called Reggie Cook.'

'Where can I find this Reggie Cook?'

Jarrett told him the address that Selena had given him moments ago.

Tomas looked past Jarrett at Matej. 'You got that?'

There was a pause, and Jarrett could hear Matej's footsteps behind him, but he kept his eyes on Tomas.

He could see his own gun out of the corner of his eye on the table but knew he wouldn't reach it before Tomas shot him.

'Thank you for your service, Jarrett Banks.' Tomas looked away from Jarrett to somewhere behind him.

Jarrett felt Matej seize the top of his head. It felt like his hair was being ripped from his skull as he resisted and leaned forward, closer to his gun. The monstrous silver blade flashed past his face and under his chin, then the cold edge of the knife pressed against his windpipe, the blade cutting into his skin. Warm blood trickled down his throat onto his chest.

He needed to get the gun, but it might as well have been on the moon. He reached up and grabbed Matej's arm, trying to pull it away, but he was in a poor position and not strong enough for Matej.

'Please,' he begged, the minor movement of his throat causing severe pain.

He felt a sudden jolt of agony, his gullet opening as the knife ripped across his windpipe. He threw both hands up to his wound to cover it and apply pressure — anything to stop the bleeding — but a lake of blood filled his hands and ran down his forearms. Coughing now, he started gargling on the blood filling his mouth. He lurched to his feet, staggering a few steps until he dropped to his knees. Still holding his throat, he lost his balance completely and fell forward. His face smashed onto the white tiles with a crack. It was the last thing Jarrett ever felt.

61

Saturday morning
West Manor, Darlington

Byrd, Tanzy, and DC Tiffin left the garage and went through Reggie Cook's office but stopped when DS Leonard and Selena Goldberg entered, appearing out of breath.

Byrd spotted something on Leonard's face. 'What is it, Jim?'

'Sir, Selena has just received a call,' said Leonard, nodding her way to expand on it.

'Jarrett Banks has just called me,' she said quickly. 'He has my husband, Alex, at gunpoint at home. He wanted to know where the girls were. I told him Reggie had them. I gave him Reggie's address.' She took a breath after getting it out as quickly as she could.

Byrd and Tanzy both frowned, digesting the information.

'Who is Jarrett Banks, and what does he have to do with the missing children?' asked Byrd.

'Jarrett's the man who brought the three girls to me,' Selena spluttered. 'He's been blackmailing me to keep them here on the quiet. He was at my house last night with a gun.'

Byrd's eyes widened with sudden worry as he realised the severity of the situation.

He turned to Tanzy and Degnan. 'Can you two head over to Selena's house, please?'

Tanzy nodded. 'Yeah. Come on, I'll drive.'

Tanzy and Degnan shot off towards the corridor. They stopped when a crackle came through the radio fixed to Degnan's belt: '*All available personnel, please respond to an urgent call. Reported gunshot fired on Collingsway, West Park.*'

Selena took a step back, raising a hand to her open mouth. 'No . . .'

Byrd nodded at them. 'You two, go, go!'

Tanzy and Degnan disappeared and raced up the stairs back to their car. Selena turned and darted for the door to follow them. 'You wait here, please, Selena!' instructed Byrd.

She stopped. 'But — But my husband?'

'Let us sort this one,' he told her, calmly raising a hand. 'Please.'

A couple of local PCs walked in, and Byrd asked one of them to take Selena somewhere quieter and give her a cup of tea.

'I don't want fucking tea!' shouted Selena, shaking her head in despair.

Ignoring her outburst, the young PC nodded and capably guided Selena out the door and out of sight.

Byrd turned to PC Weaver. 'Amy, can you and James head over to Reggie Cook's house, see if he's there with the girls?' He pulled his phone from his jeans. 'I'll call for immediate backup.'

Leonard and Weaver ran for the door. Their footsteps grew quieter as they pounded up the staircase out in the corridor. Byrd called Dispatch, letting them know two officers were en route to West Park, but further units were needed to go to Geneva Road. He gave the address.

'*Diverting all available personnel to both addresses, DI Byrd,*' replied the operator efficiently.

'Thank you.'

He returned to the garage to see how the forensics, Tallow and Hope, were getting on.

* * *

Tanzy took a right at the bottom of Barnes Road to join Staindrop Road. He powered on, putting the car in third gear, reaching the set of roundabouts at Carmel Road and Woodland Road in no time. Luckily, no cars were approaching, so he took a sharp left, the tyres screeching as he straightened out towards Cockerton. PC Degnan was silent in the passenger seat, holding onto the door handle to steady herself as Tanzy ragged the Golf around the corners like a madman. She hadn't done her high-speed training yet, so although this was something new and made her nervous, it was exciting.

There was a crackle on Degnan's radio. She leaned to the side and turned up the volume.

'*Following on from the report of a gunshot at Collingsway, two men have been seen leaving the property and getting into a dark blue Ford Mondeo.*'

'Ask if they have the registration,' Tanzy said to Degnan, who pulled her radio fully off her belt.

'Dispatch, this is PC Louise Degnan. Do you have a registration for the Mondeo?'

'There's a pen and notepad there.' Tanzy nodded to the glove box.

She leaned forward and grabbed them.

Hearing a crackle and a hiss, Tanzy and Degnan narrowed their eyes, waiting for Dispatch to reply. He slowed at the large roundabout near Lidl and powered across it in second gear, the sound of the smooth two-litre engine busy under the bonnet.

'*November. One. Nine. Echo. Victor. Bravo.*'

'Thank you,' she replied, jotting down the information.

Tanzy pulled his mobile from his pocket and unlocked it before handing it over to Degnan. 'Louise, open the phonebook and call Jennifer Lucas, please.' There was a slim chance she was working the weekend, but she sometimes did overtime.

Degnan nodded, navigated to his contact list, tapped on the number, and turned on his phone's loudspeaker.

'Orion?' she answered softly. 'This is unexpected.'

'Sorry to ring you, Jennifer, but are you at work today?'

'I am,' she replied chirpily. 'Caught me at a good time.'

Tanzy beamed. 'Good. Can you do me a favour?'

'Anything for you, Ori.'

Degnan's eyes narrowed at Jennifer's reply, but she remained looking at the phone, not daring to turn to Tanzy.

'We're looking for a dark blue Mondeo,' he said, feeling his cheeks redden. 'It was last seen on Collingsway at West Park a few minutes ago. We're heading there now.'

'What's the reg, Ori?'

He told her.

'Okay. I'll ring you back asap.'

'Thank you,' he said before hanging up.

The traffic was light for a Saturday morning, and Tanzy pulled into Collingsway several minutes later. They hadn't passed the Mondeo, so there was a chance it had gone a different way, or the message about the two men leaving the house had been slightly delayed.

'There's the house,' Tanzy said, pointing, then grabbed hold of the wheel to park his Golf on the driveway, nose first. Tanzy grabbed the baton he kept in the storage compartment of his door, jumped out, raced to the house's front door, and tried the handle. Locked. Degnan was a few feet behind, watching him.

'Shit,' he scolded. 'Ask Dispatch if backup is on its way, please.'

Degnan relayed the request.

'*Armed Response ETA two minutes, PC Degnan.*'

'Thanks. Over.' She lowered the radio back into the slot in her belt. 'Are we going to wait for them?'

Tanzy shook his head. 'We need to move now. Come on, let's try a side gate.'

They went to the left and moved silently down the side of the house. Tanzy palmed the gate open, the hinges moaning as it moved, and Degnan followed with her baton fully extended.

Tanzy's phone started ringing, startling them both for a second. 'Jesus!' he said, stopping and taking the baton in his left hand while using his right to pluck out his phone and answer it. It was Jennifer from the town hall.

'What have you got?' he asked, straight to the point.

'Found your Mondeo. Heading Southbound on Neasham Road towards Geneva Road a minute ago.'

'That from a live camera?'

'Yeah. Literally a minute ago.'

Tanzy narrowed his eyes, recognising some of his colleagues were heading for Reggie Cook's house on Geneva Road — was it the same house? 'Thank you, Jennifer. I'll call you back.'

'Okay, no p—'

Tanzy had already hung up, pushing his phone back into his pocket and feeling bad about not giving her more time. He just hoped Degnan hadn't noticed the way Jennifer had spoken to him.

'Right, come on,' he said, his grip tight on the extended baton. They rounded the rear corner and noticed a set of glass double doors, one of which was open. Tanzy slowed and silently shifted across the back of the house, peering in the kitchen window. A man was slumped in a chair.

'Stay behind me.'

'Got ya,' Degnan whispered.

He popped his head inside at the open door, looking around for any signs of anyone with a weapon. After all, there had been reports of gunfire. It was clear to the left. He panned to the right.

'God . . .' he said, stepping inside on the white tiled flooring. 'Don't get too close,' he told Degnan, who followed him, ready with her baton.

There was blood everywhere. They studied the man on the chair, leaning back, with a hole in his head, then the man on the floor with a huge slice across his throat, his head nearly drowning in a lake of blood beneath him.

'Never a dull day, even when it's the bloody weekend,' he muttered, shaking his head.

'What did you say, boss?'

'Never mind. Call Forensics.'

62

Saturday morning
Geneva Road, Darlington

Reggie raced home after leaving West Manor, shaken and worried after what he'd done to Selena. He'd known her for years. He'd never intended to kill her. If only she had stayed away and not interfered with him and his garage. She had no right to be there this morning — she never worked weekends.

It had been an adrenaline rush, certainly, but it wasn't what he did, and he hadn't covered his tracks. And Selena was different again. She was connected to him. They were friends. If she was reported missing, the police would search West Manor.

'Shit,' he whispered, sitting in his van parked on his driveway. 'What if they get into the garage?'

He'd been shady about her having a look when she'd asked, so if the police got involved, they'd definitely find a way in and see the bags. That couldn't happen.

'Fuck!' He slammed a palm on the steering wheel, making it judder for a moment. He got out, still shaken up, and went inside the house, closing the door to shut out the sounds of passing cars.

It wasn't his fault, he thought, as he stood in the kitchen. He could hear them now, up in the attic — the agents of his destruction. The drugs he'd given the girls must have worn off; they were awake and shouting, their desperation to be set free echoing down the stairs.

It was then the front door flew open with an almighty smash. Trouble was coming.

* * *

Two terrifying-looking men barged through the front door. He didn't understand why they were there, but after seeing the guns in their hands and the expressions on their faces, he knew he needed to move quickly — they didn't appear to be men that fucked around.

'Where are my daughters?' screamed one of them.

Reggie was speechless, unable to get a single word out.

'Fucking tell me now!'

A sudden desperate scream came from upstairs.

Shit, thought Reggie as he backed further into the kitchen away from them. The man raised his arm and fired. Reggie felt the bullet whizz by his ear, smashing into one of the cupboards to his left. He ran to the door at the end of the kitchen and jumped out onto the decking. He could hear them running after him.

His heart raced as he fled the house, taking long strides up the narrow garden, desperate to escape.

Just before he reached the back fence, he heard a shot and an intense, sharp pain filled the back of his right arm. A sudden flapping of wings came from a tree nearby, and four birds flew away from the startling sound. He staggered into the back fence, panting hard, trying to pull himself up despite the pain.

Another gunshot exploded, and this time the pain was in his right calf. He collapsed onto the grass in agony, rolling over to look back at the house.

He couldn't move. Didn't even try. Just rode out the pain.

'Whoever the fuck you are, you fucked with the wrong family.'

His vision was hazy. He could barely make out the big man coming towards him. The man raised his gun.

Reggie closed his eyes, waiting for the inevitable.

'Hey!' someone screamed nearby. 'Hey! The police are coming! I'm recording this!'

'Fuck this,' the man said, and then footsteps moved away, back towards the house.

Reggie sighed heavily and let himself drift into unconsciousness.

'I've called the police!' the distant voice shouted. 'Just hold on.'

63

Saturday morning
Geneva Road, Darlington

DS Leonard took a left at the roundabout, quickly pulling the Insignia onto Geneva Road, the tyres whining in complaint. A woman pushing a pram on the path scowled her disapproval at the speed he'd taken the corner.

'How far up is it?' he asked.

'About fifty or sixty metres,' replied Weaver. 'Was here last night.'

'Last night?'

'Yeah. Working late. Needed the OT,' she explained sadly.

Leonard focused on the oncoming car and the gap between the parked cars on either side, judging if he could make it through in time. He put his foot down and squeezed through, the elderly driver of the oncoming Mercedes blasting his horn and shaking his head at him.

'Which house is it?'

She leaned to the centre of the car to get a better view. 'There was a grey van parked on the driveway.'

'Ahh, there!' Leonard shouted, stabbing the air.

As they approached, they saw three girls run out of the house, followed by two men carrying guns. They got into a dark blue Mondeo and slammed their doors shut.

'That must be our Mondeo.'

'Looks like it,' she agreed. 'The two men who were seen in Collingsway too.'

'And three of our missing children.'

They were roughly thirty metres away from the car. Leonard slowed.

'Where's that backup Byrd promised us?' Weaver muttered.

A flash caught his eye in his rear-view mirror, followed by a loud siren wailing in the air. His eyes flicked to the mirror for a second, and he saw a marked car driven by PC Andrews approaching quickly, then slowing behind him. The Mondeo in front pulled away hurriedly from the kerb.

'Fuck.' Leonard dropped into second and put his foot down. 'Call Andrews, tell him to check the house. See if Reggie Cook is there. We'll follow the Mondeo.'

Nodding, Weaver picked up her radio. 'PC Andrews, this is PC Weaver. Call back.'

There was the crackle and hum of static. '*Go ahead, PC Weaver.*'

'Two male suspects and three young girls have left the property on Geneva Road in a dark blue Mondeo, the same one reported from Dispatch. The two men are armed. DS Leonard and I are giving chase. Can you check the house to see if Reggie Cook is there?'

Leonard powered into third, reaching forty-five miles an hour, the Mondeo ahead still in his sights.

'*Roger that. We'll check out the house.*'

'Dispatch, call back,' Weaver said into the radio.

'*This is Dispatch,*' the response came immediately.

'You get that?'

'*Loud and clear. What direction is the Mondeo heading?*'

Weaver brought the radio closer to her lips. 'Heading eastbound on Geneva Road towards Yarm Road.'

'*Sending all available armed units to that area. Advise if you require air support.*'

'Thanks. I'll keep everyone updated through this channel.' She lowered the radio to her lap.

Leonard kept his eyes on the road. 'Good job.' He trailed the Mondeo along Geneva Road, watching it speed over the mini roundabout near the corner shop. He slowed slightly on his approach to the same spot, ready to brake, but continued when the coast was clear.

'What we gonna do, Jim? They have guns.'

'We need to stay with them. We'll let Armed Response take over when they get here.'

* * *

Andrews stopped outside the house and jumped out the driver's door. PC Grearer got out the passenger door and turned to the house. From the left, a woman ran down her driveway, waving frantic hands above her head.

'Officer! Please help!' she shouted. 'Please help Reggie. He's been shot. He's in his garden.' She stabbed the air towards the back of the house.

Grearer raised a hand to let her know they'd handle it from there.

'Okay. Go back inside your house. We have this.'

She bobbed her head several times and backed away. 'Just make sure he's okay. There's blood.'

The PCs dashed up the drive with their batons extended and squeezed through the gap between the van and the side of the house, Grearer going first.

'Police! Police! Make yourself known!' he shouted, entering through the front door. He shifted to the left, scanned the living room, and then backed out, climbing the stairs.

'I'll check through here,' Andrews said, going right at the base of the stairs into the dining room and kitchen area.

The French doors were open. Andrews stepped out onto the decking and looked around. No sign of anyone. Hadn't the neighbours said someone was in the garden?

If there was, he was gone.

64

Saturday morning
Yarm Road, Darlington

'Is your seat belt on, Amy?' asked DS Leonard, approaching the crossroads at Yarm Road.

'Of course.' She was still gripping the door handle tightly.

The Mondeo had nipped through before the lights turned red, taking a right onto Yarm Road. Leonard approached the line of waiting cars in front and dropped into second gear, veering onto the other side of the road.

'James?' muttered Weaver.

He put his foot down and a yellow Vauxhall Corsa turned into the road.

'Jim!' she screamed, grabbing her seat in despair, expecting the inevitable.

Once past the first waiting car, he dabbed the brakes and threw the steering wheel to the left, barely missing the front of the yellow Corsa. The driver was a young, thin lad with wide, shocked eyes.

'Jesus!' said Weaver. 'You're gonna bloody kill us!'

Leonard straightened up, saw a fortunate gap in the traffic, and planted his foot, the Insignia's tyres gripping the tarmac, powering the car almost sideways as it made it across the road in front of an oncoming white transit van. The driver blasted the horn. Leonard continued along Yarm Road, passing Aldi and Lidl on the left. The Mondeo was in his sights ahead, weaving carelessly in and out of traffic. There was a dawdling queue as they approached a set of lights outside Greggs, but the Mondeo shifted to the other side of the road, hurtling past the island to a blare of horns.

'What a lunatic,' said Leonard.

'Jim?' Weaver said. 'You're not gonna do what I think you are, are you?'

He scowled. 'Can't lose 'em, Amy.'

He moved onto the opposite side of the road. A car was approaching the traffic lights from the other side, and there was space for only one car in the gap between the pavement and the traffic light island.

'Jim, there's no room this way.'

Leonard pushed his foot as far as he could, the Insignia surging forward, the engine whistling. A young girl around the age of eight or nine was waited at the crossing, looking the opposite way.

'Jim, watch that girl!'

'I see her, I see her,' he said quickly, now less than ten metres away. He pounded the horn several times. Nearby pedestrians glared his way. An elderly lady raised her walking stick in despair and shouted something. Two men dressed in orange hi-vis workwear shook their heads in utter disbelief.

'Jim?'

'Hold on . . .'

Weaver closed her eyes and bowed her head, waiting for the impact of the oncoming car.

Leonard made it through the narrow gap before throwing the car over to the left side of the road, narrowly missing the other car.

'God.' Weaver dropped her face into her hands, shaking.

'Don't see what all the panic is about.'

The Mondeo was ahead, still weaving in and out, the brake lights flickering as the driver manoeuvred.

'He can drive,' said Leonard. 'Not as good as me, though.'

'Just don't do anything daft, Jim. I have plans later.'

He frowned. 'What plans? Who with?'

'Didn't know you were my dad . . .'

He ignored it and tried to put the thought of her being with someone else out of his mind. They reached the round-about at the fish shop and went straight over, flying past Cummins on the right and the Travelodge on the left. They were thirty metres behind the Insignia and closing in.

* * *

Tomas spotted a flash of grey in his rear-view mirror and peeled his eyes from the road for a second. 'Matej, I think we're being followed.'

His brother craned his neck to see out the back of the car.

'The Insignia?' asked Matej.

'I think so. I saw it on the same road the house was on and then just now. It's keeping up with us.'

All three girls were silent, too afraid to speak.

'I'll lose him, don't worry,' said Tomas calmly, pushing his foot down as he approached a large roundabout. With no cars coming from the right, he sped over the next two round-abouts onto the A67 heading towards Middleton St George.

Matej was focused on his phone screen, studying the live map of their location. He didn't know the area very well but zoomed out, trying to find a main road where they could get some speed and lose the Insignia.

'They still following us?' Tomas pulled out and overtook a slow camper van as they passed the Farmhouse pub on the right. Raindrops started to appear on the windscreen. The sky was a dark grey, and in the distance, the clouds were black, filled with rain and thunderstorms.

Matej turned his head. The Insignia pulled off the round-about, still trailing them.

'They're far back but still there.' He lowered his gaze onto Nina. 'How you doing?'

Nina smiled at him. 'Good now. How did you find us?'

'We'll talk about it soon,' Tomas said from the front of the car. 'Let's just get rid of this car following us.'

'Go straight over the next two roundabouts, then take a left at the third,' Matej told him.

A minute later, Tomas turned left onto Mill Lane, and powered on, reaching 100 miles per hour in no time. The road veered around to the right, so he slowed to ninety to ensure he could make the bend without going onto the grass verge.

'Where to, Matej?'

His brother studied the map on his phone. 'There's . . . there's a farm coming up on the right.' He peered up, finding his bearings. 'Just before the roundabout, there's a right turn. Take it.'

'You sure?' asked Tomas.

'Trust me.'

The conviction in Matej's voice was good enough for Tomas.

'How far?'

'Start slowing. It's coming up very soon. Sixty metres or so.'

Tomas eased his foot off the accelerator. He couldn't see the Insignia anymore.

'I think we lost them.'

'Just take a right here, Tomas.'

The Mondeo slowed and turned, followed the slight bend, and took another right through an open gate into an area of old tarmac the size of a tennis court. To the left of the open space was a huge barn roughly fifty metres long, thirty metres deep, and fifteen metres high. The base of the barn was made from breeze blocks that supported the structure, a solid base roughly four metres high before it changed to metal cladding, which made up the rest of the sides and the slanted roof. The area looked empty and unused, with plenty of overgrown weeds and grass around them. At the edge was a fence roughly three feet high that ran around the perimeter of the land. Beyond that, it looked like a farmer's field. Whatever the place was used for appeared to be a thing of the past. The only vehicle was a wrecked Ford Kuga with a broken window and a flat tyre beside the barn. The state of it indicated it hadn't been driven in a long time and probably wouldn't be capable of making it very far.

'Think they saw us turn?' Matej looked behind them. The girls raised their heads like meerkats, doing the same and looking out the rear window. 'Sit down, please, girls.'

The girls nodded and did as their uncle asked.

'Let's hope not.' Tomas drove around the back of the building so they were out of sight from the road. He cut the engine and turned to the girls. 'What happened to you? I thought I'd never see you again.'

Nina told him about Jarrett Banks picking them up from school and telling them that the Molnars were in trouble and he'd been asked to keep them safe. Once they'd arrived, Jarrett had taken their phones so they couldn't contact anyone.

'The fucking bastard!' Matej was vibrating with anger. 'I can't believe he did that.'

Tomas inhaled a deep breath to control his rising anger. 'Well, he won't be doing it anymore.'

'Have you killed him, Dad?' asked Anya, her face so innocent and tone so sweet, it didn't seem possible for her to have asked the question.

'We won't have to worry about Jarrett — that's all you girls need to know,' he replied, turning back to the front of the car. 'Matej, we need to get home. Can you find us a way?'

Matej nodded. 'I'm on it.'

65

Saturday late morning
Geneva Road, Darlington

Byrd knew roughly where Reggie Cook lived based on working a missing person's case on the same road two years ago — a man called Karl Etton, an unfortunate name still featured on the list of missing people in their cold case investigations. He'd spoken to his wife at the time and gathered everything he could. Still, nothing had materialised and all the trails had gone cold.

He spotted the police car and ambulance just ahead on the left and pulled up behind the police car. He turned off the engine, took hold of the door release, and looked in his side mirror for oncoming vehicles before he opened it. Across the road, two women were standing at the edge of their small garden, interested in Reggie Cook's house and the police car and ambulance that were there. One of them, somewhere in her late fifties, was smoking a cigarette and watching Byrd.

Just as a car passed, he opened the door, and his phone rang. He pulled it out and answered it, edging the door closed so he could hear without the annoyance of the passing traffic.

'Ori.'

'Max, just a heads up so you're in the loop,' Tanzy said.

'What's happening?'

'PC Degnan and I have just left Selena's house on Collingsway. Are you still with Selena?'

'No, I'm at Reggie Cook's house on Geneva Road.'

'Is she still at West Manor?'

'She was when I left. Forensics will be there for a while yet. They'd only emptied three of the six bags, and I counted sixteen body parts so far.'

'God.' Tanzy let out a sigh. 'Whoever is with Selena needs to keep her there, mate. Her house is a mess.'

'What about her husband?'

'We found two men. One had his brains all over the kitchen table, and another one had had his throat slit. There's a very good chance her husband is one of them.'

'Fuck's sake.'

'We waited until some of the new PCs were there to watch the house. I've closed the door to preserve it the best I could and told the PCs to stay out front to make sure no one goes in until Forensics arrive. How long will they be at West Manor?'

'A while,' replied Byrd. 'Like I said, they have another three bags to get through, and when I was there, Tiffin and I saw something on the workbench and the vice. It's one big bloody mess this morning.'

'Has he been chopping up a body, trying to hide it in with the grass waste?'

'Seems that way.'

'Tell you what, Max, this isn't my idea of a Saturday morning with the family.'

'It'll be a Saturday afternoon *and* night, by the looks of things, Ori.'

'Guess I'll have some making up to do with Pip and the kids, then.'

Byrd sighed. 'We'll get through it,' he said softly.

'We always do.'

Byrd eyed the time on his watch. Almost 11 a.m.

'Is Reggie Cook at the house?' asked Tanzy.

'I haven't been in yet. There's an ambulance here and PC Grearer's car. I'm just about to go in. Where are Leonard and Weaver at?'

'Last known location chasing the blue Mondeo down Yarm Road. I'll ring them now to find out.'

'Okay. I'm heading inside the house. Speak soon.'

Byrd pushed the phone back into his jeans. He opened the car door and stepped out, feeling a drop in temperature. Dark clouds hung over Darlington like a blanket of gloom, giving Byrd not much hope his Saturday would get any better. He glanced at the two women over the road.

'What's going on over there?' one of them asked, sucking on her cigarette and blowing plumes of grey smoke above her head.

Byrd ignored her and walked around his car towards the house, squeezing between the van and the house to the open front door. 'Hello?'

'Through here.' The panicked voice came from inside, to the right.

Before he went in, Byrd put on some plastic overshoes and stepped over the lip of the door, angling right through a dining room. He found PC Andrews in the kitchen.

'Found anything?'

'The neighbours said there was a man in the garden. There's no one there now. He's gone.'

'He was shot?'

Andrews nodded. 'Yes. The neighbour said he was on the grass outside.' He pointed to the garden. 'There's no one there now, boss.'

'You checked the whole house?'

'Yeah. No sign at all. Grearer's done the same.'

'Anything else?'

'There are signs the girls were here. Small things. Hair bobbles. Reggie kept them up in the attic, by the looks of it.'

Byrd nodded, moving a few steps forward to see into the garden. PC Grearer was standing further down, looking around for the man who was recently there.

'Where's Reggie?' Byrd shouted.

Grearer turned with a shrug. There were sirens in the air, and it wasn't long until two paramedics turned up. Byrd answered the door to them, explaining that Reggie Cook had disappeared. It was a little embarrassing.

'So he's walking the streets?' asked one of the paramedics, frowning.

Byrd nodded. 'It won't be long until we find him.'

'How long?'

Byrd called Dispatch, relaying a message about the missing Reggie Cook, requesting additional support to search the area.

'*Assistance being sent to your location, Inspector,*' replied Dispatch, ending the call.

'We can't just wait here until he's found, Inspector. We have other scenes to attend to.'

Byrd understood their position and smiled lightly. 'He's been shot. He won't have got very far. We'll find him and call it in as soon as we do.'

Frowning, they returned to their ambulance and left, the siren suddenly erupting in the air and fading in the distance as it headed down Geneva Road.

Andrews was searching the kitchen cupboards when Byrd returned. Grearer was inspecting the rooms upstairs.

'He can't have gone far,' Byrd told Andrews. He went back out onto the decking and studied the garden, noting where the neighbour had last seen him. If Reggie had been shot in the leg, would he have been able to climb the fence? He'd known injured suspects to escape crime scenes before under the influence of sheer adrenaline.

He walked up the middle of the garden and peered over the back fence. Nothing but a swing set, a small slide and multiple colourful footballs. He did the same with the neighbouring gardens. No sign of the injured Reggie. On his way back to the house, he noticed a separate garage to the left. The two shabby wooden doors were closed. He pressed down the handle and pulled the door slowly towards him, the hinges moaning.

Inside it was dark, the only light coming from a dirty window. It smelled musty and damp, and was full of stuff: a lawnmower, boxes of all shapes and sizes, gardening and DIY tools, a bench piled high with more boxes. A shelf spanned both sides, roughly head height, containing bottles: white spirit, car cleaning products, battered paint tins. The back wall housed an old storage unit that looked decades old, filled with worthless clutter.

He found a light switch. The bulb hanging from the wooden beam shed a weak light that gave Byrd a little more idea of the items inside. Nothing looked out of the ordinary.

He backed out, closed the garage door, and headed for the house. On his way, Byrd studied the garden once more, including the seating area on the decking: a low-level three-seater sofa, an equally low single chair, and a wide wooden coffee table.

He frowned at the grass near the decking; it was different to the rest of the grass. Artificial grass. It didn't strike him as that type of a garden. And why have it just there? Too much shade, or something more sinister?

Byrd passed Andrews still in the kitchen and went upstairs, starting with the front bedroom. He checked everywhere: under the bed, in the wardrobe, the bedside unit, behind the radiator. He even moved items of furniture and looked behind them.

Happy he'd covered the front bedroom and Grearer was covering the bathroom, he went to the landing and peered up. The loft hatch was open, and the extendable stairs were pushed back up but visible. He leaned up, flicked the latch, and lowered them. In the attic, old pillows and quilts were spread around, signs the girls had been kept up there.

'What an animal,' Byrd whispered, shaking his head. With nothing more to see, he lowered himself to the landing and stepped into the rear bedroom. The upstairs was compact, only having two rooms. The rear bedroom was much bigger than the front, presumably due to the extension.

A king-size bed was up against the wall to the left, running from left to right across the room. Two identical wooden bedside units, with matching lamps, stood either side of the bed. Byrd had a feeling there may be a woman living here or had been recently. He knew himself that if he lived alone without Claire, he wouldn't go to the trouble of having two bedside units, let alone lamps to match.

With gloved hands, he checked the bedside unit closest to the door, pulling out the three drawers and thoroughly checking inside. The most unusual object he found was a ten-inch dildo.

'What the . . .' He shook his head and closed that particular drawer.

He rounded the bed and checked the other side. The top drawer had underwear in, the middle one catered for socks, and the bottom contained receipts for old purchases like household appliances and materials Cook had used for DIY, dating back several years. *Odd to keep those receipts*, thought Byrd.

Once he was done with the drawers, he turned to the double wardrobe that took up half the wall opposite the bed. He opened the left door, then the right, and studied all the hanging clothes, running his hand between them, but nothing looked or felt unusual. Closing the doors, he lowered to the carpet, feeling something click in his knee. Ignoring it, he pulled open the drawer and peered inside at the number of A4-sized folders.

'Hmmm.' He took out the first one, placed it on the floor and opened it up. Mortgage and utility bills, correspondence from the DVLA, and MOTs and service records seemed to make up most of it. He pushed the file to the side, picked up the next one, and placed it on the carpet.

The first page was a newspaper article, dating back nearly ten years. Byrd frowned, picked up the folder, and brought it closer to his face. The article covered the disappearance of Phillip Jones, born in Darlington and last seen in the centre of town. The man's name was familiar to Byrd: his own department had covered the case and found nothing. He opened the stiff ring binders and removed the single A4 pocket, which seemed too heavy for a single document. Then, he opened the top, pushing his hand inside to remove its contents.

He laid out everything inside the single wallet on the carpet: the *Northern Echo* newspaper article, a driver's licence, and three photographs of Phillip Jones taken from a distance without him knowing.

The last photo made Byrd freeze and raise a hand to his mouth. 'What the fuck?'

The photo was taken somewhere familiar, and it took Byrd a few seconds to realise it was the garage back at West Manor. On the workbench he and DC Tiffin had been looking at less than an hour ago, dozens of body parts were all laid out, captured in that one single shot.

He returned to the file and slowly turned the other A4 pockets, counting dozens of them.

He left everything where it was, descended the stairs, and walked out the back onto the decking. PC Andrews was standing at the front of the garage to the right, peering in. 'I haven't checked in here yet.' He turned to Byrd. 'You okay? You look pale.'

'I need some air,' explained Byrd.

'Found anything?'

Byrd smiled, looking away from him to the garden. 'You could say that.'

'What is it?' He frowned.

Scowling, Byrd moved slowly across the decking, then down onto the first patio stone of the path.

'What you doing, boss?'

Byrd examined the artificial grass to the left and then stepped onto it. It felt harder than it should have — there should be a layer of sand and dolomite underneath artificial grass. He lifted a foot and stomped, hearing a hollow thud. It definitely wasn't dolomite and sand.

'What's that?' asked Andrews, also hearing the unusual sound.

Byrd moved in a slow arch, occasionally tapping the grass with his foot, the hollow sound following him wherever he seemed to go. He returned to the patio stones and bent over, nipping the edge of the fake grass between a thumb and finger, then lifted it, but it was secured down.

'Josh, step on that grass.' Byrd pointed to it. 'Tell me if that feels right.'

Andrews did as he was asked, stamping in different places, before he shook his head. 'Something's not right here, boss.'

'Are there any tools in there?'

Andrews bowed his head, seemingly on the same wavelength. 'Something to grip with?'

'Yeah.'

The PC disappeared into the garage for thirty seconds and returned with some water pump pliers, a plumbing tool generally used to tighten fittings.

'Try these.'

'Thanks.'

Byrd pinched a small area and pulled upwards, ripping the edge of the grass up over the screws that pinned it down. He took hold with two hands and stood, pulling more of the edge up until the grass was free along one side.

'Josh, go to that side and pull it up.' Byrd went to the decking end and gripped the outside part, then yanked it with some strength. Andrews did the same on the other side, and they both moved backward, lifting away the grass in one piece.

Once the grass had been fully removed, they carried it further down the garden so it was out of the way and dropped it.

'Well, that's interesting,' said Andrews, looking at the large sheet of wood with four small hatched doors built into it.

Byrd stepped back onto the wooden floor and lifted the closest hatch.

The smell that hit his nose knocked him sick.

66

Susan Brown pottered around the house most of the morning after Steve Mitchell had left, thinking about him as she tidied. She felt so sorry for him, losing a wife and struggling to cope with his missing daughter. Who could blame him? It was awful.

With her husband out with his friend playing golf, she decided to start painting the decking. He'd said he would do it today, but it was obvious his priorities were very much on a golf green somewhere. She shook her head as she carried the tin of decking paint to the back door.

The morning was bright, the sky peppered with white and grey clouds, the rising sun shining its light on the first day of the weekend. She looked forward to summertime, sitting out here, lying flat on her recliner, soaking up the rays, a reminder of the holiday home they used to have in Greece all those years ago. They'd talked about going back, but Susan didn't fancy it. She wanted to experience other parts of the world. Life was too short to not enjoy life and make the most of it.

She rearranged a few items on the decking so they were down on the grass out of the way to give her more space. Starting at the end where the dividing fence was seemed a logical choice, so she could go from left to right and move back towards the door. That way, she'd avoid stepping on anything wet.

Removing the lid from the paint tin and grabbing a brush, she placed the rubber kneeling pad down on the decking, readying herself to make a start. But, before she did, she wanted some music on, so she went inside to grab her iPad that she'd been charging since Steve Mitchell had left. As she unlocked it, she noticed the folder with the CCTV clips was still there. She frowned, wondering whether to quickly scan through the footage after Ella Mitchell had disappeared up until now or whether to close the app and play some eighties classics and crack on with the job. If most of the painting was done by the time her husband got back, he'd not only be impressed, but she'd have one over on him because it was him that was meant to be doing it today.

She decided to check the footage quickly. Even if she scanned through the videos at a 5x speed, it would still show anyone who it had picked up.

She reached Friday evening, when she saw the next-door neighbour's French doors open, and a girl ran out onto their decking, closely followed by her neighbour, Emma, who dashed out, grabbing her and pulling her back inside quickly.

'That's weird.'

She turned back and watched it again, confused as to why Emma had not wanted her niece in the garden last night.

'What's going on here?' she whispered, watching the clip for the third time.

The small girl was wearing a dark grey T-shirt, leggings, and pink trainers, and looked scared as she ran out, even more so when Emma raced out and grabbed her.

'The poor thing.'

She hadn't known that Emma had a niece; she hadn't seen her before. Why she was there, she didn't know, but the clip had disturbed her.

Her eyes widened. 'Hold on a minute . . .'

She closed yesterday's file, searched through the folder, and found another one from Tuesday night. She watched it over five times, scowling at the footage and making sure she was right.

'I don't believe this . . . This can't be right.'

67

Saturday late morning
Geneva Road, Darlington

Leonard was approaching the roundabout at over 100 miles per hour, the spinning tyres causing a drone on the damp road below. Weaver was stone stiff in the passenger seat, grabbing the side of the door and the edge of her seat so tight her knuckles were white. She glanced left momentarily, the blur of green and brown whizzing by her window, before focusing back on the road ahead. With the clouds darkening, the persistent rain became heavier. Leonard had increased the wipers' speed and could feel the effects of the rain when he cornered, the tyres losing traction. The Mondeo had taken a left turn at the upcoming roundabout moments ago.

'We're gonna lose them,' said Weaver, frowning but not wanting Leonard to drive any quicker. How they hadn't crashed since leaving Reggie Cook's house was a stroke of better luck than winning the bloody national lottery.

'Just leave that to me,' replied Leonard evenly. He adjusted his aching grip on the wheel, then dipped the clutch, dropping the Insignia from fifth gear into third as he made the sharp turn, the car sliding uncontrollably.

Weaver tensed up and closed her eyes, expecting them to slide right into the road sign, but somehow, Leonard saved it.

'Jesus, James!'

'Told you I'm good.'

She shook her head and saw the Mondeo up ahead. 'There it is.'

'I see it.'

The Mondeo had gained distance now, roughly eighty metres up the road. In the time it took Leonard to climb through the gears and reach any sort of speed, the Mondeo had increased the gap.

Leonard pushed his foot down and turned the wipers up a notch. They flicked back and forth across the screen, dismissing the rain effectively, but it made driving trickier. The road veered towards the right up ahead, and the Mondeo nipped out of sight.

Leonard sighed, not liking the idea of being unable to see it.

'Do we need air support?' asked Weaver.

'Good shout. Call it in, please.'

Weaver used the radio and asked Dispatch to request NPAS.

'*Air support will be with you within a few minutes, Constable Weaver,*' the operator said. '*They'll be contactable through channel twelve.*'

'Thank you.'

'A few minutes? They must be on standby,' said Leonard. 'Normally based at Newcastle.'

Weaver lowered the radio as they veered around the bend at eighty miles per hour, Leonard keeping the car away from the grass verge and in one piece.

He frowned. 'Doesn't make sense.'

'What's up?' she asked, looking his way.

'Where've they gone? They weren't going that quick.'

Weaver thought about it and agreed. 'I think you're right. Is there a turn earlier than the roundabout?'

'Where the hell is Armed Response at?' Leonard slapped his wheel in frustration.

Weaver lifted the radio to her mouth. 'Dispatch, can we have an update on the ETA of Armed Response?'

'*With you in five minutes. Confirm your location, please.*'

'Travelling down Mill Lane towards the A66. We think the suspects have taken a turn somewhere. Hold tight. I'll update soon. Over.' She lowered the radio to her lap and leaned forward, trying to find her bearings. If she remembered rightly, there was a right turn fifty metres before the mini roundabout. 'Slow it down, Jim, slow it down.'

'What?' Leonard lifted his foot off the pedal, the roaring engine becoming quieter. 'Where do you—'

'Take a right here. Here!'

Leonard slammed his foot on the brakes and barely managed to turn into a minor road at just over thirty miles per hour, the car sliding and clipping the kerb as he did so, sending Leonard and Weaver to the left in a sudden jerk, but he kept the car on the road.

'That's the fucking alloys gone, then!'

Weaver winced and said nothing.

'Where'd they go?'

Weaver saw a large farm up ahead on the right. 'Turn in here. Go right.'

Leonard did as she suggested, turning into the farm and stopping in an open concrete area. 'Now what?'

'There!' Weaver pointed at the side of the building, catching a glimpse at the rear quarter of the dark blue Mondeo before it went out of sight. 'Behind there.'

***

Tanzy took the left onto Mill Lane and powered through the gears until he reached ninety miles per hour.

'*Dispatch, this is Weaver. Come in,*' they heard Weaver say through channel two.

'*Go ahead, Weaver.*'

'We've turned into a farm just off Mill Lane. The Mondeo has gone behind the big farm building. I don't think there's a way out. How far away is Armed Response?' Weaver asked.

'ETA three minutes.'

'Okay, we'll sit tight.'

'Air support is three minutes out,' confirmed the operator.

Tanzy frowned. 'Message Weaver and ask where this turn-in is, please, Louise.'

Degnan lifted the radio and pressed the button. 'PC Weaver, this is Degnan. Where's the farm?'

There was a short crackle.

'Louise, take a right fifty or so metres before the roundabout, then follow the road a little bit, and you'll see it on your right.'

'Okay. We'll be there in a minute,' Degnan replied.

Tanzy spotted the roundabout up ahead but couldn't see any turn. His eyes dropped to the dash. He was still going too fast, so he lifted his foot and dabbed the brake, expecting it any second.

'Here it is, coming up now,' she said, seeing it better from the passenger seat.

Tanzy slowed the Golf as he cornered the winding road, then straightened out. 'There's the farm.' He took the right, saw Leonard's Insignia parked in the middle of the open area, and pulled up beside him, lowering Degnan's window.

Leonard lowered his. 'Boss.'

'Where've they gone, Jim?'

'Behind there. This is the only way in and out by the looks of it.'

Tanzy looked through his windscreen, studying the size of the building. Its double door was locked with a padlock the size of a shoebox. Down the side to the left was another single door and a window. 'This place looks deserted.'

'It does, doesn't it?' Leonard studied it and opened the door. 'Backup are coming now.'

'Where you going?' asked Degnan.

Tanzy moved to the front of the Golf and observed the barn, assuming the same as Leonard that the turn-in they'd just used was the only access point. To the right, there was a low, rumbling drone. Tanzy peered up to the sky and watched the incoming helicopter. He ran and opened his door. 'Give me the radio.'

Degnan did.

Tanzy tuned the radio to channel twelve. 'NPAS, come in.'

'*Go ahead,*' replied the distorted voice.

'This is Detective Inspector Orion Tanzy. Can you see me waving?' Tanzy waved theatrically towards them as they approached, the sound of the chopper blades growing louder.

'*Yes, Inspector. We can see you.*'

Tanzy took a few paces forward. 'Can you see a blue Mondeo round the back of the farm?'

There was no reply, only the sounds of the rotating blades whirring above him.

'NPAS, come in?'

No reply.

'Fuck's sake!' Tanzy hit the side of the radio with his other palm, frustrated with the poor signal. 'What's the fucking point in radios if we can't use them . . .'

Leonard opened his door and climbed out, joining Tanzy. 'What's happening, boss?'

'This stupid radio.'

'You on channel twelve?' asked Leonard.

Tanzy made a what-do-you-think face and pressed the radio button again. 'NPAS, call back.'

'*We read you, Inspector,*' replied the voice, although still crackly.

'I don't think the signal is great.' Tanzy peered up, seeing the chopper hovering above them. 'Can you see the Mondeo?'

'*We see the Mondeo . . . tive. Other . . . of . . . you are.*'

'Goddamn thing!' Tanzy shouted. He turned to Leonard. 'Come on.' He walked towards the corner of the farm with the radio in his hand.

'Shouldn't we wait for Armed Response?' Leonard shouted.

Tanzy couldn't hear him because of the spinning chopper blades in the sky.

Leonard followed Tanzy to the corner while Weaver and Degnan remained in the cars, watching them where they felt safe. Just before Tanzy reached it, he peered up at the chopper, seeing the two pilots looking down on them.

He tried again with the radio. 'Can you see the Mondeo?'

The pilot was talking, but nothing but static was coming through on the radio. He turned to Leonard and shrugged. 'We can't stay here all day, Jim.'

Leonard frowned, the whirring machine above them drowning everything out. 'What, sir?'

Tanzy stood an inch from the corner, put his back against it, and removed his phone. He found his camera app and turned, lowering to his knees. He placed the phone against the side of the breeze blocks and slowly moved it so the camera could see what was happening around the corner of the building.

Before the camera had a chance to focus, they heard a gunshot and a bullet whizzed by Tanzy's phone, hitting the concrete a few metres behind them, lumps of it breaking from the ground. He pulled back and shouted, checking to see if he'd been hit.

'Jesus!' gasped Leonard, jumping against the breeze blocks for cover.

Tanzy put the radio to his mouth. 'Can you hear me?'

Nothing.

Tanzy couldn't risk peeping around the corner again — they were obviously waiting with their guns. He glanced back at the entrance to the grounds and saw a police van arrive, pulling in next to his Golf. Three armed officers jumped out and soldiered towards them.

'About time too.'

The first armed officer, with the badge number PK665 pinned to his shoulder, all suited and booted with a stab vest

and a helmet, carried what looked like a standard Heckler &
Koch 416 assault rifle. These guys meant business.

'How many?' he asked Tanzy.

Tanzy raised his hand and opened it, indicating five
people. He thought about only putting two fingers up, but
there was a chance the girls had been given a gun too and he
couldn't take the risk of playing the situation down.

The armed responder indicated to the other two there
were five people. They nodded and tucked in behind them.

'Go back to the cars!' he shouted to Tanzy.

Tanzy and Leonard nodded and ran back to the cars, got
in, and closed their doors.

'What's going on?' Degnan asked.

'The big boys are taking over.' He lifted the radio to his
mouth. 'NPAS, do you copy?'

'*Go ahead,*' crackled the voice.

'What's happening?'

The armed officers sneaked around the corner. Two gun-
shots were fired, followed by another three in quick succession.

'*Officer down,*' said the pilot from the helicopter.

'Shit,' said Tanzy, desperate to help but knowing he
couldn't do a thing.

Another gunshot was fired, immediately followed by a
smash of glass, then a high-pitched scream.

'The fuck's happening round there?' Tanzy asked no one
in particular. He spoke into the radio: 'NPAS, what's going
on?'

'*Officer down. Another one has been shot.*'

Tanzy banged his palm on his steering wheel. 'We need
to do something,' he said to Degnan.

'*Suspects are back in the Mondeo. They've driven through the fence
into the fields,*' the pilot informed them.

Tanzy turned on the engine, put the gear in first, and
raced around the side, seeing the gap they'd made. They passed
two injured officers down on the ground, the other officer
aiding them. Tanzy grabbed the radio, changing the channel

to number two. 'Dispatch, requesting medical assistance to the farm on Mill Lane. Two officers are down. One looks critical.' He passed the radio to Degnan, pulled the steering to the right, and guided the car through the gap. Through his rear-view, Leonard was following him in the Insignia.

Up ahead, they could see the back of the Mondeo.

'Let's get these bastards!'

68

Saturday late morning
Mill Lane, outskirts of Darlington

Tanzy followed the track the Mondeo had made, his hands tight on the steering wheel, keeping the Golf steady across the uneven terrain as the car bounced and juddered. The sounds of the helicopter blades above followed them as they raced across the farmer's field, reaching almost forty-five miles per hour on the muddy terrain.

'Be doing the suspension no good at all, this, Louise,' muttered Tanzy, checking in the rear-view, seeing Leonard still on his trail.

'Where are they going?' asked Degnan.

'Put the radio channel on twelve and pass it to me.'

'Here you go.'

He took the handset and pushed the button. 'Where is the Mondeo heading?'

'*There's a road running down the side of the field you're on. The car is angling across to an opening to join the road.*'

Tanzy passed the radio back to Degnan and pushed his foot down. Once the Mondeo turned a little, he could see the opening in the hedge diagonally across the field. He dropped it a gear and planted his foot, causing the Golf's wheels to spin until they gained traction on the damp soil.

'Remind me never to do this again, Louise.'

Degnan winced, gripping her seat to stop herself from bouncing out of it.

The Mondeo nipped through the gap in the hedge and joined the road. Tanzy went through seconds after and, for a moment, thought he'd lost control as he attempted to straighten because of the wet, dirty wheels on the drenched road surface.

'Shit,' he said, keeping the car under control. 'Ask the chopper what's up ahead.'

Degnan spoke into her radio and listened to the response.

'There's a sharp left turn coming up in forty metres or so. It's tight, so don't go too quick.'

Tanzy nodded — mainly for his own benefit — dipped the clutch, pushing the gear into third, and accelerated forward.

'Sir, there's a turn coming up,' Degnan reminded him.

With focused, narrowed eyes, Tanzy watched the back of the Mondeo and noticed the brake lights flash a few times, the driver obviously weighing up the corner that the helicopter pilot had mentioned.

'Sir?' said Degnan, worry creeping into her voice as they approached the car in front too quickly.

'Hold on,' advised Tanzy.

As the Mondeo slowed and shifted to the right to take the left turn, Tanzy maintained his speed and moved to the left. The Mondeo slowed right down and veered to the left sharply to take the turn.

'Tanzy, what are you—'

At the last second, Tanzy shifted the car to the right and hit the rear quarter of the Mondeo, spinning the car around to face the direction they'd just come from. Tanzy slammed his foot on the brake, but the Golf continued through a wooden fence, pieces of wood flying all over, until he skidded sideways to a halt into another field.

'You okay, Louise?'

'Feel like I have bloody whiplash.'

Peering around the front of the shaken Degnan, Tanzy spotted the driver's door open, and one of the men got out of the Mondeo. He tilted his neck as if relieving pain from the collision, then turned to Tanzy's Golf with a raised gun.

'Shit — get down!' screamed Tanzy, leaning over and pulling Degnan down into him to protect her. The passenger window shattered, a sea of glass exploding over their heads.

Holding her tightly, Tanzy opened his eyes, thankfully feeling no pain. The bullet had missed him.

'Are you okay?'

Silence.

'Louise?'

Beyond her, the big man stood on the road, holding a gun. Tanzy frowned, watching Leonard speed towards him in the Insignia. He winced as the Insignia catapulted the man up over the car so his body flipped and landed with a dull thud. Leonard continued, struggling to stop his car as it powered into the field through the broken fence and moaned to a halt near Tanzy.

'Fucking hell,' Tanzy gasped, edging back, then focused on Degnan once again. 'Louise, are you okay?'

She moved slightly and groaned. 'It hurts,' she whispered.

Tanzy leaned over. There was blood on her back. She'd been shot.

He searched for the radio. It was in the passenger footwell, and he awkwardly bent down, careful not to move Degnan too much. He changed the channel to number two.

'Dispatch, I need emergency medical assistance. Officer down. A bullet wound to her back. She's in a bad way.'

He watched the other man get out of the car with a gun in his hand and fury all over his face. Tanzy left Degnan for a moment and opened his door, climbed out, then leaned inside, gripping the top of Degnan's stab vest before he dragged her across the centre of the car away from danger. She wailed in pain.

'I know, I'm sorry,' he said softly. 'I need to get you on this side of the car away from him.'

Once clear, he laid her down gently on the mud beside the car.

'Help is coming, Louise. Sit tight.'

He peered through the driver's door. The man with the gun was charging over.

* * *

'Dad!' screamed Anya from the rear of the car. 'They ran over Dad!'

Luna screamed in rage, and Nina remained silent, not believing what had happened.

Matej Molnar kicked open the passenger door and jumped out. 'You fucking bastard!' he screamed towards the Insignia, and dashed over to his injured brother.

'Tomas?'

Tomas Molnar was still on his back. His left arm was crooked, clearly broken, and had come away from his shoulder joint. His knees were painfully bent, and one of his ankles faced the wrong way. His eyes were open but were still, staring into the dark grey sky. Raindrops fell on his lifeless face.

'Tomas?' said Matej, lightly slapping his brother's cheek. 'FUCK!' he screamed, his anger ripping through the air. He stood straight, scowled at the Insignia, and set out for revenge.

* * *

Tanzy rose from his crouched position and saw Leonard in the Insignia driver's seat. The airbag had gone off. Leonard was slumped forward, not moving.

'Jim, fucking move it,' Tanzy whispered.

He saw the man to the left stomping towards Leonard with his gun raised.

'Fuck, fuck.'

Tanzy's heart was pounding in his chest, and he heard the ringing in his ears over the sound of the chopper blades in the sky. He had to make a decision, and quickly. The baton was in the passenger footwell. He leaned in, grabbed it, and backed out.

'Stay here,' he said to Degnan, but knew she wasn't going anywhere soon.

He kept low and moved to the corner of the Golf, catching a glimpse of the man with the gun heading for the Insignia. He was a few metres from him. With the man almost to Leonard's car, Tanzy jumped to his feet and sprinted with the extended baton above his head, using the sounds of the chopper blades as cover.

The man was level with Leonard's window and raised the gun. Weaver screamed from the passenger seat. As Tanzy grew close, the man cocked his head towards him and raised the gun.

Tanzy swung hard, smashing the baton across the man's wrist. The gun bounced away, nestling into the soil with a thump.

The man gritted his teeth and lunged at Tanzy, catching him off guard before he could raise the weapon to strike again, and speared him into the side of the Golf with a metallic thud. An excruciating pain shot up Tanzy's back as he crashed to the ground. The man had the advantage now, climbing on top of Tanzy and punching his face repeatedly with his meaty fists. Tanzy's head jolted with each impact, stars swirling in his blurred vision. The punches were hard, but Tanzy shielded his face the best he could with his arms, hoping the psychopath would tire.

After the tenth punch, he could feel the blows becoming less effective. He managed to throw a quick jab to the man's nose, which disorientated him long enough for Tanzy to grab the back of his hand and pull him close. Tanzy expertly placed his left forearm under the man's chin, pressing hard against his throat, and with his right hand behind the man's head, pulled him close into him, compressing his throat and cutting off his air supply.

The man threw countless punches to Tanzy's ribs and hips. Each blow rattled Tanzy and hurt like hell, but he held on, riding out the blows, feeling each attempt getting weaker until the man's body eventually became limp and he lost consciousness. With everything he had left, Tanzy shoved the dead weight of the unconscious man off him and gasped in desperation for some air.

'Never a dull day in this fucking town,' he panted, staring up at the helicopter hovering in the dark, grey clouds above him. Somewhere in the distance, sirens filled the air. Help was on its way.

69

Saturday late morning
Geneva Road, Darlington

Byrd made two phone calls before further backup arrived. The first call was to DCI Corbridge, giving his boss an update on an eventful day so far, particularly the discovery of what they'd found in the garden at Geneva Road, along with the documents, photos, and articles in the wardrobe in Reggie Cook's bedroom.

'Has there been any sign of Reggie Cook?' the DCI asked.

'Nothing yet. We have teams searching the area.'

'How long's he been missing?'

'Long enough to get far away from here,' replied Byrd.

'I'll see you soon.'

The second call was to the lead coroner, Peter Gibbs. Byrd felt Peter would want to see what they'd found before anyone interfered with it.

It had started raining, so Byrd and Andrews decided to put artificial grass back over the wooden structure to preserve it as best they could until it stopped. Ideally, they'd need to set up a tent for Forensics to examine this one thoroughly. This was a significant find.

Watching the garden from the open French doors, the rain seemed to ease and finally stop. The dark grey clouds had passed, and the sun came out, shining a light on the garden that made the grass glisten. A faint rainbow appeared in the distance, making Byrd think of home. He pulled out his phone and sent Claire a text message.

I love you x

He pressed send, put his phone away, then turned to Andrews, who'd just walked back into the kitchen.

'Everything okay?' he asked him.

Andrews nodded. 'Tanzy and Leonard got them, boss. One of the men is dead, and the other has been arrested.'

'The girls?'

'Medics are checking them over but it sounds like they're uninjured.' Andrews went on. 'Three Armed Response members were there. Two of them were shot.'

'They okay?'

'One of them has been taken to hospital. The other was patched up on the scene. Nothing too serious.'

'Everyone else all right?'

'Yeah, although James has a minor concussion from a crash. The airbag came out but was ineffective, so he cracked a tooth on the steering wheel. Medic reckons he'll be fine with rest. Tanzy said he's heading back here. He wants to see the scene. He said he won't be long.'

Byrd nodded. 'Never a dull . . .'

'What?'

'Never mind.' He took his phone back out and called the senior forensic tech, Jacob Tallow.

'Hey, Max.'

'What's happening on your end?'

Tallow explained they'd emptied all six binbags at Reggie Cook's garage at West Manor and laid everything out neatly on plastic sheeting. He said he and Emily Hope had counted over thirty-seven body parts.

'They all from one victim?'

'Looks that way.'

'Great work.'

'We've had a look at the workbench and vice too. There are traces of all sorts on there, Max. Blood. Body fluids. Hairs. Fibres. Some of the marks are old, indicating the bench has been used for various activities for some time.'

Byrd thought about what they'd discovered under the artificial grass and didn't doubt that.

'How long will you guys be at West Manor?'

'Few more hours yet, I think.'

The Forensics team was aware of the double murder at Selena's house and knew they'd need to attend that scene too.

'Okay.'

'You have more work for us, don't you?'

'Let's just say it will be a long night for us all.'

70

Saturday morning
Haughton Road, Darlington

Susan Brown sat on the sofa in the living room, rocking back and forth, peering down at the iPad in her hand. She wasn't one hundred per cent sure, but she had a terrible feeling about something that she couldn't shake from her mind.

She watched the footage again. This time, she was sure. She had to do something about it.

She placed the device down and slowly stood, unsure whether to ring Jeff about it or not. No doubt he'd only tell her to relax and stop overthinking — she was terrible for that.

'No,' she told herself, 'I need to do this.' Confident, she left the living room and walked out of the front door. The day had perked up a little, warmer than before, a glimmer of the summer to come.

She knocked on Emma's door twice before she took a step back. The car was on the drive, so there was a good chance her neighbour would be in. It wasn't long before the door opened, revealing a nervous-looking Emma wearing a black top, blue jeans, and nothing on her feet apart from socks.

'Susan,' Emma said. 'Are you all right?'

Susan smiled thinly. 'I am. Are you?'

Emma nodded. 'Yeah, thanks.' A moment of silence passed, and Emma frowned. 'Is everything okay?'

Susan scowled. 'Can I come in? I need a word about something.'

The neighbour's frown deepened. 'I — I was just in the middle of something. What's this about?'

'I think you know.'

Emma's eyes narrowed. 'I . . . know what?'

'Let me in, Emma.'

Susan was ready when Emma attempted to slam the door closed, and barged forward with her shoulder, stopping it from fully closing. She then pushed the door hard, allowing enough space for her to enter the hallway. Emma was behind the door, eyes wide, and charged for Susan with her arms out. Susan felt the woman's nails clutch at her face and the sharp scratch was hellishly painful, but Susan, being slightly plumper than Emma, grabbed her neighbour's arms and turned, dragging her hard into the wall with so much force that she screeched in agony.

'Where is she?' Susan demanded.

'Just leave!' Emma screamed, falling to one knee. The sudden blow to her shoulder prevented her from getting up.

The cry from upstairs made Susan look up. In that split second, Emma climbed to her feet and punched Susan in the gut, knocking the wind out of her. Susan staggered back, colliding with the closed front door with a thud.

'You're not going up there,' Emma told her. 'You're not taking her! She's mine!'

Susan breathed heavily, trying to ease the pain in her side. She nodded slowly, her eyes focused and determined. 'I have to. I have to see.'

'Just leave us alone, Susan. It's got nothing to do with you. Leave!'

Shaking her head, Susan charged at Emma and flung her thick arms around the woman's waist, using her weight to shove her onto the stairs. Emma's back bounced off them, each stair edge digging into her back. She yelped like a cornered animal. With the outside of a clenched hand, Susan pounded down on her neighbour's face several times until her fingers felt numb, using her weight to her advantage.

Emma's head flopped to the side, and her body went limp.

Susan caught her breath. It had been her first fight in decades, the last being a dispute at a christening that the family would rather forget. She stepped back and watched Emma slip into a hazy, semi-conscious state, taking deep breaths.

A patter of feet sounded above her head.

Wasting no time, she dashed up the stairs as quickly as her size would allow, turned right at the top, and headed for the closed bedroom door at the front of the house, which was secured with three tower bolts.

'What on earth . . .' she whispered as she approached it.

Unlocking the bolts, she grabbed the handle and opened the door. The smell of faeces and urine hit her immediately, and she covered her mouth and nose. In the corner of the small room, cowering under the windowsill, was Ella Mitchell, her face half hidden between her knees.

'Ella!' Susan raced over, lowered to her knees, and wrapped her arms around the girl. 'You're safe now, Ella.'

71

Saturday afternoon
Haughton Road, Darlington

Stepping out of his car into the gentle breeze, Byrd walked to Susan Brown's open front door and knocked. 'Anyone here?'

'In the living room, sir,' replied the familiar voice of PC Timms. 'The door on the right, boss.'

Byrd turned right into the living room and smiled at the gangly PC Timms, sitting on the arm of the nearest sofa as if minding the doorway. Byrd moved further into the room and saw Emma Slater on the sofa to the right, her hands together in cuffs, tears streaming down her face. Beside her was PC Tramer, one of the new recruits Byrd had had the pleasure of meeting a few weeks back. He was young, clean-shaven, and doing well since he'd joined, showing initiative that hadn't gone unnoticed by his superiors. His hair was short, and Byrd saw something in the young recruit that reminded him of his younger self, but couldn't pinpoint exactly what. Perhaps the northern twang to his accent, with him coming originally from Durham.

'DI Byrd,' the PC said, nodding courteously.

'Where's Ella?' asked Byrd.

Timms pointed behind him, indicating the kitchen diner. 'Through there. Susan's with her.'

Byrd entered and took a seat on the other sofa. He could see from Emma Slater's body language that she was deeply ashamed of her actions. 'Mrs Slater, can you please explain why you've been keeping Ella Mitchell locked up in your house?'

'I didn't mean to,' she started, almost in a whisper, her eyes fixed on the carpet. 'It just happened. Me and my husband. W-We had five miscarriages in six years. We wanted kids so much, you know.' She finally looked up and met his gaze. 'If you've never lost a baby like that, you can't know what it does to you.'

Byrd nodded gently, listening closely. He could see the pain she was feeling as she spoke about it, but he was way off feeling sorry for her.

'The doctors didn't know why, said it was just one of those things.' Emma wiped away her tears with her sleeve.

'What happened with Ella?' he asked.

'Late Tuesday afternoon, I walked out of the house and saw Ella run out of hers. She was upset and shouting, saying a man was trying to get her. Another girl was with her but ran off in a different direction. I asked if it was her dad but she said it wasn't. I immediately ran back into my house with her and locked the door. She told me what had happened to her mum and that her dad was working away.'

Byrd nodded. It made sense so far.

'What happened next?'

'I was about to call the police, but I needed to make sure she was okay. She was shaken up, as you could imagine.'

Byrd waited.

'I took her upstairs to hide, in case the man came looking for her.'

'And did he?'

She shrugged. 'I didn't go outside to check. I kept the door locked.'

Byrd frowned. 'So you kept her here?'

'With my husband dying last year, I figured this was my only chance.'

'Only chance for what?'

'To be a parent,' she explained like it was obvious. 'I'd never get the chance again.'

'That's no excuse for what you did, Mrs Slater.'

The room went silent for a moment.

'So, what did you tell Ella?' Byrd went on. 'Surely she knew something was going on.'

'I told her that I'd spoken with the police and that they'd said she could stay with me until her dad got back. So she spent her time downstairs with me, watching telly. I'd make her food and comfort her because of what had happened with her mum. But then she changed, demanding to see her dad. I told her he was still away. She wanted to talk to him on the phone, but I couldn't let that happen. It wasn't long before she said she wanted to go. So I told her to stay the night and she could go the next day. When she slept, I put locks on the bedroom door and never let her out again until Susan found her.'

Byrd was struggling to digest this, knowing he'd spoken with her the following morning and she'd lied to him. Come to think of it, the figure he'd seen in the window must have been Ella.

'Mrs Slater, you've done something truly awful here. I hope you know that.'

She curled her bottom lip, as if the realisation of her hideous actions weighed heavily on her.

Byrd shook his head. 'Thank God for Susan.' He turned to Timms. 'Take her down to the station.'

Susan Brown was sitting at the table next to Ella Mitchell with her arm around her, watching something on an iPad. Looked like a cartoon of some kind, but it wasn't familiar to Byrd. No doubt when his son Alan got older, he'd know all about what was going on with TV programmes.

'Hi, there,' Byrd said softly, stopping near them. 'Ella, I'm Detective Inspector Max Byrd. I'm so very glad to see you.'

Ella craned her neck towards him. Byrd could see happiness and sadness in her eyes, somewhere between exhaustion and relief.

'Where's my dad?'

'He's on his way.' He pulled out the chair beside Susan. Steve Mitchell had been spending all his waking hours walking the streets and parks of Darlington searching for his child, and now he would be rushing home to be with her. He was a good father, thought Byrd, and his heart broke for the family again.

Susan smiled at him. 'Nice to see you again, Inspector.'

'Thank you so much for finding Ella.'

Susan placed a gentle hand on the girl's head. 'It's okay. I'm just glad to have been able to help.'

'Ella, is it okay if I speak with Susan for a bit?'

Ella nervously looked at Susan, who beamed at her, an indication that she was safe. Ella slipped off the chair, shuffled across to the corner with the iPad in her hand, and plonked herself on the single-seater near the French doors. Byrd played back in his mind Wednesday morning, when he and Tanzy had spoken with Emma about what had happened to Mia Mitchell, and he had seen the indistinct form of the girl up in the front bedroom window. If only he'd questioned it then. Ella had been hidden in plain sight, and no one had had a clue about it.

'Let me see if I understand this,' he said to Susan. 'You thought you recognised Ella on your CCTV and you didn't call the police?'

'I wasn't totally sure,' Susan explained, looking sheepish. 'You've seen the quality of the footage before — the clothes and build looked the same. And then Emma reacted oddly when this "niece" was outside — as if she wasn't supposed to be. Let's just say it got me thinking about things. In the time I've known her, I never knew she had a niece. So I thought I'd just go over, meet the niece, set my mind at rest. But Emma was guilty to the high heavens when I knocked on the door and set on me as soon as I came in.'

'But you won the altercation.' Byrd grinned.

'Seen my fair share of scraps over the years,' she explained. 'Then I found Ella upstairs, locked in the front bedroom.'

Byrd absorbed the story and stood. 'I'm just going to take a look.'

She nodded. 'It isn't pleasant, Inspector. She must have been kept in there the whole time, if you know what I mean.'

72

Saturday afternoon
Darlington police station

Byrd was tired and hungry. It had been the most stressful day of his career so far. Tanzy had already written up his reports and left, telling Byrd he'd promised Pip and the kids they were going for ice cream at the beach. Byrd had told him to enjoy his day with his family and that he would stay on and get things wrapped up.

Before he commenced any interviews, he decided to feed his stomach, and grabbed a twelve-inch hot shot pizza on his way to the hospital, which he scoffed as he drove. It was the nicest pizza he'd ever had.

It turned out the sisters he'd been looking for were called Molnar, not Deacon. *That* name had set the Warrington police alight. He suddenly had stacks of files about the Molnar family on his desk — drug dealers with a bit of gunrunning on the side, mostly. It was clear now why these missing children had not been reported to the police — it had all been part of some turf war, one that had gone wrong. Poor kids, to have got caught up in that. The mother seemed a nice woman, despite her gangland husband. She had readily agreed when Byrd had asked if he might interview her children. Even so, he knew he was interrupting a family reunion, and a grieving family at that.

He found the four of them in a private room in the children's ward of the hospital. The kids looked tearful and undernourished. The youngest one had a tight hold of her mother's hand.

'Hello, Anya,' he said. 'I'm not sure if you remember me? My name is Detective Inspector Max Byrd. We met a few days ago when you were last in hospital. I'm very sorry for your loss.'

'I remember you,' she said. 'My memory's all right again now.'

'I'm glad to hear it. We've been very worried about you.'

He leaned over, pressed the button on the recording device, then said his name, the time and date, the names of the children he was interviewing, and on what grounds he was interviewing them.

'So, can you explain why you're in Darlington?'

Byrd was surprised at how honest the children were during the interview: they told him about Jarrett collecting them from school, telling them that their family in Warrington was in danger and that he was getting them to safety.

'How did you come to leave West Manor?'

She told him about Reggie helping them, telling them to hide in his van, and getting out that way.

'And how did you come to know Reggie? You weren't there very long.'

'Reggie told us he'd help us escape, set us free. He told us we could go home to our parents if we went with him.'

'But that wasn't the arrangement, was it?'

Anya shook her small head, her dark hair shifting side to side. 'He told us he wanted to show us things similar to those he was shown growing up. But then things got weird.'

'How?'

'He said he was sorting us a lift out so we could go home. Then he walked in with a man.'

'Who was the man?'

Anya Molnar shrugged.

'Then what happened?'

'He injected him with something and tied him to his kitchen table and told us to kill him.'

Byrd was lost for words for several moments. 'And then?'

'We're not killers.' She looked away, tears filling her eyes. 'He got angry with us, started shouting at us, and told us to get upstairs. He locked us up in the attic.'

'And the man on the kitchen table?'

'I don't know, I'm sorry.'

'There's no need to be sorry. You're doing great.' Byrd smiled at her for reassurance and moved on, going back in time to the first meeting with Ella Mitchell. 'So, can you explain what happened with Ella?'

Anya scowled, then remembered. 'Oh, yes, so when Reggie locked us in the attic, he was angry, then he came up later that day and said we had a way to make things right, a way to make him less angry.' She paused, collecting the thoughts in her little head. 'He wanted me to help him kill them. He said if I could get in the house he'd knock on the front door, and get inside. If I did that, I could go back home.'

'Then what happened, Anya?'

'I would never hurt anyone, never in my life. I went into the house, and her mummy was making me tea. Reggie knocked at the door, and we hid upstairs. He pretended to be my dad when he knocked, and Ella's mum let him in. That's when I told her he was there to kill, and they had a fight. Me and Ella got out and ran away.'

'So, where did you go?'

'I — I don't know. Like I said, Reggie hit me on the head. I got dizzy and stopped behind some bins and passed out. When I came round, it was dark. Ella and Reggie were

313

gone. Then I saw my necklace was gone and I went back to the house.'

'And that's when Corey Timms turned up looking for you? How did he know you were there?'

She shrugged. 'I have no idea.'

'Thank you, Anya, you've been so helpful.'

Byrd wanted to know more about Luna's story about Reggie taking her to a random house on Edinburgh Drive.

'What happened with you, Luna?'

'He told me he was disappointed in Anya and said he'd give me a chance to make things right. So, he found a woman in front of her house, pulling weeds from her driveway. He told me to put fake blood on my face, pretend I'd been beaten up, and go inside, make sure the door was unlocked. A minute later he came in. We were upstairs in the bathroom. I couldn't help it, but I told the old lady he was here to cause trouble and he heard me. He killed her. It was awful.'

'Why did he kill her?'

'I don't know. She panicked and was trying to call the police.' Another small shrug. 'He didn't even stop to ask questions, just came in and attacked her.'

Byrd thought about it. There was something about this last death, he thought. The other attacks, although frenzied and panicked, were different to Josh Carter's death, because it seemed more based on chance rather than planning. And why leave his body out in the open so it could be so easily found? Was he getting bored on his usual methods of deposing of them like previous victims? Did he want to raise the stakes? Nevertheless, Reggie had intended on killing each of the victims in some way, and had planned to use the girls to help him do that.

* * *

As he came out of the hospital, Byrd felt exhausted. He watched the bright headlights of the passing cars on St Cuthbert's Way and wondered how there could be so much evil in the world.

The disappearance of Reggie Cook weighed heavily on him, knowing he was still out there, unpunished and free to roam the streets. Based on what he knew, Reggie had been shot and was injured, but no hospital reports had indicated he'd been anywhere to get patched up.

Byrd sighed. He must be somewhere.

Had they missed something? Something at the house that would give them a better clue as to where Reggie may have gone?

Desperate to go home and sleep for days, he knew he wouldn't be able to. He started the car, but instead of heading for home, he set off for Reggie Cook's house.

73

Saturday evening
Geneva Road, Darlington

Byrd received a call from Claire, asking when he'd be home. She wasn't in a cooking mood and fancied a takeaway. Byrd said he had to make a stop somewhere first, and promised he wouldn't be long.

'Okay, don't be. I'm starving,' she said before the call ended.

Byrd parked directly outside Reggie Cook's house. He keyed off and the headlights faded, the street falling into almost darkness due to several broken street lights near Reggie's house.

He spotted the outline of PC Timms sitting in the under-cover car parked across the road in case Reggie turned up unannounced. It was possible that Reggie could be at the other end of the country by now, but there was always a chance he'd return if he needed something important.

Timms leaned closer to the driver's window, half of his face visible from the nearby dim lighting, and smiled, giving Byrd a small wave. Byrd wandered over, and Timms lowered his window. 'Boss. What's going on?'

'Just doing another check in case there's something we missed earlier.'

'Need any help?'

'No, you stay out here, Eric. Keep a lookout. Ring me if you see anything.'

Byrd pulled out a torch and stepped onto the driveway, using the light to illuminate the shadowy walkway by the side of the parked van. Ducking under the police cordon that had been set up earlier, he made his way past the van.

With the key he'd collected from evidence, he opened the front door and edged it open. The torch beam lit up the familiar staircase, but somehow, the house felt different now. Quieter, emptier. Colder, darker.

He stepped in and turned on the hallway light. The living room was to the left, and the dining room was to the right. He thought about where he'd searched earlier. If he was Reggie and wanted to hide something, where he would put it?

'The attic,' he whispered. He switched off the light, and climbed the stairs. If Reggie was to return and noticed a light on, he wouldn't enter, that's for sure. At the top, he looked up at the open hatch. The steps were folded up. He pulled them down and slowly climbed them, his torchlight bouncing off the angled ceiling above.

The attic was surprisingly big, spanning the width of the house, the highest point in the centre. Each side sloped to the attic floor to match the pitch of the roof, with a strip of yellow insulation around the edge, and the floor was boarded. Forensics had given the all-clear for this particular space, so Byrd knew he wouldn't contaminate any important evidence by being here.

Other than a few boxes he'd already checked earlier, the attic appeared to be empty. Byrd wasn't so sure.

Carefully, he slowly moved around, shining his torch so he didn't trip and end up crashing through the hatch to the floor below. The boards felt firm, but he remained cautious.

The torch beam brushed over where the girls had been sleeping. The stained quilts they had used gave off an odour of mustiness and neglect. They must have huddled together, no doubt comforting one another during their time trapped here.

He lowered the torch a moment, snapped on some nitrile gloves, and searched through the covers, finding nothing but a hair bobble one of the girls must have left behind.

He stood, careful not to knock his head on the sloping roof, and turned, allowing the torch to lead the way. The open hatch was to the left near the solid brick party wall, so he angled to the right, squinting to focus on anything out of place — a box he hadn't seen, a part of the attic with a hidden compartment, a floorboard that was—

'Ahh, what's that?' he whispered. In one corner the insulation was slightly out of line. Had it been moved on purpose? He kneeled and leaned closer, lifting it up cautiously.

His ringing phone made him jump. 'Jesus!'

He rocked back, pulled it out. It was Tanzy.

'Ori,' he answered.

'Hey, Max. What a day, eh?'

'How was the beach?'

'Yeah, good. I was thinking . . .'

'Let me call you back, Ori,' Byrd said. 'I'm in Reggie Cook's attic.'

'What on earth are you doing there?'

'I'm not sure, to be honest. I'm making sure we haven't missed anything.'

'I see. Is Timms still there?'

'Yeah. Parked up outside.'

Byrd put the call on loudspeaker and placed the phone down to his left. 'Hold on, Ori. Might have found something here.'

'I'm through Darlington now, picking up some food for Pip and the kids. I'll pop over.'

'See you soon, then.'

Byrd ended the call with a tap on the screen, leaving his phone where it lay. With both hands, he rolled back the sheet of insulation and discovered a metal box, approximately eight by ten inches.

'What do we have here?'

He picked it out and set it down near him, then carefully prised the lid open to discover several wads of money, all different currencies, along with three passports and a set of keys. He opened the first passport, the thin spine slightly cracking. It belonged to a male called Henry Garmin. He placed it down and tried the next one, which belonged to another man, Jack Thornley.

'Clever bastard.' The photos in each passport were the same. The third one had the same photo too, but the man was called Liam Abbott. He put the passports back in the box, closed the lid, and stood up. He made his way back to the hatch and descended until he touched down on the landing carpet. Moving to the side of the steps so he could turn for the stairs, he came to an immediate halt. Something sharp was pressing into his back.

'Easy now,' said the voice right behind him. 'No sudden movements or this knife goes through your spine.'

Byrd froze. 'Reggie Cook?'

'That's me. Who the fuck's asking?'

He was unable to move. His torch lit up Reggie's bedroom, but nothing behind. If he'd been a little to the right, he could have seen a reflection in the bedroom window, got a good look to see Reggie's position. He breathed deeply, thinking about what to do.

'I'm a detective inspector with Durham Constabulary. You can call me Max.'

'Well, detective inspector with Durham Constabulary, you see that little box in your hand?'

'Uh-huh,' replied Byrd.

'Hand it over.'

'You won't get out of the country with any of those, Reggie. Why not just pop down to the station to have a chat about what we found in the garden? We have the best coffee there.'

The knife pressed a little harder into his back. 'I bet you do, Inspector.'

319

Byrd needed to bide his time and come up with something to keep Reggie talking. 'I bet you didn't expect me to be here tonight.'

Reggie laughed hard. 'I knew you wouldn't make it easy for me. But yes, I thought the coast was clear. Never mind.' His voice had no emotion, just acceptance of what he'd done. 'I knew one day, sooner or later, you'd catch up with me.'

'What I will say here, Reggie,' said Byrd, 'is that the more cooperative you are, the better your chances of a reduced sentence.'

Reggie laughed again. 'You're talking like *you're* the one holding the knife in *my* back.'

Byrd winced as the knife tip penetrated his jacket. It was terrifyingly sharp. He tried to edge forward to ease the pressure but Reggie grabbed his shoulder with a strong hand and held him still. The knife continued to press against him.

'It doesn't need to end this way, Reggie.'

'How else can this possibly end, Inspector? Tell me.'

'You could lower the knife, and we can talk about it. Get some closure for the families of those people buried in your garden.'

'Got to give it to you, you're a trier.'

'They do say God loves a trier.'

'Not today, they don't. Now, give me that box. Do it slowly.'

Byrd paused. He was dead either way: Reggie would stab him if he gave him the box, he was sure. But he could stab him and take the box too. So why was he taking so long about it? Reggie was a talker, thought Byrd. He needed to draw the man out, buy himself some time.

'Just tell me,' he said, 'why the girls, Reggie?'

'I needed help with what I was doing.'

'You seem pretty capable enough without bringing three young girls into it.'

Reggie sighed. 'I guess I needed company.'

'How do you mean?'

'My sister passed away,' Reggie explained.

Byrd considered his meaning. 'And she used to help you?'

'She did, just the same way I was trying to get the girls to help me.'

'Why did you need help from the girls?'

'Because it's fun, plain and simple. It's fun. What's the point in doing something fun on your own? There's no risk in that, is there?'

'So you promised the girls if they helped you, you'd let them go back home to Warrington. Did you ever intend to do that, or were you going to kill them too?'

'I'd never kill a child, Inspector. That would be crossing the line.'

Byrd rolled his eyes, although Reggie couldn't see his face. 'How very noble of you.'

He needed help, and soon. When would Tanzy arrive? he wondered. Or would PC Timms decide Byrd had taken too long in the house and come to check on him? He assumed Reggie had sneaked in through the back of the house, otherwise Timms would have seen him. But there was no way to signal to them, let them know he needed help, without putting himself in danger. He just needed to keep Reggie talking.

'Now, give me the box!'

'I will, I will,' Byrd replied softly. 'I just want to know why. Why the body parts at West Manor? Why the bodies in the garden? Why, Reggie? There must be a motive here. Tell me why, and I'll hand it over.'

Byrd felt Reggie's warm breath on his neck as he sighed once more. 'You don't fucking give up, do you?'

Byrd didn't reply, not wanting to break the spell.

'Three weeks ago, I brought a man back to my house and drugged him before I took him to West Manor in the van. It was getting too risky burying them in the garden — too many prying neighbours wanting to talk over the fucking fence because they have nothing better to do with their lives. Anyway, I needed a different method. I just had to make sure the body parts were small, then mix it all in with the grass cuttings. The council usually comes and collects the waste, and then it's gone. It goes to a waste site, gets churned up in a shredder, makes the finest fertiliser you'll ever see.'

'How many, Reggie? How many people have you killed?'

'I have no idea. And I don't really care.'

Fucking monster, thought Byrd, but didn't want to piss him off by saying it. 'Why, Reggie? What's this all about?'

'It all started because I hated my father,' Reggie said. 'What he used to do to my mother was awful. He used to beat, whip, and smack her with a belt. It was fucking horrible.'

'What happened to him?'

'My father? I killed him. When I was old and strong enough, I killed my dad. I wanted him gone. I stabbed him in his sleep when my mother was working nights, dragged him into the garage, and cut him up with a saw.'

Byrd gulped. 'How old were you?'

'I was twenty-two. I remember it like it was yesterday. I put his body parts in the bins and let the binmen take them away as if nothing had happened.'

The tip of the knife penetrated Byrd's skin in a hot, sharp nip. Reggie was clearly becoming excited reminiscing about the story.

'Right, enough fucking talking.' Reggie's tone had become impatient. 'Give me the box. Last chance, Inspector.'

Byrd couldn't wait for Timms or Tanzy. He needed to make his move or Reggie was going to kill him. With the box in one hand and the torch in the other, he darted out of Reggie's grasp, brushing the wall at the top of the stairs with his shoulder, and ducked under the angled steps before bolting into the back bedroom, using the torch to guide him. He grabbed the edge of the bedroom door and slammed it, but Reggie's shoulder bounced into it, knocking Byrd backward onto the bed. He shunted himself off to the floor, now on one knee.

Reggie pushed open the door and turned the light on. The bedroom erupted in light, temporarily blinding Byrd as he stood and backed off. He shuffled back, rounding the bed, and backed into the corner near the window.

'I'm not playing games. Give me the fucking box!' Reggie pointed the knife at him.

Byrd quickly studied the room around him, looking for something to use as a weapon, realising the four-inch torch in his hand was not much of a match against the butcher's knife getting closer by the second.

* * *

Tanzy spotted Byrd's X5 outside Reggie's house. Across the road, he saw Timms parked up, his car nestled in the darkness of the street. He went over.

Timms lowered his window. 'Boss, Max is in there.'

'Just been talking to him on the phone,' Tanzy said. 'Anything to report?'

'No, nothing yet.' Timms appeared a little bored, no doubt pissed off he'd been chosen to watch the house for an overtime shift that hadn't been optional.

'How long's he been in there?'

'Not long. Said he was having a look around in case we missed anything.'

Tanzy studied the dark house. No lights on inside. 'Okay. I'll go see what he's up to.' Tanzy crossed the road, slid down the side of the parked van, and stopped at the front door. Through the tinted glass, he could see a torch beam at the top of the stairs, pointing upwards. He watched it for a while, noticing it was still.

'Strange,' he whispered. Was Byrd checking something out?

The longer the light remained still, the worse the feeling in Tanzy's stomach became. He put his face up to the glass to see clearer. Was that Byrd holding the torch? Why was he so still?

'What are you doing, Max?'

The light then moved erratically, followed by a collection of thuds, and then a more prominent light turned on. He could see a shadow on the landing, moving slowly.

Tanzy grabbed the handle, slowly opened the door in silence, and stepped inside. The bedroom light was spilling out onto the landing and stairs. He heard multiple footsteps.

'I'm not playing games. Give me the fucking box!' someone said. It definitely wasn't Byrd.

* * *

Byrd edged back as far as he could, clutching the box, the back of his legs hitting the windowsill by the radiator. He was trapped and had nowhere to go.

He frowned. Was that the faint sound of a handle being pressed? The mechanical locks sliding within a door? These were followed by an almost imperceptible shift in the air and the distant sound of the outside world.

Someone had opened the front door.

Judging by Reggie's face, he hadn't heard anything, although he was closer to the bedroom door.

Byrd had to do something to distract Reggie, throw him off. He gripped his torch and started slapping it against the radiator quickly, the sound of the metallic claps filling the room and the rest of the house.

'What the fuck are you doing?' asked Reggie.

* * *

Tanzy approached the stairs and, as silently as he could, started to climb them, the wood creaking under his weight. He didn't know who was up there with Byrd, but he knew it wasn't good.

The sudden sounds of metallic banging rang out, echoing around the house.

His eyes widened, knowing it was a sign. A distraction of some sort. Whatever it was, Tanzy needed to shift himself.

He grabbed the handrail and propelled himself up to the top, then shot into the rear bedroom.

He saw the situation in a moment: Reggie Cook, knife in hand, was going for Byrd. Byrd was in the far corner of the room, still slapping the radiator with his torch. He looked over Reggie's shoulder and locked eyes with Tanzy.

Reggie must have seen Byrd's glance. He stopped and turned. By that point, Tanzy was halfway around the bed, darting towards him. He caught Reggie mid-turn, shoulder colliding with his ribs, sending him flying towards the back window. Byrd ducked out of the way.

They flew through the window, glass erupting around them, and landed on the sloped roof with a clatter. Tanzy lost his hold on Reggie and rolled a little, but managed to stop on the slope before he hit the end. Reggie carried on falling, rolling uncontrollably down the roof until he dropped off the end and landed on the decking with a series of mighty hollow thuds.

'Tanzy!' screamed Byrd from the bedroom behind him.

Tanzy edged forward, peering over the guttering at the dark decking below. Under the dull shine of the moon above lay Reggie's twisted body.

'I'll call Timms,' Byrd said.

Tanzy managed a silent nod, the events of what had just happened going over in his mind and what could have gone wrong. Had he known there was a sloped roof above the kitchen extension? He hadn't given it any thought — he'd just seen red and had desperately needed to help Byrd.

Tanzy groped his way back towards the smashed window, glass digging into his hands. Byrd was shaking his head at him.

'I can't wait to get home and have some pizza. I'm bloody starving,' Tanzy said.

Byrd laughed.

74

The sun had made the afternoon warmer, so warm that Tanzy removed his parka and left it on the passenger seat of his car when he got out to wait for Byrd and Selena to arrive. They could have come together in one car, but Tanzy had needed to nip home for something while Byrd collected Selena from the station.

Tanzy stood, leaning back against the bonnet of his Golf, soaking up the afternoon rays and feeling the heat on his tanned, almost bald head. He opened his blue eyes, and his focus fell on the bush where they'd found Corey Tills on Thursday morning, strangled. Their number-one suspect for that was Reggie Cook, a topic they'd discuss with him in detail later this afternoon. Reggie had suffered a broken arm during his fall from the sloped roof when he'd hit the decking. He'd also twisted his ankle. Tanzy had a few bandages and stitches — he'd cut his forearm and hands when he'd gone through the window, though he hadn't felt it at the time.

Less than five minutes later, Byrd pulled up. Tanzy watched him guide the car into the space near the front, a couple of spaces from where he'd parked. Selena's head was bowed in the passenger seat, her face buried into a tissue.

In silence, they left the car park and crossed the road, walking through the main entrance of the Memorial Hospital. It took them only three minutes to reach the pathology department. After signing in at reception, the double doors opened automatically, and they went down the corridor to Dr Arnold Hemsley's office.

Tanzy took the lead, knocked on the door, waited a few seconds, and opened it.

'DI Tanzy,' the doctor said, standing behind his desk. 'Is she here?'

Tanzy nodded and waited for Hemsley to walk out into the corridor. A faint smell of cigarette smoke lingered from him.

'Follow me.'

In the harsh bright lights of the examination room, two bodies lay on separate trolleys, both covered with white sheets. Selena padded into the dark room nervously and gasped, using the crumpled tissue in her hand to dab her sore eyes again.

'Thank you, everyone, for coming,' the doctor said to them. 'Mrs Goldberg,' he said softly, 'this will be challenging for you, but we must go through this process.'

Selena nodded twice, her eyes filling with tears again.

Dr Hemsley stood at the head of one of the bodies and peeled back the cover, revealing the man underneath it. 'Is this your husband?'

She nodded slowly. 'Yes. That's Alex.'

Dr Hemsley smiled thinly, admiring her ability to hold her emotions in. He covered Alex Goldberg and moved over to the other body.

'Selena, can you identify this man, please?'

She sniffed loudly and pulled away from Byrd, wiping her eyes again.

Hemsley pulled back the cover.

She took a deep breath. 'That's Jarrett Banks. He's the man that threatened me and my husband.'

Tanzy jotted the name down, nodding. He turned to Hemsley. 'Thank you, Doctor.'

Hemsley accepted the thanks with a nod and covered him up. The detectives then left him to it, leaving the hospital and returning to their cars.

'Thank you for doing that, Selena,' said Byrd. 'I know how difficult that must have been.'

Byrd had been through it repeatedly, especially when he'd identified his dead sister all those years ago.

'We need to go to the station and get the full story,' Byrd said to Selena, lightly nodding.

'Yes. I need to tell you everything.'

Back at the station, under interview conditions, she told them about what had happened in Warrington last month when she'd knocked down the elderly man. Jarrett had told her to leave, but because he'd captured the footage on his dashcam, he'd threatened to go to the police with it unless she helped him with something.

Based on what the detectives had gathered from speaking to Anya, Luna, and Nina, and what they knew from Cheshire police, it seemed that Jarrett had planned for Selena to look after the girls while he pretended that another rival family or gang had captured them, in an attempt to con the family out of the drug game so he could have Warrington to himself. Pure greed, the detectives thought.

Byrd and Tanzy then asked her about Reggie Cook and what he was like. She told them she'd known him for years and considered him a close friend. When they told her about what had been happening in the basement and what he'd asked the girls to do, she was gobsmacked, unable to speak. They then told her what they had found at his house. The decomposed bodies they'd found under his artificial grass had made her gag and throw up all over the interview room.

'Can you get some water, please, Max?'

Byrd stood and left the room, returning a few minutes later with some water and cleaning equipment.

Eventually, she said, 'I — I can't . . . No, I don't believe this.'

Byrd nodded to indicate the story was true. They spoke some more about the girls and what would happen to them.

She hung her head in shame. 'If only I'd known about Reggie and what he'd done. God, I'd never have agreed to looking after the girls if I'd known he was such a monster.'

'Thank you for being honest with us, Selena.' Byrd stood. 'We'll let the CPS decide what happens next.'

EPILOGUE

DCI Corbridge held a national television press conference about finding Reggie Cook, the man responsible for Darlington's recent murders along with a string of previous murders, as evidenced by the discovery of the victims in his garden. He praised his team, especially DI Max Byrd and DI Orion Tanzy, stating that without them, Reggie Cook would have no doubt gone on to murder dozens more innocent people.

Reggie Cook was put in front of a packed-out court, the families of those victims identified through DNA analysis all there to see him burn, along with the media and at least a dozen police officers in case things got out of hand. The court presented the evidence against him, spanning from his first murder twenty years ago to his most recent. The room was shaken by his actions. Without question, all twelve members of the jury deemed him guilty, and the judge gave him a life sentence thirty-two times over. Reggie showed no remorse, smiling as he left at the families whose lives he'd ruined over the years.

Matej Molnar had his day in court. Evidence from Durham and Darlington Constabulary helped to convict him for first-degree murder, multiple cases of GBH and ABH, and importing and supplying drugs. It was certain he wouldn't set foot outside a prison again.

The Molnar girls went home to live with their mother, safely away from the mess their father and uncle had brought to their door. According to Cheshire police, Maria decided to move away from Warrington and start somewhere fresh, just her and the girls. It would give them the best chance at life.

Selena Goldberg stood trial at Teesside Crown Court for the manslaughter of Jack Benton, the elderly man she'd killed in Warrington. She'd not only been charged with manslaughter, but the court deemed the way she'd fled the scene inhumane, whether persuaded to or not. She was also found guilty of child neglect relating to the Molnar girls and sent away for a very long time.

Emma Slater was sent to court for kidnapping and imprisoning Ella Mitchell. The court heard of the horrible story and the way she'd cruelly kept Ella against her will. She was sacked from her job as a lawyer and faced eighteen months in prison.

DI Max Byrd was recognised for his diligence and hard work in recent cases, especially his discovery of the victims in Reggie's back garden. Assistant Chief Constable Edward Johnson awarded him with a token of their appreciation and asked DCI Corbridge to put a photo of Byrd in their hallway to go with the previous officers from years gone by who had shown excellence in their roles. Byrd continued as DI for the next few months, working hard but making sure he put his family first. Alan started sleeping better, which gave Max a few months of rest, although he still suffered from insomnia, and often used Amaretto as a medicine to get some sleep. He and Claire made some big plans for the following year, including trying for another baby — it was Claire's idea, not his, but if it made her happy, then why not.

DI Orion Tanzy took a few weeks off after the Reggie Cook case and went to Tenerife with Pip and the kids to escape it all. On his return, he received an award for excellence. His photo went up next to Byrd's in the hall of fame corridor. Eric and Jasmine thrived in school, topping their classes in every subject. Tanzy was so proud of them and thanked Pip for all the work she'd done with them while he was busy working.

A few months later, Pip told Tanzy she needed to speak with him. So, on that particular Tuesday night, after another long day at work, Tanzy returned home to find her in the living room, lost in a daze. There was definitely something on her mind. As he sat beside her, she took his hand and placed it gently on her stomach.

'Are you ready to be a daddy again?' she asked him.

Tanzy hugged her and cried with happiness for the first time in years.

THE END

ACKNOWLEDGEMENTS

In a world full of amazing fiction, talented writers, and an endless galaxy of books, I want to personally thank you, the reader, for choosing this to read — I really hope you enjoyed it. Thank you, C.J.

THE JOFFE BOOKS STORY

We began in 2014 when Jasper agreed to publish his mum's much-rejected romance novel and it became a bestseller.

Since then we've grown into the largest independent publisher in the UK. We're extremely proud to publish some of the very best writers in the world, including Joy Ellis, Faith Martin, Caro Ramsay, Helen Forrester, Simon Brett and Robert Goddard. Everyone at Joffe Books loves reading and we never forget that it all begins with the magic of an author telling a story.

We are proud to publish talented first-time authors, as well as established writers whose books we love introducing to a new generation of readers.

We won Trade Publisher of the Year at the Independent Publishing Awards in 2023 and Best Publisher Award in 2024 at the People's Book Prize. We have been shortlisted for Independent Publisher of the Year at the British Book Awards for the last five years, and were shortlisted for the Diversity and Inclusivity Award at the 2022 Independent Publishing Awards. In 2023 we were shortlisted for Publisher of the Year at the RNA Industry Awards, and in 2024 we were shortlisted at the CWA Daggers for the Best Crime and Mystery Publisher.

We built this company with your help, and we love to hear from you, so please email us about absolutely anything bookish at feedback@joffebooks.com.

If you want to receive free books every Friday and hear about all our new releases, join our mailing list here: www.joffe-books.com/freebooks.

And when you tell your friends about us, just remember: it's pronounced Joffe as in coffee or toffee!